DYING

GASP

Blood of the Wicked
Buried Strangers

DYING

GASP

Leighton Gage

First published in the United States by
Soho Press, Inc.
853 Broadway
New York, NY 10003

Library of Congress Cataloging-in-Publication Data

Gage, Leighton.
Dying gasp / Leighton Gage.
p. cm.
ISBN 978-1-56947-613-0 (hardcover)
1. Silva, Mario (Fictitious character)—Fiction. 2. Police—Brazil—
Fiction. 3. Missing persons—Fiction. 4. Brazil—Fiction. 5. Snuff
films—Fiction. 6. Psychological fiction. I. Title.
PS3607.A3575D95 2010
813'.6—dc22
2009032706

10 9 8 7 6 5 4 3 2 1

For Tony, Patrick, and J. Michael,
more and better friends than any guy has a right to have.

". . . escape will elude them; their hope will become a dying gasp."

JOB 11:20
(NEW INTERNATIONAL VERSION)

Chapter One

AMSTERDAM, THE NETHERLANDS

THE BOMB ABOARD THE number nine tram claimed seventeen lives. Sixteen were passengers.

The seventeenth was the driver of a nearby postal truck. Mail from his shattered vehicle littered the cobblestones in front of the Museum of the Tropics and fluttered, like tiny flags, from the branches of the linden trees.

An hour later, in a shaky VHS video delivered to the studios of Al Jazeera in Dakar, a masked man, posing in front of a green banner, took responsibility for the outrage. A group calling themselves Justice for Islam, he said, had acted "in reprisal for Dutch support of the American crusaders' continuing occupation of Iraq." The Dutch had withdrawn their last troops from Iraq long since, but that was something the terrorists chose to overlook.

The incident took place on a glorious April day, chilly but without the usual breeze. The absence of wind ensured that much of the scattered mail stayed in the area of the blast instead of littering the neighboring streets and being blown into canals.

As soon as the authorities liberated the area around the truck, postal employees moved in and gathered up what they could. The salvaged mail was stuffed into canvas sacks and carried away to the Central Post Office on the Oosterdokskade, where a team under the leadership of Postal Inspector Marnix Gans started sorting it.

Some of the letters and packages were relatively undamaged.

These were immediately fed back into the system and sent on their way. Some pieces had suffered the effects of the explosion, the resulting fire, and the water that had been used to put the fire out. Wherever addresses were still legible, tape was used for repairs and that mail, too, was sent on its way. Finally, Gans's team got down to the hard part: trying to piece together fragments and subjecting charred remnants to ultraviolet and infrared lights in an attempt to decipher addresses unreadable to the naked eye.

A few of the mystery envelopes had the same characteristics. They were square, made of a manila paper almost as strong as cardboard and lined with a protective plastic permeated with tiny bubbles. One of them had been torn open by the explosion. It contained a digital video disk. The DVD itself was neither damaged nor labeled. There was nothing else inside the envelope.

Jeroen Velder, the only sorter on the team who was still young enough to be taken for a student, gathered the envelopes containing DVDs, put them into one of the plastic sorting boxes, and deposited the box on the desk of Inspector Gans.

"What's this?" Gans said.

"Unreadables, *mijneer*. Fourteen of them, all alike. All DVDs, I suppose."

"You *suppose*?"

"One of the envelopes is torn, mijneer. I didn't want to open the others without permission."

"Quite right. No return address either, eh?"

"*Nee*, mijneer."

Always "mijneer," never "Marnix." Unlike most youngsters of his generation, Velder expressed proper respect for his superiors. As long as Marnix Gans was in charge, Velder's future prospects were bright.

Gans stared at the contents of the box. What he obviously

needed was a DVD player. But if his superiors drew the conclusion that Gans wanted the player as a permanent addition
to the employee's lunchroom, with the attendant risk that
Gans and his buddies might fritter away their time in there
watching American movies, the authorities would feel com-
pelled to look into the matter. Approval of the requisition, if
it came at all, could take weeks.

Gans was a proponent of order, a man who took deeply to
heart his mandate to rapidly dispatch the queen's mail. The
thought of having those DVDs hanging around for weeks,
maybe months, was anathema to him. Yet it was strictly
against the rules to take anything home. If a piece of mail
not his own was found on his person when he was leaving
the building, he'd be in trouble.

Gans decided he'd take the risk. He'd bring the DVD back
to his house, pop it into his player and see if the content
could give him a clue to the addressee or the sender.

As was his custom, Gans left promptly at five, the damaged envelope containing the DVD in the pocket of his
nylon ski jacket.

Sun in Amsterdam, rare in April, seldom brings warmth.
As Gans walked the few hundred meters westward toward
the entrance to the Central Station, a cool breeze was blowing from the east. He pulled up his hood, tightened the cord
at his throat, and reflected that if the wind had been blowing
earlier in the day they wouldn't have recovered half of what
they did.

He caught his usual train and disembarked in Haarlem at
5:31. He went to the rack at the back of the station,
unlocked his bicycle, and pedaled home to his apartment on
the Ambonstraat, arriving well before dark. He locked his
bike in the storage shed and climbed the two flights of stairs.
The television in the flat below was blaring in some

unintelligible language. He thought it might be Turkish. His was a mixed neighborhood with more than its share of unassimilated immigrants. An exotic meal, something offensive to his sense of smell, was being prepared in the kitchen of the apartment next door. He wrinkled his nose.

Gans was a Haarlemer born and bred. He resented the invasion of his territory by swarthy-skinned foreigners, and he especially resented them after the events of the day. Noise, foul smells, and now a bomb on the streets of Amsterdam. Could it get any worse?

His immaculately clean little flat of just over forty-five square meters was divided into four spaces: a small bedroom, an even smaller kitchen, a truly tiny bathroom (with a shower, no bathtub), and a reasonably spacious living area with a balcony. The balcony he seldom used, because it was usually too cold and overlooked the playground of a school where the kids were always shouting at each other in whatever damned language they spoke back home in Northern Africa or wherever they came from.

Gans took off his jacket and hung it on the peg to the left of the door. Then he went into the kitchen, piled some *boeren Kool*—chopped cabbage—onto one of his microwave-resistant plastic plates and added a piece of smoked sausage. While he was waiting for it to heat, he remembered the DVD and returned to the hall to fetch it. Then he went back into the kitchen and picked up some utensils, a bottle of Oranjeboom, a glass, and a paper napkin. The utensils and the napkin he put on the coffee table. The beer he poured into his glass. The DVD he loaded into his player, pressing the pause button to make sure it wouldn't start until he was ready.

Five minutes later, his dinner in one hand and his half-empty glass of Oranjeboom in the other, Gans went back into the living room and sat on the couch. He put down the food and drink, picked up the remote control, and hit the PLAY button.

Fourteen minutes after that, Marnix Gans stumbled into his bathroom and vomited everything he'd just eaten into the toilet.

Then he called the police.

Chapter Two

BRASILIA, BRAZILIAN FEDERAL DISTRICT

NELSON SAMPAIO PUSHED AWAY from his desk, distancing himself from his chief investigator. "They're doing *what?*"

"Raping Nardoni five or six times a day," Mario Silva repeated, "which is exactly the reason I put him there."

Sampaio, the director of the Brazilian federal police, held up a faultlessly manicured hand. The gesture reminded Silva of a traffic cop.

"Wait a minute," he said. "Are you telling me you *expected* the man to be sexually abused?"

"More than 'expected,' I *counted* on it."

"Explain yourself."

Silva looked out of the window. A buzzard was flying lazy circles over the roof of the Ministry of Culture across the way.

"I'm waiting, Mario."

Silva narrowed his eyes, redirecting his attention to his boss.

"The other prisoners in that cell aren't there by chance," he said. "They're all animals, just like Ercilio Nardoni, but they're a different breed. They don't go after children; they prey on other men."

"If we treat felons the way you're treating him," Sampaio said, "there's no difference between them and us. Frankly, Mario, there are times when I find these methods of yours revolting. You're my Chief Investigator, not judge, jury, and executioner. The old days are gone. This is a democracy now. People, even the worst kind of people, have rights. Take a lead from the Americans."

"If we had the Americans' forensic capabilities, we might be able to use their methods."

"All right, we don't. And I admit we have to do some things differently, but it still doesn't justify the torture of prisoners."

"Not even in a case like Nardoni's?"

"Not even then. I want you to—"

"I *know* the bastard's lying," Silva said, before his boss could complete the thought. "I just need his confession. Technically, we're not laying a finger on him. What's happening to Nardoni is being perpetrated by the other lowlifes in his cell. You have total deniability."

"I'm not talking about deniability. I'm talking about what's right. It's demonic to put pressure on someone that way."

"He's a demonic man, Director. My intention is to leave him there until you specifically order me to return him to solitary."

"Then I specifically order you to—"

"And before giving me that order, I'd like you to reflect on what he did. Not what I *think* he did, but what I am absolutely, positively *sure* he did."

Sampaio stopped short, closed his mouth, opened it again, closed it again. The action made him look rather like a fish.

"You don't have to remind me," he said at last. "I remember well. But you don't need his confession. You have evidence. You have photographs."

Either Ercilio Nardoni, or his late roommate, Clovis Borges, always made Polaroid photographs of the faces of their terrified victims. They'd kept those trophies, along with the stuffed animals, along with the cotton panties stamped with cartoon characters and teddy bears, along with the little pieces of jewelry—rings just big enough for little girls' fingers, crucifixes with chains just long enough for little girls' necks.

"The photographs will be useless in court," Silva said.

"Why?"

"Nardoni claims they belonged to Borges. He claims Borges did all the raping and all the killing. We can't prove otherwise. They used condoms. They washed the corpses. The trophies were wiped clean of prints."

"That confounded Borges," the director said petulantly, "you shouldn't have killed him." There was a time when Sampaio would have said "goddamned," not "confounded," but not any more.

"Self-defense," Silva said.

"I read your report." Sampaio leaned forward and looked Silva in the eye. "But we're alone in my office, Mario, just the two of us. Did Borges really threaten you with that pistol?"

Silva didn't blink. "Of course he did." He waited for the director to say something more. When he didn't, Silva continued, "If Nardoni doesn't confess, he isn't going to be convicted, and if he isn't convicted, he's going to go out and do the same thing all over again. With that in mind, does your order still stand? Do you want me to take him out of that cell before he signs a full confession?"

The director finally said, "Leave him where he is. Let's move on. There's something else I want to talk to you about."

He picked up a pencil and started to toy with it. Sampaio fumbled with pencils when he was about to say something his listener wouldn't like. This time, he appeared to be going for the world record.

Silva braced himself.

"How can I put this?" Sampaio said, temporizing.

Silva glanced around Sampaio's recently redecorated office. His boss had retained his big wooden desk and the two flags that flanked it. There was still a portrait of the president of the republic to the left of the window, but now it was lower and situated off to one side, ceding precedence to an image of Jesus.

Jesus held his right hand in the air, as if he were administering the Boy Scout oath. From Silva's perspective, it looked like He was administering it to Nelson Sampaio.

The director was, of course, anything but a Boy Scout. The oath he'd set his sights upon was of an entirely different nature. For almost three years, Sampaio had been angling to secure himself a seat in the Chamber of Deputies, and now he'd hatched a scheme to do it. That scheme involved embracing a new religion; but for a man with as much ambition as Sampaio, that was no obstacle.

It hinged on a statistic: since the previous election, Evangelicals in Brazil had been multiplying like rabbits. They now formed a very significant voting bloc. Given a choice, Evangelicals voted for other Evangelicals, and there was no Evangelical running in Sampaio's home district. With the election only five months away, the votes in São Paulo were still up for grabs. All Sampaio had to do was to declare that he'd been born again in Jesus—and make sure he made the announcement early enough to get the word out.

He'd already made the declaration.

Hence the redecoration of his office. Devotional plaques with excerpts from the Scriptures were a feature of the décor, beginning with the Ten Commandments and running through the Twenty-Third chapter of Luke: "Father, forgive them; for they know not what they do."

Silva was studying the scrollwork around that one when his boss began to speak. "You know I don't hold with people who apply political pressure for personal objectives, or to obtain favorable treatment," he said.

Silva didn't know any such thing. He regarded the statement as an outright lie.

"But this time," Sampaio continued, "I'll have to make an exception. Not for me, of course, but for the good of this department. Do you know *Deputado* Roberto Malan?"

"Not personally, no," Silva said, "but I know of him. Isn't he a deacon in your . . . uh, church?"

"A bishop, actually," Sampaio said, "but that's not the point."

"So what *is* the point?"

"The point," Sampaio said in a steely voice that implied he didn't like Silva's attitude, "is that he's head of the Appropriations Committee in the Chamber of Deputies."

"Ah," Silva said.

The new budget was coming up for discussion. There were hundreds, probably thousands, of ways the pie could be sliced, and every head of every department in Brasilia was busily engaged in efforts to get a bigger piece of it. Sampaio was just like all the others.

"I see," Silva said. "So there's something we might be able to do for Deputado Malan, and in return he may look favorably on our budget proposal for the next fiscal year?"

"Exactly," the director said. "You're always talking about having more money to invest in resources. Look at this as a chance for us get some of those fancy forensic tools you go on and on about. One hand washes the other, you know."

"What does Malan want?"

"His granddaughter's missing. He wants us to find her."

"Kidnapped?"

The director looked down at his desk, and then went back to fumbling with the pencil. When next he spoke, it was with a touch of embarrassment.

"Probably not," he said. "Most likely, she's just a runaway. She's fifteen, and she's done it before."

Silva raised his eyes to the ceiling. The director looked up just in time to notice.

"I know what you're thinking," he said. "I know it's not normally a job for the federal police."

"Normally?" Silva said. Then, when it became clear that Sampaio didn't intend to respond, "How about 'never'?"

Sampaio dropped his pencil and rested his forearms on his desk.

"Stop being difficult, Mario. Look at it from the deputado's point of view. It's not just a missing girl; it's also a political thing. The deputado has to get her back before it's known she's gone. Otherwise, people might start asking themselves what she's running away from, might draw the conclusion that there's something dysfunctional about the household of the deputado's son and daughter-in-law, or odd about the deputado himself, which of course there isn't."

"Which of course there isn't," Silva echoed. "With all due respect, Director, I can't imagine that Deputado Malan has so little influence with the cops in . . . where's he from again?"

"Recife."

"In Recife, that he can't get them to find her and be discreet about it."

"That's just it. They tried, and they *can't* find her. Malan knows we're better at that sort of thing than the locals. He wants us to look into it."

"And if we say no?"

"We're not going to say no," the director said. "I've already told him yes. He's waiting for your call."

Chapter Three

DEPUTADO ROBERTO MALAN WAS a scion of one of the great landholding families of Brazil's Northeast, people who'd wielded considerable power since colonial times. Originally, they held their estates in fiefdom to the King of Portugal. After the declaration of independence, they transferred their loyalty to the emperors of Brazil. Then, in May of 1888, Dom Pedro II, by Imperial decree, abolished slavery throughout the country. Slaves had been as much a part of the economic equation as sugarcane and coffee. Five times more Africans had been shipped to Brazil than to North America. Their value as property had been reduced to nothing by a few strokes of the monarch's pen.

The powerful barons of Bahia and Pernambuco, owners of more than 90 percent of the arable land in those regions, managed to survive the blow by hiring their former slaves as employees. But the price of rent and food was deducted from wages. And the price of both was determined exclusively by the landlords. Deductions always exceeded wages. What's more, the landlords no longer had the obligation to care for sick and infirm slaves. So, in the end, the landlords were better off than they'd been before. They came to accept, indeed embrace, a slaveless society.

What they couldn't accept was a continuing subjection to Dom Pedro II. Their newfound distrust, and in some cases hatred, led them to work assiduously for his downfall. The traitor to his class, the last emperor of Brazil, was overthrown and sent into exile. A republic was established.

Within a year, Pedro Malan (named after the emperor he'd worked so hard to depose) became a duly elected senator in the new federal government and Malan had been in the legislature ever since. Roberto, the current patriarch of the line, the grandfather of the missing girl, had been there for over thirty years.

Now, at sixty-four, his was the name most often cited as the next president of the Chamber of Deputies, a job that would put him third in succession to the Presidency of the Republic. He'd become accustomed to treating federal employees much as he treated his workers back home.

"Sit," he said, pointing Silva to a chair, as if he was issuing instructions to a household pet.

The deputado offered neither his hand, nor an apology for keeping Silva waiting. He was a man with a florid face, bushy white eyebrows, and a habit of leaning forward when he spoke.

Silva did as he was bade. The legs of his chair were unusually short, while Malan was sitting on something that raised him up. The politician's diminutive stature was a feature well known to, and exploited by, caricaturists and cartoonists. He'd taken steps to compensate for it.

Ostensibly in the interest of keeping the inquiry under wraps, the deputado had asked that their meeting take place in his home on Paranoá Lake. The lake, an artificially constructed body of water in the center of Brasilia, was largely surrounded by imposing mansions like Malan's. Behind him, through an open window, Silva could see an expanse of green lawn and the dock where the deputado's gleaming white motor yacht was moored. A sailor in white shorts was polishing one of the cleats. There were two gardeners at work among the rose bushes, and the fragrance of the flowers permeated the room. Across the blue water of the lake the national flag waved lazily from its huge flagpole on the Praça dos Três Poderes. The room would have been a pleasant place had it not been for the presence of the man who owned it.

Silva took out his notepad, turned to a blank page and uncapped his pen.

Malan offered no refreshment, made no attempt to indulge in small talk. He got right down to business: "Sampaio tell you what this meeting is about?"

"Your granddaughter," Silva said. "I understand she's missing."

"You understand right."

"I've been told she's gone missing before."

"Right again."

"What's her full name?"

"Marta Nascimento Malan." The deputado said it slowly so that Silva could make a note of it. "Her mother was a Nascimento."

Silva was obviously expected to know the name, and he did. The Nascimentos also owned great estates in Pernambuco.

"Was?" he asked.

"Was," the deputado repeated. "Now, she's a Malan."

Possessive, Silva thought.

"How long has she been missing?" he asked.

Malan had to rifle through the calendar on his desk to answer the question. When he found the annotation he was looking for, he tapped it with his finger.

"My son first told me about it on the fourth of this month," he said. "So she must have gone missing four or five weeks before that."

Silva lifted his head from his notebook and stared at the deputado.

"Five weeks before the fourth of April? More than two months ago?"

Malan wrinkled his nose and sniffed, as if he could detect criticism by scent alone. He glared at Silva. "I know how to count, Chief Inspector."

It was the first time he'd used Silva's title, but there was no respect in it. He said "Chief Inspector" much as he might have said "waiter" or "driver."

Silva masked a flash of anger. "When did your son report her disappearance to the authorities?"

"On the same day he notified me, the fourth of April. He called a friend of ours in Recife, the mayor, Arlindo Venantius. You heard of him?"

"No," Silva said.

"You will before long," Malan said. "We're talking about making him governor."

Not running him for governor, *making* him governor. Malan paused long enough for Silva to draw the obvious conclusion, then said, "And Arlindo called his chief of police."

Not *the* chief of police, *his* chief of police.

In many places in the North, true democracy was little more than a distant dream. The real power was in the hands of feudal families, and it had been that way for four hundred years. Silva was glad he hadn't been obliged to deal with people like Malan when he was growing up in São Paulo. Back then, he had been accustomed to telling people what he thought.

"Why did your son wait for more than a month before talking to the mayor?" he said.

Malan waved an impatient hand.

"I *told* you. She's gone missing before. Why fuss about it if she's going to come crawling back with her tail between her legs? One time, she was gone for almost three weeks. My son figured it was the same *merda* all over again. But this time it was different. This time she didn't come back." He shifted in his chair, considered for a moment, apparently decided to be candid. "Personally, I don't care whether she comes back or not, but my son's wife was nagging him, then she started nagging *me*, so I've got to do what I can. It's family."

"The police in Recife found no trace of her at all?"

"Obviously not. Otherwise, why would I bother to talk to you?"

Silva took a deep, calming breath.

Malan seemed to enjoy trying Silva's patience. A smile creased a corner of his mouth.

"What's the name of the police chief in Recife?"

"Norberto Venantius."

"Same last name as the mayor. Pure coincidence, I suppose."

The deputado pulled his eyeglasses down to the tip of his nose and glared at Silva over the top of the frame.

"You trying to be a wise-ass?"

"No, Deputado, certainly not. I'll need a photo of your granddaughter."

The deputado grunted. "I'll get you one," he said, but he didn't rise.

"Now?" Silva prompted.

"Not now. I'll have to get one from my son. My secretary will call you when it arrives. You can come over and pick it up."

"You don't have a photo of your granddaughter?"

Malan started to redden. At first, Silva thought it was embarrassment, but it wasn't. It was anger.

"Not a recent photo, no. I don't want to have anything to do with her any more. She's turned into a disrespectful little bitch. I don't know how her mother puts up with her. Her father and I sure as hell don't. What else do you need to know?"

"Do you have any idea why she left?"

"No."

He looked straight into Silva's eyes when he said it.

And Silva was sure he was lying.

Chapter Four

MANAUS,
BRAZILIAN STATE OF AMAZONAS

MARTA MALAN LEANED CLOSER to the mirror above the sink and studied her lip. The magazines she was fond of reading called that kind of lip "beestung." Sometimes the effect was natural, sometimes achieved by injection. In Marta's case it had been created by a blow from a fist, a huge, hairy, disgusting *male* fist. And that fist belonged to a bastard they called The Goat.

When Marta pulled the lip away from her gums and curved it over she could see a cut on the inside. The cut corresponded with the edge of one of her lower front teeth. She'd been cursing at him when he hit her. He must have caught her with her mouth open.

It wasn't only her lip he'd damaged. There was a bruise on her cheek, and her nose was swollen. Gingerly, she touched it with a fingertip and moved it from side to side. It hurt, but it didn't seem to be broken. That one, thank God, had only been a glancing blow.

She was tilting her head back, trying to look at the crusted blood inside her nostrils, when she heard a key in the lock. She spun around and faced the door. The deadbolt was sliding back.

Marta was adept at *capoeira*, the Brazilian martial art, but she couldn't use it here. There was no room for a decent kick. She raised her fists. The animal had done something to her arm as well. No, not her arm, exactly, more like her shoulder.

She wondered if she'd be able to throw a punch. Maybe not, but she was sure as hell going to try.

He didn't come in right away, seemed to be having trouble with the bottom lock, the one on the doorknob.

The door was covered with steel sheeting, unpainted, and with traces of rust where it met the lower jamb. There were scratch marks on the metal, marks that might have been made by someone's nails. The light in the little room was dim. There was no window and only one lamp, the one above the mirror. The bulb was tiny, barely enough to read by—*if* they'd given her something to read.

At last the door swung open. The fluorescent lights in the corridor cast the person standing in the doorway into silhouette.

Marta breathed a sigh of relief. It wasn't The Goat. It was Rosélia, his bitch of a girlfriend, the one who'd lied to her and Andrea, the one who'd gotten them into this mess in the first place.

Rosélia came in cautiously. When Marta didn't make any aggressive moves, she smiled, locked the door behind her, and put the keys in her pocket. She had something in her right hand, and she held it up for Marta to see: a wooden club.

Marta flinched.

"Don't make me use it," the bitch said. "I really don't like hitting people."

"Your boyfriend does."

"Not really. And I certainly don't."

"So why did you bring it?" Marta asked.

"Because I'm not dumb enough to walk in here without it," Rosélia said. "You're quite the little wildcat, aren't you?"

Marta didn't reply.

"You shouldn't have talked to him like that," Rosélia said. "You made him angry."

"Where's Andrea?"

Rosélia's smile was more like a smirk.

"She's getting fucked. Third man today."

"I don't believe you. She wouldn't."

"She didn't have any choice. Neither do you. You just don't realize it yet. Andrea's okay, because she isn't stubborn like you are. She never threatened to bite and scratch the customers."

"I meant what I said."

Rosélia let out an exasperated sigh.

"Look, *querida*," she said, "why don't you just be reasonable? It's not that bad. Every girl has to go through it, sooner or later."

Marta didn't like the bitch calling her "querida." That's what Andrea always called her.

"Not every girl," she said. "I told you. Until I came here, there was no way I was going to let a man put his thing in me, not ever. You can force me, I know that, but I'm going to fight you every centimeter of the way."

"Sooner or later," Rosélia said, "you're going to get sick of bread and water. Sooner or later, you're going to get sick of sitting here on your own with nobody to talk to, nothing to read, no TV to watch. You'll change your mind. It's just a matter of time."

"I'll never change my mind."

"I'll talk to you again in a week."

She put her hand into the pocket where the keys were and turned toward the door, but Marta suddenly didn't want her to go.

Rosélia was right, maybe not about her giving in, but certainly about how bad it was to be alone with no one to talk to. Somebody, anybody, was better than just staring at the wall, or into the mirror.

"Why didn't he rape me?" she said in a low voice, less aggressive this time.

Rosélia turned around, a triumphant gleam in her eyes. She must have thought Marta's resistance was crumbling.

"How do you know he didn't?" she said. "You were unconscious, weren't you?"

"No. I wasn't. I just pretended I was."

"Aren't you the clever one?" Rosélia walked over and sat on the bed, making herself comfortable, as if she was a friend who'd just dropped by for a chat. "Why don't you come over here and sit down next to me?"

"I'll stand. Why don't you put down that club?"

"I'll hold on to it, thank you very much."

"Why didn't he do it? Rape me, I mean."

"That would be like owning a candy store and eating your finest chocolate. The Goat is a businessman. He saves the best for his customers."

"But I'm not the best. I'm not anything."

"No, querida, of course you aren't. You know that, and I know that, but the customers don't. They think you're something special because you're a virgin."

"And The Goat—"

"Knows better. The Goat has had plenty of virgins. Nowadays, he doesn't even like virgins."

"But his customers do."

Rosélia nodded.

"It's the idea that appeals to them. That, more than the fuck. They all want to be the first, the one they think you're going to remember. They're willing to pay through the nose for the privilege. In this business, querida, you'll never be more valuable than you are right now."

"How does he—"

"Do it? He holds an auction. The bidders are mostly the kids with rich fathers. It's a prestige thing for them, coming up with the money to be the first and bragging about it later, like they won a race or something. Stupid, I know, but that's the way the little bastards think. And you can stop looking at me like that. I don't make the rules. I'm just telling you the way it is."

"Who would even want me?" Marta said. "Who would want me when I look like this?"

She pointed to the bruise on her cheek.

"They don't care about your face, querida. They care about what's between your legs. Anyway, that bruise is your own fault. The Goat was reasoning with you, trying to get you to see his side of it. Then you had to get snotty. You tried to kick him. You tried to bite him. What did you expect him to do? Stand there and suck it up? You made him lose his temper. By the way, he told me to tell you no hard feelings."

"No hard feelings?"

"Not on his part. It wasn't personal. Just business."

Marta snorted, and gave Rosélia a look that would freeze water. "You lied to me," she said. "You lied to both of us."

"Yeah," Rosélia said, "I lied." She didn't seem to be in the least embarrassed. "Mostly, I just tell the girls I have jobs for them in hotels and restaurants. But I knew that wouldn't work with you and your friend. You had too much class. I still can't figure out why you were sleeping on that beach. Want to tell me?"

"No."

"Not even if I tell you where your girlfriend is?"

Marta thought about it. "Then, yes," she said. "You first."

Rosélia stared at her for a long moment as if she was reflecting on the benefits of honesty.

"Okay," she said at last. "The Goat sold her."

"Sold her? *Sold* Andrea?"

Rosélia nodded.

"Almost every new girl we get tells us she's a virgin. They think it will protect them. It doesn't, but we always check."

"What's that got to do with Andrea?"

"She wasn't a virgin, so there wasn't going to be any auction. Then, too, she was too old for—"

"Old? Andrea's eighteen."

"Yeah, like I said, too old. Men come to us for the younger girls. It's our specialty, so to speak. Your turn. Why were you sleeping on that beach?"

Marta took a deep breath. "My parents locked me up," she said. "They didn't want me to see Andrea again, said I was too young to commit myself. And Andrea's parents didn't approve of our relationship. They wouldn't let us stay at her place."

"So you ran away, and you had no place to sleep except for the beach?"

Marta ground the sole of her sandal into one of the dead cockroaches on the floor and nodded.

"And now you're wishing you'd stayed home," Rosélia said.

Marta looked up and met her eyes. "No," she said. "I'm wishing you'd left us alone."

"Too late for that, querida."

Rosélia's smile had a sharp edge.

"Not too late," Marta said. "The cops are looking for me, and when they find me—"

Rosélia laughed out loud.

"What a little dreamer you are," she said. "You've been gone for a couple of months. By now, the cops have forgotten all about you."

Marta shook her head.

"They haven't, and they won't. They'll keep looking, because my grandfather will make sure they keep looking."

"And who's he? The President of the Republic?"

"He's Roberto Malan."

She expected Rosélia to look shocked, but Rosélia gave her another one of those smiles.

"Malan the big-time deputado?"

"Yes."

"And I'm Princess Diana," Rosélia said.

"I'm not kidding."

"Me neither. That whole business about me being killed in Paris was a lie. Dodi and I have an apartment on the square in front of the *Teatro Municipal*, and after you've been auctioned off, maybe I'll let you fuck him. Meantime"—she got up and fished her keys out of her pocket—"you'll be sitting here playing with yourself, eating bread, and drinking water. Pound on the door when you change your mind."

"I'm not going to change my mind."

"Oh, yes, you are. Believe me."

This time, Marta didn't say a word when Rosélia got up to go. She was damned if she was going to let the bitch know she was starting to cry.

Chapter Five

AMSTERDAM

ASPIRANT JAN BENTINCK WAS twenty-two and in his third and final year at the police academy. The current stage of his training involved a series of one-on-one sessions with an experienced officer. When Bentinck's instructor told him he'd drawn Piet Kuipers, he also told him it was a stroke of luck. Kuipers was thought to be the best investigator in the whole *Korps Landelijke Politiediensten* and known as a man who enjoyed sharing his knowledge.

Kuipers worked out of a cramped space in the headquarters building on the Elandsgracht. His tiny cubicle had only one redeeming feature: a window with a view over the canal and the busy Nassaukade.

Kuipers offered Bentinck coffee, then began a lengthy lecture into which the investigator wove examples from past successes. But when he saw the young man's eyes glazing over, he took pity upon him.

"What I'm about to tell you is confidential. You're to keep your mouth shut on this one."

"Ja, mijneer," Bentinck sat up straighter in his chair. Kuipers had his full attention.

"The bomb that blew up that tram took a postal truck along with it."

"I saw the pictures in *De Telegraaf*, mijneer. Mail was all over the street."

"It was, and much of it was recovered. Among the stuff gathered up were a number of envelopes, each containing a single DVD. They were being shipped to addresses all over the world. You know what a snuff video is?"

"Snuff videos? I think I might have heard something, but . . ."

"It's a video where a person's life is snuffed out," Kuipers informed him.

"I thought that was an urban legend."

"It's not. The Russians have been doing it for some time and so have the Thais. The DVDs we apprehended begin with a man and woman engaging in sex. They end with her murder."

Kuipers described the murder in some detail.

Bentinck blinked. His pale skin turned even paler.

"We discovered the crime quite by chance," Kuipers continued. "A few of the envelopes were badly damaged, their addresses illegible. A postal inspector took one of them home in the hope that, if he played it, it might give him enough information to return it to the sender. The poor fellow made the mistake of watching it while he was eating dinner."

"Were you able to trace the material?"

"There were no return addresses, and there was nothing else inside the envelopes, just the DVDs."

Kuipers opened his desk drawer and took out a plastic evidence envelope. "This," he said, "is one of them."

Bentinck took the DVD and studied it. The grooves reflected a rainbow of light. He turned it over to look at the other side.

"No label," he said.

"And here's what it was being shipped in," Kuipers said, handing him another plastic sheath.

Bentinck examined both sides of the manila envelope through the plastic. The side with the address was scorched.

Kuipers leaned back in his chair and made a steeple with his fingers.

It was time to drive the lesson home.

"Name the five most important elements in the resolution of any crime," he said.

Kuipers turned red and proffered, "Persistence, good forensics, deduction . . ."

Kuipers smiled and said, "Good. But here are the two most important: dumb criminals and dumb luck. The operative word is 'dumb'. Dumb criminals talk about what they did. Dumb criminals don't cover their tracks; they leave things behind, they leave witnesses."

"And dumb luck?"

"Dumb luck is what we need when the criminals aren't dumb. Take a look at these."

Kuipers bent over and took four mailing envelopes, each in its own protective cover, out of a cardboard box. He lined them up in front of Bentinck as if he was laying out a game of solitaire.

Bentinck studied the envelopes. Each of them was scorched in the area of the address, but otherwise . . .

And then he got it. "They were all franked at the same post office."

Kuipers beamed. "Bravo. They were. It's on the Kloveniers-burgwal, just off the Nieuwmarkt. It's one of the smallest post offices in the city. All the envelopes were part of the same mailing."

"So you . . . we went to the post office?"

"We did. Dumb luck: a clerk remembered."

"He was actually able to remember a single customer based on the mailing envelopes alone?"

"Dumb luck," Kuipers repeated, "The individual in question was a *flikker*. The postal clerk shares his sexual preference.

The suspect has been making shipments at the same post office for the last couple of years. The clerk remembered his name, a first name only: Frans."

Kuipers tapped an identikit composite that had been on his desk all the time. He twirled it around so that Bentinck could get a better look.

"That's him," he said.

Bentinck studied the likeness. Frans looked to be in his late twenties or early thirties. He had curly blond hair combed straight back, an earring, a weak chin, and a petulant mouth.

"We figured he had to be living in the neighborhood of the post office," Kuipers said. "It helped that he had a penchant for wearing bright pink. People remembered him. His last name is Oosterbaan. We tracked him to a canal house on the Oudezijds Voorburgwal."

"And arrested him?"

"Not yet. We're going to roust him out of bed in the dead of night. It's more of a psychological shock that way, makes people more likely to tell us things. Want to come along?"

THE FIRST report shocked Arie Schubski awake, causing him to sit bolt upright. Then there was another *bang* followed by a clatter. Arie threw the covers aside and leaped out of bed.

By the time he'd opened the bedroom door, dark figures were already sprinting up the staircase: men in police uniforms, carrying guns. He slammed the door and tried to lock it, but he wasn't quick enough. They forced it open.

The guns had spotlight-type devices mounted above the barrels. Two of the beams focused on him. The cop behind one said, "Hands up. Don't move unless you want to get shot."

Arie lifted his hands.

Frans stared straight in front of him like a deer in head-lights. He held the covers up to his chin as if for protection.

"We're talking to you too, mijneer. Hands up." The polite form of address didn't match the speaker's tone of voice.

Hesitantly, Frans raised his hands, dropping the covers, exposing his hairless chest.

They pulled him out of bed, put him next to Arie, and slapped handcuffs on them both.

"How many other people in the house?" one of the cops asked.

Frans spoke in a high-pitched and terrified voice. "No one. No one else," spilling his guts before the cops had even started serious interrogation.

Arie knew right then that Frans was going to cause serious problems.

THEY SPLIT them up, keeping Frans in the bedroom, lead-ing Arie into his office where windows overlooked the street. The street was in the heart of the Zeedijk, Amsterdam's red-light district. The house had been standing there for well over three hundred years. The law wouldn't allow Arie to make any modifications to the facade, but he'd gutted the interior and rebuilt it to suit his tastes and needs.

He was going to miss it.

On the floor above him, the top floor, was the heart of his business: one large room with tape players, format convert-ers, DVD burners, and computers that controlled them all. He could make copies from DVDs, but he could also make them from Betacam tapes, both SP and digital, and in Secam, PAL, and NTSC. And that's all he did: copy and mail. Once they found that out, the cops were going to grill him for the names of the producers, but the cops were going to be disappointed. And that meant they were going to get angry, which meant that the judge would probably throw the book at him. He might get as much as ten years, but he was prepared for that, prepared as anyone could be without it actually having happened.

You couldn't run a business like Arie's without confronting the reality that, someday, you were going to be raided by the police. Well, now it was over. Now, he could relax. No more fear. The money was safely squirreled away. A few years in jail wouldn't kill him. He might even get away with less than ten, if Frans would only keep his mouth shut.

MARTIN SMIT lived in a spacious apartment about three kilometers away from Arie Schubski's canal house. The duplex was just off the Leidseplein and had cost him just short of three million Euros, all paid in cash.

Smit had been born in Suriname, but he harbored no memory of the place, nor any desire to go back.

During the last few weeks leading up to the 25th of November, 1975, the day the country would receive its independence, the government of The Netherlands, in a gesture typical of a land famed for political correctness, offered Dutch citizenship to those inhabitants of the colony able to reach the Fatherland prior to Independence Day. Half of the population of Suriname took them up on their offer, and much of the other half might have done so if they'd had money to pay for a flight.

Before 1974, a black face like Smit's had been a rarity on the streets of Amsterdam; by November of the following year, there were neighborhoods, like the Bijlmermeer, where you saw nothing else.

Smit arrived speaking only *Sranang Tongo*, but he quickly mastered Dutch and breezed through the country's school system (ten years of it, anyway) before he got bored and quit.

By then, his speech was indistinguishable from that of any other Amsterdammer.

At fourteen, he'd already begun dealing drugs. By the time he was thirty, Smit, now known to most as The Surinamer, had become the head of a criminal enterprise called the Rakkers, an organization almost as international as Royal Dutch Shell or Philips.

The Rakkers' main business was the production and distribution of methylenedioxymethamphetamine, better known as Ecstasy, but they also served as middlemen for criminal enterprises across the globe. If you wanted something, they were the people who knew where to find it. A murder for hire? They could locate the man (or woman) who'd commit it for you. Drugs of any nature? They knew where to go. They profited by putting criminals into contact with criminals and by promoting transactions. That was how the Surinamer had come to be acquainted with Arie Schubski.

Arie, who had begun his business dealing exclusively with pornography, had been receiving an ever-increasing number of requests for snuff videos. No one would be crazy enough to try to make them in The Netherlands. The country was too small, the cops were too good, and the disappearance of protagonists would quickly be noticed. But if Arie could find foreign producers, the potential for profit was great.

He called the Surinamer and invited him for coffee.

Smit used the Rakkers to put the word out. As a worldwide supplier of Ecstasy, the gang had relationships far and wide, contacts in Thailand, in Russia, in Brazil, all of them places where people might be able to get away with killing people for other people's amusement. And, when Schubski met their price, some of them started doing just that.

The producer in Moscow was a nightclub owner who ran girls on the side. The one in Bangkok was an opium exporter, who drew his protagonists from across the border in Cambodia. The woman in Manaus was someone Smit had sold a number of false passports to, who'd indicated she was open to any profitable proposition.

But now the shoe was on the other foot.

Arie Schubski's arrest had made the front page of *De Telegraaf*. The Surinamer hadn't found it necessary to read the whole article, just enough of it to discover what the cops had found.

Arie and his little friend Frans would obviously be going away for a long time. They wouldn't need The Surinamer's help any more.

But the suppliers would. If they were going to stay in business, they were going to need a new distributor. And Martin Smit, The Surinamer, intended to furnish one.

Chapter Six

THE SMELL OF FRESH coffee, beer, and *poffertjes*—sugared pancakes—hung over the terrace of the American Hotel on the Leidseplein. The place was packed, but the Surinamer had been lucky. He'd captured a table that put his back to the wall of the building, as far as was physically possible from the passing streetcars. A hundred meters to his right, tourists were lining up for the canal tours. Others were flocking over the bridge toward the Rijksmuseum on the Stadhouderskade. Amsterdammers, enjoying an unprecedented seventh straight day of sunshine, were on the terrace in force. Most of the voices around him were Dutch and, like him, many were talking on their cell phones.

"They busted Schubski and Oosterbaan," The Surinamer said, cupping a cautious hand over his mouth.

"I don't want to know anything about their personal lives," the banker in Riga snapped. "The only thing that concerns me is their accounts. Anything else?"

"No. That's it for today."

The banker grunted and hung up without saying good-bye.

The employees of the Latvian Overseas Bank didn't go out of their way to be cordial. They didn't have to be.

The Surinamer lifted a finger to summon a waiter.

"Mijneer?"

The Surinamer ordered a beer on tap.

The waiter returned three minutes later with a brimming glass of Amstel. The Surinamer didn't usually drink beer when he was making his calls; it was too diuretic. But the day was warm and talking had made him thirsty.

The call from the woman in Brazil came in right on time, at 11:25. She started talking as soon as she recognized his voice.

"Where's my money?"

"We've got a problem, Carla. The cops busted Arie Schubski."

Carla—or whatever her name really was—remained silent for a moment. The line didn't. The Surinamer could hear static and crackling.

"You still there?" he said.

"Yes," she said. "Is he likely to talk?"

"Not Arie."

"How about that little princess he lives with?"

"Frans Oosterbaan." The Surinamer snorted contemptuously.

"Yeah, him."

"One time," The Surinamer said, "I dropped by to pick up some of our money. Arie wasn't home, so I had a little chat with Frans, told him if he ever shot off his mouth about me, I'd get him, cut off his balls, and let him bleed to death. Before our conversation, I was worried he might break if the cops bent him far enough. That's why I figured we had to talk."

"And now?"

"Now, I'm no longer worried."

"Good. How about finding me another distributor?"

The Surinamer had been waiting for the question. He took another sip of beer, letting her think he was considering it.

"Now that the heat is on," he said, "the new guy's gonna want a bigger percentage."

"Why am I not surprised?"

"What do you mean by that?" The Surinamer said sharply, even though he knew exactly what she meant by that.

"Now that the heat is on," she said, "the price of my work just went up by fifty percent. Go ahead and find me somebody. We'll work it out."

"I'm on it," The Surinamer said.

THE DUTCH cops were on it too.

That morning, all of Smit's calls were being recorded. He'd been tripped up by an instance of what Hoofd Inspecteur Kuipers liked to call dumb luck.

A LITTLE over four weeks earlier, a water pipe had broken in the apartment where The Surinamer kept his answering device. After repeated and unsuccessful attempts to contact someone living in the apartment, the manager of the building asked the police to force the door.

After a short discussion between a judge and the landlord's lawyer, the proper paperwork was issued. The cops called a locksmith. Why break down a door when you don't have to? The locksmith made short work of getting them into the place. The maintenance people repaired the broken pipe and departed.

The police stayed. They were intrigued by the sole contents of an otherwise empty apartment: an answering machine sitting in the middle of the living room floor.

Research revealed that the individual who'd rented the flat had been doing so for nineteen months and had been dead for a year and a half. The rent, however, was still being paid directly into the landlord's *postgiro* out of a numbered account in Riga.

It was time to bring in Hoofd Inspecteur Kuipers.

Kuipers listened to the greeting on the machine, a teenage voice reciting a series of numbers in English. The numbers began with the digits zero and six and totaled ten in number, leading Kuipers to conclude (1) that the digits were the number of a cellular telephone, (2) that the answering device was an anonymous way of divulging it, and (3) that anyone who took such precautions was up to no good.

Kuipers tried calling the number, but a recorded voice informed him that the phone was either switched off or out of service. There was no voice mail.

Rather than meddle with the equipment, he gave instructions to keep the place under discreet surveillance, to make a duplicate key for the lock and to erase all evidence of a visit. Two days later a kid showed up and recorded a new number. They followed him back to his home and put a man to watch him, but they didn't pick him up. They made a note of the new number, but they didn't dial it. They simply put a tap on it.

Within a week, Kuipers had discovered (1) that his suppositions were correct, (2) that the man using the phones was Martin Smit, aka The Surinamer, and (3) that he was switching the phones on only minutes before using them.

"MARTIN SMIT, eh?" Kuipers said after he'd studied the transcript of the first series of calls. He was talking to Inspector Guus Hein, his principal assistant. "Well, well. Not just drugs any more. That lowlife scum has diversified. And now we know why we never get any useful information from the taps we have on his other numbers. The scumbag set up a whole alternative system of communication. His associates call the answering device and get a new contact number every week."

"You want to put surveillance on Smit?" Hein asked.

"Certainly not. It might spook him."

During the following weeks, they recorded Smit receiving calls to four successive numbers. He took care to make few outgoing calls and kept the incoming ones to a minute or less. On the fourth of May, they registered an incoming from a woman he addressed as Carla. She began by dunning him about money and went on to pester him about a distributor, an affair in which he told her he'd made little progress. He asked her to drop her price. She said she wouldn't, but that didn't mean she wasn't working. She was stockpiling material, and if he didn't get his ass in gear she'd take measures to find someone else.

The police managed to get a trace, but it led to a prepaid cell phone in Brazil, which wasn't a lot of help.

As soon Kuipers had finished reading the transcript, he picked up the phone and asked for a few minutes with his boss, Albertus Montsma.

TWO HOURS later, Kuipers and Montsma were sitting across a desk from each other.

"I think you can safely assure the *burgemeester*," Kuipers said, "that the videos aren't being produced here, only the copies."

"Thank God for that," Montsma said.

Amsterdam depended heavily on tourism. Sex and drugs were among the attractions, but the city fathers underplayed them. They preferred to present the city as a family destination and would not look kindly upon a revelation that snuff videos were being produced in their midst. Distribution of the damned things was bad enough.

"Some of the worst," Kuipers said, "are coming from Brazil."

He told his boss about the telephone call, adding that the woman had spoken in English and that her English was fluent.

"That young fellow, Costa," Montsma said, "Is he still here?"

"The Brazilian? Yes, he's still here. I just saw him downstairs, talking to Hugo de Groot. You want him involved?"

"I know his uncle," Montsma said.

"His uncle?"

"Mario Silva, Chief Inspector of the Brazilian Federal Police. He's a good cop."

Kuipers grunted. Coming from Bert Montsma, *a good cop* was high praise.

"You think Costa might be of some help?" he said.

"I don't know," Montsma said, "but I'm sure his uncle will be. Let's get the young man up here, shall we?"

HECTOR COSTA was a slim fellow of slightly below average height. His mother was Mario Silva's sister and only sibling; Hector, her only child.

His father, Claudio, an architect, had been thirty-four years old when he was shot to death. Hector, now thirty-two, looked nothing like him. Claudio's eyes had been blue. Hector's were black. Claudio had been fair-skinned. Hector, like the rest of the Silva family, was dark, so dark that his mother's ancestors had been suspected of Moorish blood. And Moorish blood had not been a good thing to have in sixteenth-century Portugal.

In those days, the country was under the Spanish yoke and subject to the Spanish Inquisition. Moorish blood was regarded as a sign of less than complete devotion to the true faith, and less than complete devotion to the true faith could be fatal. To escape distrustful inquisitors, the Silvas had left their native country and moved to Brazil, a melting pot where the prejudice against darker skin was less strong and the Inquisition less pervasive.

They chose São Paulo as their new home. It wasn't a city then, not even a village, just a frontier outpost founded by the Jesuits for the express purpose of converting the Indians. The place grew little over the next one hundred and fifty years, remaining a sleepy hamlet well into the eighteenth century. That changed when the Europeans developed a passion for coffee. The soil and climate around São Paulo were found to be ideally suited to the new crop. The great coffee barons became cash-rich. They had money to invest, and many of them invested it in manufacturing. By the mid-twentieth century, the city had become the premier industrial center, the largest city in the country.

And the most dangerous.

Hector's maternal grandfather had been shot to death by bandits in 1978, just two years after Hector was born. His grandmother, raped by the same individuals and forced to watch her husband's murder, lost all interest in life and didn't survive the year.

The incident motivated Mario, Hector's uncle, to give up a promising career as a lawyer and join the federal police.

Nine years later, his nephew had been moved in the same direction.

On a sunny Saturday morning, Hector's parents were driving to a shopping center. His father, Claudio Costa, was behind the wheel. Hector was in the back seat. He'd been playing with a toy, a Rubik's cube, when he heard a voice.

"Hand over your watch."

A man was standing just outside, pointing the barrel of a gun at his father's head. They were stopped at a traffic light, locked in by other automobiles. The day was hot. The car had no air-conditioning. The windows were open.

The watch, his mother told him later, was a family heirloom. His father was reluctant to give it up. Twenty years on, as an experienced cop, Hector would have recognized the man with the gun as a drug addict, trying to gather enough money for his next fix. At the time, he just thought the man was scary. His mother folded the newspaper she'd been reading over her lap, thereby concealing her wedding ring. The ring was the only jewelry she ever wore on the street.

"Claudio," she said, keeping her voice low and steady, "give him the watch."

Almost everyone in the extended family had been robbed at one time or another. If it wasn't some kid threatening you with a sliver of glass, or a gang with clubs and rocks, it was someone like this: a frightened little man with bloodshot eyes, a two-day growth of beard, and a revolver that was trembling in his hand.

Claudio took his hands off the steering wheel, as if he was going to unfasten the clasp on his watch, but then he swiveled to his left and made a grab for the revolver. The man stepped backward. There was a loud explosion, louder than any firecracker Hector had ever heard. His father flew backward, as if someone had given him a push.

Hector stared at the shooter, and for a moment they locked eyes. Then the man was putting the weapon into a canvas bag and backing away.

He looked down at his father. Blood covered the front of his shirt. Sucking noises were coming out of a hole in his chest. Hector's mother was saying "Oh, God, oh, God, oh, God," over and over. Hector leaned over the seat, buried his nose in his mother's neck, and tried to comfort her.

The sucking noises stopped.

KUIPERS ASKED Hector how he liked Amsterdam. Hector said he liked Amsterdam very much. Montsma asked him if the conference on the suppression of the drug trade had been useful. Hector said it had. Then, unlike Brazil where the pleasantries would have gone on for at least another five minutes, they got down to business.

"You heard about that bomb, the one set off by a group

calling itself Justice for Islam?" Kuipers asked.

Hector nodded. "Terrible thing," he said, wondering why they wanted to talk to him.

"The bomb," Kuipers said, "also took out a mail truck. The explosion blew mail all over the street." He paused.

Hector waited for him to get to the point.

"Among the scattered envelopes," Kuipers continued, "were a number of DVDs. The newspapers are calling them 'videos that are pornographic in nature', but that's not the half of it. They were snuff videos. The action was all covered in one shot, no cuts, and at the end there was something . . . convincing. Proof that the action wasn't faked."

Hector frowned. "Proof? What kind of proof?"

"After the murderer strangled her," Kuipers said, "he cut off her head with an ax."

Chapter Seven

MANAUS

MARTA AWOKE TO FIND her door ajar, a crack of light spilling in from the corridor. At first, she was too wary to approach it. What if they were toying with her, what if someone, maybe The Goat, was standing on the other side?

She sat up, legs together, fighting the urge to urinate. After a while she could stand it no more. She stood, reached for the knob and drew the door toward her.

No Goat.

She stuck her head into the corridor.

Nobody.

She went to the bucket and used it.

No one disturbed her.

She pulled up her panties, washed her hands at the sink, and resumed her seat on the bed.

Reason told her the open door was no accident, no mistake. But it *might* have been, and so she'd be foolish not to take advantage of it.

When they'd brought her in, there'd been a dusty burlap sack over her head. She hadn't seen anything of the building, and had little idea of its floor plan, except for the location of the shower. That was about ten meters down the corridor to the right. Rosélia took her there every other day in the small hours of the morning when the rest of the house was asleep. The soap was brown and smelled like medicine. The water was lukewarm, never hot. She only got two minutes, and she was expected to dry herself with a rough fragment of terrycloth; but after the grinding monotony of her prison, every shower felt like a holiday.

When it was over, Rosélia would throw some clean clothing at her and push her back to her cell where she was permitted to dress.

But it wasn't the bathroom she was thinking of at the moment. She was thinking about another door she'd seen in the corridor, bigger and heavier than all the others. She just *knew* it led to the outside.

Gingerly, she stepped through the doorway. To her left, she could hear voices. Except for the choice of words, they could have been coming from the playground of an all-girls' school

One girl said, "I told her she could kiss my ass."

Another was saying she didn't care about how many other girls he'd done it to, there was no way she was going to let him do it to her.

Still another exclaimed ". . . three hundred Reais. Can you imagine? Three hundred Reais?" As if that was a fortune, when it wasn't even *half* of what Marta used to pay for one of her dresses.

The whores. It had to be them.

Marta turned the other way, to the right, toward the bathroom, toward the door that led to freedom. As she scurried along, a random thought popped into her head: her uncle had once given her a pair of hamsters for Christmas. By Easter, they were dead, but she remembered how there'd been a maze inside their cage. They'd scurry back and forth along the corridors of that maze. They'd gone on scurrying, every waking hour, until they died.

Her heart gave a leap. She'd been right about the door. It *did* lead to the outside. She could see daylight shining through a gap at the bottom.

Cautiously, she reached out a hand and turned the knob. The door didn't budge, but a loud bell began ringing with an ear-splitting clang.

She ran back to her cell and sat on the bed. A moment later, she heard a door open and a woman's unhurried steps coming along the corridor to her left. The steps paused. The ringing stopped. The girls, too, had fallen silent.

Rosélia appeared in the doorway.

"Tomorrow," she said, with a triumphant grin, "try going the other way."

She slammed the door, and Marta heard the key turning in the lock.

Chapter Eight

BRASILIA

THE DAY AFTER HER delivery, Irene Silva's obstetrician came into her hospital room, sat down in the chair next to her bed and gently told her she'd have no more children. She and Mario had planned on two. They were disappointed, but not devastated. Their newborn son got a clean bill of health from the pediatrician. They knew couples who didn't have any children at all. One baby was surely enough to make their happiness complete. And he did, for the next eight years.

There was a photograph from that happy time: all of them crowded together on a couch. On the far left was Irene, radiant and smiling with her arm around little Mario. Next to her was the youngster himself, proud of his new school uniform, pointing at the crest on his white shirt. Next to him, leaning against his shoulder, Clara's son Hector, five years older than little Mario, his face serious, as if he could look into the future and see the trouble lurking there. Lastly, on the far right, Mario Silva himself, his hair and moustache still black, without a sign of gray.

In the photo his son had a grin from ear to ear. He looked robust and healthy, but the sickness had been in him even then. Four months later he was dead, struck down by leukemia thirteen days before his ninth birthday. He died on the eighth of May, 1989.

The next day Silva put the photo into his desk drawer, and there it sat.

When he'd become a chief inspector, they'd offered him a

modern glass desk, with an accompanying credenza, and no drawers. He'd turned it down, just so he could have the photo close to him, but in a place where no one could see it.

And what he did with the photo, he did with his memories: locked them away, never discussed them with anyone.

It hurt too much when he did.

Irene handled her grief in a different way.

She drank.

Most days she'd sleep until noon. Then she'd get up and spend a few hours working at the orphanage to which Silva sent twenty percent of his salary. That, too, was something he never discussed.

Sometimes the children at the orphanage could coax a smile from Irene's lips, just a smile, never a deep, full-throated laugh like the ones that bubbled out of her in the old days. When he could, Silva would take an afternoon off and stop by, just to see her like that, smiling, with the kids, before she went home and got drunk.

She usually started at five o'clock in the afternoon. Five o'clock exactly, trying to prove to him that she wasn't really an alcoholic, just a woman having a cocktail at the end of the day. She'd insist that alcoholics drank in the morning. She didn't drink in the morning, only at night.

But it was every night. And it was always to excess.

When Silva was on a trip, he'd try to ring home before eight P.M. If he called much later he'd hear Irene's slurred speech and know she wasn't absorbing half of what he said. But he'd call anyway, because he knew she needed to hear his voice, even if they weren't going to have a coherent conversation. He worried about what would happen to her if someone were to kill him. He'd taken to being more cautious. For her sake.

* * *

AND NOW, here it was, the eighth of May come around again. On the night before the anniversary of her son's death, Irene Silva hadn't gone to bed at all.

At seven-thirty A.M., her husband found her on the couch in the living room, an empty vodka bottle on the coffee table in front of her, clutching little Mario's teddy bear in her arms. She didn't wake when he carried her into the bedroom and tucked her in.

At ten, Hector called from Amsterdam. It was five hours later there, and Hector sounded more awake than Silva felt.

"Today's the day," were the first words Hector said.

"Yes," Silva said.

"How's *Tia* Irene?"

"Sleeping. I hope."

"But she didn't sleep last night?"

"No. Not last night. How was the drug conference?"

Hector knew the signs. His uncle wanted to talk about something else, anything else. "Like being inside a bag full of cats," he said.

"The Americans blaming the Bolivians and Colombians for growing it; the Bolivians and Colombians telling them that it's their own damned fault for creating a market?"

"And the other Europeans all ganging up on the Dutch because they think they're too soft. It didn't help, either, that the Dutch have cornered the world's Ecstasy market. These days, they've got more labs than windmills."

"And we import more of it than their cheese and their chocolate. You pick up any promising leads?"

"Not as far as drugs are concerned, but there's something else. I have to see you."

"Personally?"

"Personally. My flight from Amsterdam arrives in São

Paulo tomorrow morning at seven. I'll catch a connecting flight and come right to Brasilia."

"It's that serious?"

"Yes."

"Then you'd better bring Arnaldo."

Agente Arnaldo Nunes was about Silva's age and had been a cop for almost as long. The fact that he hadn't achieved a lofty position in the hierarchy had nothing to do with being irreverent and sarcastic, which he was, nor to do with his abilities and competence, both of which were considerable. But he'd come from a poor family, married young, and had never been able to raise the money to go to law school. Without a law degree, the statutes governing the federal police blocked him from becoming a *delegado*, which was the first step to every other position of major responsibility. So on paper, Arnaldo remained a lowly *agente*. In practice, he wielded far more power and influence.

"What do you mean, bring Arnaldo?" Hector asked. "Isn't he there with you?"

"He's in São Paulo at the moment. I'll call him and tell him to meet your flight."

"It's Air France."

"Not KLM?"

"No. I connect in Paris."

"Number?"

"AF 0454."

"Consider it done. Now, tell me."

Hector gave his uncle a rough overview of the situation, and then described his conversation with Montsma and Kuipers. He finished by saying, "There are tapes from Russia and Thailand, too, but the Brazilian ones are the most disturbing. They made me sick, Tio, physically sick. They all have titles in English. One is called *Killing the Vampire*. The killer uses a sledgehammer to drive a sharp stake through the woman's chest."

"Ouch," Silva said.

"All of them cover the murder in one shot. And they all end with either dismemberment or severe mutilation of the victim. Kuipers thinks that's to prove to the buyers that what they're seeing is real, not faked. That it's proof of death. Another one was entitled *The Lumberjack's Revenge*. The killer takes a chain saw and—"

"That's enough. I get the picture. How can they tell which ones came from here?"

"They've all got live sound. It appears that the . . . clients like hearing what's going on."

"Sick bastards. Any luck following the money?"

"None. They were using a bank in Riga."

"Riga?"

"Capital of Latvia. Apparently, Latvian banks are much tougher to deal with than the Swiss. Montsma says they won't violate their security for anyone."

"How about the master tapes? Any fingerprints?"

"Only Schubski's and Oosterbaan's. But I got a list of their clients. It was password protected and encrypted, but Oosterbaan gave it up."

"Any Brazilians?"

"A few."

"Addresses?"

"Mostly post office boxes and E-mail addresses so they can be advised about new releases."

"Send them to me. I'll have Arnaldo lean on the Internet service providers, get us names and addresses for the account holders."

"The Dutch don't have a law that makes it illegal to buy

the stuff, only to sell it. They can't prosecute the customers in their own country. It's got them hopping mad."

"I'm not sure we can prosecute either. I'll have to check. How about the killers? More than one?"

"Different in every DVD."

"You get frame blowups?"

"Being made as we speak. But there's something more. There's a Brazilian woman whose phone call was taped. She seems to have been a supplier."

"The woman. Is her voice in the background on any of the DVDs?"

"The last one. She spoke English with Smit, and Portuguese on the DVD, but they did a voiceprint analysis. Same person."

"What did she say?"

"It sounded to me like she was operating the camera and directing the action at the same time. She tells the murderer to hold the victim still, because there's too much movement to zoom in and get a tight close-up of her eyes. Later, she tells him to get out the ax and do what she told him to do."

"And he did it? Just like that?"

"No. Not just like that. He looks at the camera and shakes his head. He tells her it isn't worth the trouble, that the woman is already dead."

Hector paused. His uncle could hear him swallow as he remembered.

"And?" he prompted.

"She told him he was a cretin and to do it anyway."

Chapter Nine

MANAUS

WITH CONSCIOUSNESS CAME FEAR.

Marta turned her head and looked at the door.

Ajar.

She toyed with the idea of not playing Rosélia's game, but the alternative, another day of being alone, caused her throat to constrict and made it hard for her to breathe.

She inhaled deeply, kept on inhaling until her heartbeat settled down. Then she stuck her head into the corridor.

Empty.

She crossed the threshold and turned left. The sound of high-pitched voices got louder, the smell of frying onions and garlic stronger, as she approached the green door at the end of the corridor.

She turned the knob and pushed.

A head turned in her direction, then another. Conversation stopped dead. Marta found herself in a bar filled with girls. Several wore T-shirts, others nightgowns. The youngest, a brunette with big eyes, looked to be no more than twelve. A *mulata*, taller than the others by half a head, and with dirty blond hair the texture of steel wool, opened her mouth to say something.

But then she froze like a nocturnal animal caught in a searchlight.

Marta spun around. The Goat, a menacing figure almost six-foot-two in height and an obese two hundred and sixty pounds, was less than a foot behind her. She flinched.

He smiled at her reaction, brushed her aside and headed for a raised platform in the center of the room. Like dogs with their master, the girls' eyes followed him every step of the way.

Light on his feet for such a big man, he mounted the platform. Muscular biceps stretched the sleeves of his T-shirt. His blue eyes were set close together and seemed out of place in a face as dark as any Indian's.

"Good morning, my children," he said.

One and all, except for Marta, they murmured a response.

"You girls over by the bar," he said, "come closer. This is important."

He waited until they'd rearranged themselves, until he could see the entire group. Then he pointed a stubby finger. "This," he said, "is Marta. She's eating my food, she's sleeping in one of my beds and she hasn't done a damned thing to work off her debt. What do you think about that? You, Topaz?"

Topaz, the girl with the steel wool hair flinched. "*Senhor?*"

"You think that's fair, Topaz? You think it's fair she's eating my food and sleeping under my roof, and she isn't doing a damned thing to earn her keep?"

The mulata looked down at her bare feet.

The Goat cupped a hand behind an ear. "I can't hear you."

"No, Senhor," the mulata said, almost inaudibly.

"You're goddamned right it's not." The Goat's voice was a whip, but when he spoke again his tone was almost gentle. "I'm a reasonable man. You know that, don't you girls? You know I'm a reasonable man?"

No one said a word.

"I'll take silence as agreement," he said. "So, as a reasonable man, here's what I'm going to do. I'm going to leave her here all afternoon. You girls are going to reason with her and get her to change her attitude."

Marta shook her head. "I'm not—"

"Shut up," The Goat snapped. "I'm not talking to you; I'm talking to them."

Marta glared at him.

He ignored her and let his gaze sweep over the other girls. "If you're not successful," he said, "I'm gonna be unhappy, and all of you know what happens when I'm unhappy."

He walked back through the green door and slammed it behind him.

Topaz was still shaken. She'd risen to her feet when addressed, but now she sank back into her chair and put her head in her hands. The other girls turned, as one, to stare at Marta.

Marta braved it out. She swallowed and said, "I came here with another girl. Her name is Andrea. Has anyone seen her? Anyone heard anything about a girl named Andrea?"

No one had.

They had lunch right there in the *boate*: rice, beans, and fried fish, cooked and served by an old woman the girls called *Dona* Ana. No one invited Marta to share a table, so she ate standing at the bar, keeping to herself, knowing they'd be at her before long. Under the circumstances, it was no use to try to make friends. She wasn't about to give in, and they'd hate her for that. Not only because they feared The Goat, but also because they were all *putas* and she wasn't about to become one. They'd take that to mean she thought she was better than they were. And they'd be right.

She was still eating when the door opened again, and a man with a broken nose stuck his head into the room. He beckoned to the little brunette with the big eyes. She went to him, still chewing a mouthful of rice and beans. There was a rustle of relief from the other girls as soon as the door had closed behind them.

Lunch over, the girls turned their backs on Marta, drew their chairs into a circle and started talking in hushed tones. Every now and then one would turn her head to make sure Marta was keeping her distance. While they were at it, Marta took one of the vacated chairs on the far side of the room.

The talking was still going on when the big-eyed girl came back, a cigarette dangling from her lower lip. She looked longingly at the group. A few girls saw her, but no one invited her to join. She took another puff on her cigarette and sat down across from Marta.

"This girl you mentioned," she said.

"Andrea?"

"Yes, Andrea. How old is she?"

"How old are you?"

The little girl took another drag on her cigarette.

"Ten," she said, exhaling smoke.

Marta didn't know how to respond. After a moment, she said, "Andrea is eighteen."

"Oh," the little girl said. "Well, then, it's plain."

"What do you mean by 'plain'?"

"The Goat doesn't keep anybody as old as that unless they look younger, or they have lots of regular customers. Your friend, Andrea, does she look younger?"

Marta thought before answering. "No," she said.

"See? That's why we never met her. When they're old like that, and haven't been brought up in his house, The Goat gets rid of them. Sometimes he lets them work the street, but then they have to give him money until they pay back what they owe."

"Owe? What do you mean, *owe*?"

"Well, he brought you here, didn't he?"

"He didn't. Rosélia did."

The little girl sighed at the need to explain something so obvious.

"Rosélia works for him, but The Goat has all the money. So it's him you owe, not her."

"Rosélia told us she had modeling jobs for us."

When she'd finished laughing, the little girl said, "You fell for that? I'm only ten, and I wouldn't have fallen for that. Where did you come from?"

"Recife."

The girl looked surprised.

"All the way from Recife? How long did that take?"

"Not long. We flew."

"In an airplane?"

"In an airplane. Of course."

"I always wanted to fly in an airplane. Tell me what it's like to fly in an airplane."

"Later. Does the Goat think I owe him money?"

"Of course, you do," the little girl said impatiently. "You owe him for the airplane, and for the food you ate, and for anything he gives you, like perfume. Did he give you any perfume?"

"No. He didn't give me any perfume. The only thing he gave me was a beating. I'd love to pay *that* back."

The girl put one of her little fingers on Marta's lips.

"Don't say things like that," she said. "If you say things like that, and he hears you, he'll do it again."

"Why does he get rid of the older girls?"

The little girl shrugged. "They aren't chosen. If you don't get chosen, you don't earn him any money. The Goat doesn't keep you unless you earn him money."

The girl had smoked her cigarette almost down to the filter. She contemplated the ash for a moment and then ground it out in the empty margarine can she'd been using as an ashtray.

"How did you get here?" Marta asked.

"I tried living on the street, but it's hard, you know. When you're little, like me, they fuck you, but they don't pay you. They say they're going to, but when they're finished they don't care. I started asking for the money first, but then they'd pay me and take it back afterwards."

"Why didn't you go to the police?"

"Why? So they could fuck me too?"

"Why do you have to . . . fuck anybody? Are you an orphan?"

A cloud passed over the little girl's face. "No, but we never had any money. When you're really hungry, and you only have one thing to sell, you sell it. And it wasn't like I was a virgin any more. My stepfather took care of that."

"Don't you just hate it? Being here?"

The girl shook her head. "It's not so bad. There's always food, and the men who come here, they like me."

"*Like* you?"

The little girl looked hurt. "It's true," she said, defensively. "You saw Osvaldo just now."

"Osvaldo?"

"Osvaldo." She pointed to her face. "The one with the broken nose. He chose me. He could have had any of the other girls, but he chose me."

"I'm sorry. I didn't mean I didn't believe you, I just meant—"

"What?"

"Well, that you're so . . . young."

"That's what the other girls say, that I'm too young, too young to be their friend. You don't want to be my friend either, do you?"

"I *do* want to be your friend. I didn't mean too young for me. I meant for the men."

The little girl shook her head.

"But that's just it," she said. "I've got something the other girls don't have. Guess what it is."

Marta looked at her. She wore a T-shirt that was so big on her, it served as a dress. She wasn't particularly pretty, not even particularly clean. The stench of the man she'd been with still clung to her.

"I have no idea," Marta said. "What?"

"This," the girl said, lifting her T-shirt to expose her bare chest.

For a moment, Marta didn't understand. Then she did.

The little girl's breasts hadn't yet begun to bud.

Chapter Ten

BRASILIA

HECTOR COSTA LOOKED LIKE hell.

There were dark circles under his bloodshot eyes, and the long hours he'd spent inside windowless Dutch conference rooms had bleached his customary tan.

"You sure you want to do this now?" Silva said. "You could go over to my place and take a nap first, you know."

"I told him the same thing," Arnaldo said. "But he's stubborn, like someone else I know."

Silva raised an eyebrow. "And just who might that *someone* be, Agente Nunes?"

"My uncle Eustacio," Arnaldo said, without missing a beat.

"You haven't got an uncle Eustacio."

Arnaldo opened his mouth to refute that, but Hector interceded. "If I was going to sleep," he said, "I would have done it in São Paulo and in the loving arms of my *squeeze*."

"Squeeze, is it?" Arnaldo said. "Does Gilda know you call her that? And where did you pick up a word like 'squeeze'?"

"She doesn't know it, not yet, because I have yet to see her since I got back," Hector said. "As to the word, it's a bit of European sophistication that I learned from my new friend, Chief Inspector Lane of Scotland Yard."

"That does it," Arnaldo said to Silva. "You got to stop sending the kid off on conferences. Every time he gets back, I have to scrape the sophistication off. It smells bad, and it gets under my fingernails."

"Is that what it is?" Silva said. "I always thought the stuff under your fingernails was a consequence of poor personal hygiene."

There was a knock on the door of Silva's office.

"Come," Silva said.

A guy in a white lab coat appeared in the doorway.

"Where do you want it, Chief Inspector?"

"Over there, Soares," Silva said. "Turn the screen toward us."

Soares went out into the hallway and returned, wheeling a metal cart almost as tall as himself.

The top shelf of the cart was entirely occupied by a large TV monitor. The two shelves below it contained three tape players, VHS, Beta SP, and digital Beta. There was also a DVD player and a computer with a couple of disk drives.

"DVD, right?" Soares asked.

Silva looked at his nephew.

"DVD," Hector confirmed.

The technician unplugged a cable, plugged in another one, toggled a switch, pressed a button and held out his hand for the DVD.

Hector didn't surrender it.

"Confidential," he said.

Soares shrugged, pushed another button. With a click and a whirr, the DVD player stuck its tongue out at the cops.

"Enjoy the movie," Soares said. And left.

Hector put the DVD onto the extended tray, gave it a gentle push, and hit the PLAY button.

Fourteen minutes later, the girl's severed head hit the floor with an audible *clunk*.

"Enough," Silva said.

Hector reached out and pressed a button, stopping the DVD at almost exactly the same point where Marnix Gans, the Dutch postal inspector, had sprung to his feet and gone running into his bathroom to vomit.

"Fuck," Arnaldo said unsteadily, his usual sarcasm momentarily suspended. "You hear that? The person calling the shots, the one behind the camera, was a woman."

"I heard it," Silva said.

"She's some sick human being. She reminds me of—"

Silva said it for him. "Claudia Andrade."

NELSON SAMPAIO, Silva's boss, did not believe in sharing glory for success or in taking blame for defeat. When there were victories, they were always *his* victories. When there were debacles, he always looked for a scapegoat.

One such debacle was a famous case involving a team of rogue physicians who specialized in the transplantation of vital organs. *Doutora* Claudia Andrade and her associates were often able to prolong and increase the quality of life in patients wealthy enough to pay for the privilege. In that there was nothing amiss.

What *was* amiss was their source of organs. They harvested them from living, breathing human beings. Scores of innocent people had been murdered in the process.

And, in the end, Claudia Andrade had gotten clean away.

In an exclusive interview in the *Folha de São Paulo*, Sampaio spun it this way: it wasn't the federal police who'd failed to apprehend her. No. It was one man: Mario Silva. He'd been in overall charge of the case, had been given all of the resources of the state to back him up and had failed miserably. If it hadn't been for Silva's ineptitude, the psychopathic lady doctor would never have been able to escape incarceration and judgment. Silva's actions clearly required a review, and Sampaio, for one, would welcome an investigation by an independent body.

The day after Sampaio's comments appeared, droves of reporters descended on Silva's office. He fled down a back stairway, but others were waiting for him at home, milling around in the basement parking lot, clustered in front of the building, packing the hallway in front of his apartment. By the time he'd elbowed his way through the throng and reached his front door, all three groups had joined together into an insistent, jostling mob, shouting questions and demanding explanations.

A particularly strident young brunette—Silva took her for a newspaper reporter or someone from a radio station, because she was casually dressed in hip-hugging yellow jeans—inserted a sandal-clad shoe between his front door and the jamb and told him she was going to keep it there until he answered her questions.

Silva asked her to remove it. When she didn't, he brought down the sole of his shoe on her exposed toes, not hard enough to break anything, but with sufficient force to discourage her. With a screech of pain and an expletive her mother never taught her, the brunette pulled back her foot. Before a hardier soul could take her place, Silva slammed the door, locked it and went to look for Irene.

He found her curled up on the sofa, breathing heavily, although it wasn't quite four in the afternoon. An attack on the man she loved, her only anchor, was all it took to get her to break her five o'clock rule, but it took a great deal of drinking to render her unconscious. She must have been at it since early morning.

Later, after he'd tucked her into bed, he found the copy of the *Folha*, crumpled and folded back to the op-ed page. She'd stuffed it into the garbage compactor next to the kitchen sink. The cartoon was the first thing that caught his eye. It showed Claudia Andrade as a bird of prey, flying off into the sunset with a human heart in her beak. Down below, hanging out of a tiny, ineffectual paddy wagon, were the Keystone Kops, wearing tall hats, blowing whistles, waving billy clubs. The sergeant leading the Kops bore a striking resemblance to Silva. The accompanying editorial went on to excoriate him and those who served under him. It didn't seem to matter that the organ-theft ring had been broken up and that all of the other members, save only Claudia, were either imprisoned or dead. What mattered, apparently, was that Doutora Claudia Andrade, one of the cardiovascular surgeons who'd plucked hearts from the healthy and poor to transplant them into the critically ill and rich, was still at large.

Physically, Claudia was an attractive woman. The photograph that circulated in the press had been shot head-on, foreshortening her rather prominent nose and thereby enhancing her features. Press and public alike were intrigued by the fact that someone who looked like *that* could have been directly responsible for killing tens, maybe hundreds, of innocents.

Silva survived the attack, and the ensuing independent inquiry, only by a stroke of luck: a string of call girls serving a group of prominent politicians made for even juicier news. The pack of journalists that had been hounding Silva went off to sniff and bark elsewhere. Fortunately, the gentlemen of the board of inquiry were no friends of Nelson Sampaio. Freed from the necessity of pillorying someone whom the director disliked, they closed their sessions without issuing a reprimand.

The relationship between Silva and his boss suffered, but both were practical men. It helped, too, that the Chief inspector had never had any illusions about his boss in the first place, so there was nothing for him to be disappointed about. In time, scar tissue formed over Silva's wounds.

But not Irene's.

"You have to catch her, Mario."

In the year and a half that followed, she'd say it at least once a week. Irene didn't believe that her husband's honor could be vindicated until Claudia Andrade was behind bars, or dead.

From time to time, Silva would take out the photo he carried in his wallet. The image, lifted from her driver's license application, showed Claudia smiling at the camera, a picture of innocence, displaying not a trace of the dark soul that nestled within.

He'd stared at that photo so often, showed it to so many people, that he could have made a sketch of her from memory, accurate down to the little mole on her left cheek.

But that was all he had, a photo and bitter memories. Of the woman herself, there hadn't been a single trace. She seemed to have vanished into thin air.

"CLAUDIA ANDRADE," Arnaldo repeated, still staring at the empty screen. "You think it's her?"

"Maybe not," Silva said, "Maybe it's just wishful thinking on my part. We still have a score to settle between us."

"And me," Arnaldo said. "I'll never forget waking up on that table of hers."

Claudia had nearly succeeded in making Arnaldo Nunes her final victim prior to disappearing.

Hector said, "I have to ask myself how many women like Claudia this country could produce in a generation."

"Damned few," Silva said. "Maybe only one, but let's not get our hopes up. Not just yet." He turned to Arnaldo. "When can we expect some answers from those Internet people?"

"Got the list right here," Arnaldo said, pulling a paper from his pocket. On it were the E-mail addresses obtained by the Dutch police, typewritten and in alphabetical order. Each was followed by a handwritten annotation.

Silva started reading at the top, running his finger down as he went.

On the eighth line his finger stopped.

He raised both eyebrows.

"I'll be damned," he said.

AT A quarter past seven that evening, the telephone in Silva's office rang. Camila, his secretary, was long gone. Ditto Hector, probably already sleeping in Silva's apartment. Silva was in the washroom at the end of the hall. Arnaldo picked up the receiver.

"*Pronto.*"

"Mario Silva?" a no-nonsense female voice said.

"Not here," Arnaldo said. "Who wants him?"

"This is Deputado Malan's office."

"Wow," he said, "a talking office. Do you have brother and sister offices? Are your parents buildings?"

There was a short pause while she digested the attempt at humor.

"Who's this?" Now she sounded bitchy.

"Nunes. I work with Silva."

"Nunes," she said, as if she was making a note of it. "Inspector Nunes?"

"Agente Nunes."

"Ah. Agente Nunes."

An office, particularly the all-important Deputado Malan's office, didn't have to be polite to a mere agente, and when next she spoke, she wasn't.

"Get in touch with the chief inspector," she snapped, "and tell him he's to be here tomorrow morning at ten. Suite four-forty-one, Congressional Office Building," the woman said, and hung up.

No sense of humor at all.

* * *

SILVA WAS ten minutes late.

Malan's secretary had a sharp chin and a long nose, and she wore no wedding ring. She looked to be in her midfifties.

When Silva gave his name she looked pointedly at her watch.

"Didn't that Nunes person inform you that your appointment was for ten?"

Silva admitted that the Nunes person had told him exactly that. He didn't try to explain that he'd been trapped in traffic for almost an hour. The first city in the world designed for the automobile, the city that had once boasted the complete absence of traffic lights, had become a vehicular chaos just like all the other major cities in the country. Knowing that, Silva had allowed a full hour to cover eight kilometers. But that morning a demonstration in front of the Ministry of Agriculture, one that included about a hundred and fifty farmers on tractors, had introduced a further complication into the gridlock.

The woman pursed her thin lips, stared at him over a pair of steel-rimmed reading glasses, and waited for him to apologize.

Silva didn't. He figured she was going to make him wait anyway.

She did. For nearly an hour.

DEPUTADO MALAN'S inner office was decorated partly in nineteenth-century French colonial and partly in twenty-first-century Brazilian egomaniac. There were photos of the deputado with every recent President of the Republic, there were trophies for raising prize livestock, there were honorary degrees and diplomas, there was a glass-topped case full of medallions. The office reminded Silva of the one his boss had boasted before turning to the One True Religion for spiritual sustenance and votes.

The deputado motioned Silva to a chair, one of normal height this time, but the deputado's head was still higher than his guest's. Malan's desk stood on a little platform.

The deputado shuffled through the clutter on his desk, found the photos he was looking for, and handed one to Silva.

"Marta," he said.

A brown-haired girl in pigtails—not ugly, but sullen—stared at the camera as if it was an enemy. She appeared to be about twelve.

"You said she was fifteen," Silva said. "She doesn't look it."

Malan scowled.

"Take this one then," he said, handing Silva another. "It's more recent."

The second photograph showed the same girl, now looking her age. She was no longer in pigtails and had her arm around another girl, who appeared to be two or three years older. Both were smiling. When Silva saw the face of the girl next to Marta, he took in a sharp breath.

"What's the matter?" the deputado said.

"Nothing. Who's her friend?" he said.

"I'm only interested in Marta. If you need to show that photo around, have it cropped."

Silva repeated the question, keeping his inflection exactly the same, acting as if Malan might not have heard him the first time.

"Who's her friend?"

The deputado fidgeted and finally spit it out. "Her name is Andrea de Castro. She's a fucking bull dyke."

"A lesbian?"

"What did I just say?"

"They were lovers, Marta and Andrea?"

"My son caught them at it, rolling around in Marta's bed, right there in his own house. He threw the dike out and gave Marta the beating of her life."

"And then?"

"And then he locked her in her room." The deputado snorted. "She had some tools in there, screwdrivers and chisels. She was always fucking around with stuff like that, doing boy things instead of playing with dolls. She managed to get the hinges off the door. When her parents got up the next day, she was gone."

"I see."

"I doubt that you do. Let me spell it out for you: I'm a Northeasterner. Where I come from, men are men, and women are supposed to be women. If my political enemies found out about this, they'd have a field day."

"I know how to be discreet, Deputado."

"See that you are. No need to bother my son or daughter-in-law with this. You got any questions, you come back to me. That's all I have to say. Go to it. On your way out, tell Maria to send in the next visitor."

Silva stood.

"Just one more thing, Deputado. What can you tell me about this girl, Andrea?"

"She's missing too. Maybe they're together, maybe not. The cops in Recife have no idea what happened to her."

But Silva did. He knew exactly what had happened to her. Andrea de Castro had been raped, strangled, and decapitated with an ax.

Chapter Eleven

"So what did you do then?" the director asked.

"Nothing," Silva said. "I left."

Outside, a tropical downpour was lashing the windows. Lights in the offices of the Ministry of Culture, just discernible through the curtain of rain, were little flags of cheer punctuating the gloom.

But there was no cheer in Sampaio's office. A single desk lamp with a green metal shade was the only source of illumination. The light pooled in a yellow circle on the uncluttered desk.

"You just *left*? You didn't tell the deputado that his granddaughter's girlfriend was the star of a what-did-you-call-it?"

"A snuff video."

"You didn't tell him that?"

"No, Director, I didn't."

"In the name of heaven, why not?"

"I don't want to go public at this point. It could drive the people who did it even further underground."

"Informing the deputado isn't exactly 'going public.'"

"I beg to differ with you, Director. He'd be bound to tell someone, his son and his daughter-in-law at least, and *they'd* tell someone else, and the next thing we know it'll be all over the media."

"So what? The girl's dead already."

"Not necessarily."

"Explain."

"The Dutch have thirteen videos made by the same woman. They have a tape recording of a telephone conversation where she declares her intention to make more. But, right now, she doesn't have a supplier. Her most recent work, according to one of the men apprehended by the Dutch police, is the one of Andrea being beheaded. Andrea and Marta disappeared at the same time."

"So you think there's a possibility they haven't gotten around to Marta yet?" The director looked doubtful.

"A slim possibility," Silva admitted, "but still a possibility. And if they haven't, and if her abductors discover we're pulling out all the stops to find her, they'll kill her at once."

"*Uma queima de arquivo*," Sampaio said, knowingly. Literally, burning of the files, this was cop slang for the destruction of evidence. Sampaio loved to talk the talk.

"I *am* right. And Director . . ."

"Yes?"

"It would be best if *you* didn't mention this to anyone."

The light was too dim for Silva to be certain, but he thought he saw Sampaio flush.

"Of course not," the director snapped. "It never crossed my mind. What's your next step?"

"Now that we have the murdered girl's name, and a photo to go with it, we'll be able to track down her parents. They'll be listed on the forms she filled in to get her national identity card. She didn't look to be any more than twenty when she was killed, so the odds are she didn't have the card very long. With luck, she was living with her parents when she got it, and with luck, they'll still be at the same address."

"And when you find them?"

"Depending on the way they dealt with their daughter's

homosexuality, they may have maintained contact with her and might have something to contribute."

"All right. What else?"

"We have some enhanced frame blowups of the man who killed Andrea. Someone who casually strangles a woman, then cuts off her head with an ax, probably has a record of previous offenses. We'll go through the archives, try to match the blowups with mug shots."

"How long is that likely to take?"

"There's no central database. We'll have to check municipal and state police files as well as our own. Many of the local databases aren't computerized, particularly in the Northeast where Andrea came from."

"I don't want a lecture; I just want a simple answer to my question. How long?"

"A couple of weeks, minimum."

"Anything else you can do in the meantime? How about broadening the search, trying to identify the other thirteen victims?"

"The more we ask local police departments to do, the more time it's going to take them to get back to us."

"And time," the director said, "is something we're running out of."

"Exactly," Silva said.

WHEN ANDREA de Castro applied for her national identity card, she'd lived on the Avenida Boa Viagem in Recife. The telephone number still existed and was still listed to Otávio de Castro, her father.

When Silva called, a woman answered. As soon as he told her he was a cop, she started asking if he had news about her daughter. He told her he didn't, that he was a federal, new to the case.

She asked why the federal police were now involved.

Silva lied. "If your daughter was kidnapped, and taken across a state line, then it's a federal offense."

"Of course," she said. "How stupid of me. Well, I'll be grateful for anything you can do. This is *so* unlike Andrea. Frankly, I'm scared to death."

"I'll send an agent," Silva said. "His name is Arnaldo Nunes. He's going to want to speak to your husband as well."

"Of course. Today? Tomorrow?"

"Tomorrow. He'll fly up from Brasilia."

"My husband normally gets home at seven, but I can ask him to be here earlier."

"No need, Senhora. Seven will be fine."

Silva summoned Arnaldo.

"I spoke to the mother of Andrea de Castro. You've got a meeting with her and her husband tomorrow evening at seven, in Recife."

"Jesus Christ, why do you always save the best stuff for me? What am I supposed to tell them?"

"As little as possible. Just pump them for information."

"Sometimes I *hate* this job."

"The only thing we can do for them is to track down the people who did it."

"And what a comfort that will be."

"Not much, I know. But if it was your daughter—"

"I'd want the bastards to pay. All right, what about the cops in Recife? You want me to talk to them?"

"I do. I'll call the chief up there, tell him you're coming. Handle him with kid gloves. He's related to the mayor, and the mayor is a buddy of the deputado."

"That's one of the things I love about the North. All of those people who manage to get where they are on their own merits. It restores my faith in democracy."

"I'll try for a noon meeting at the *delegacia central*. The chief's name is Venantius, Norberto Venantius. If he can't see you at noon, or if he wants to meet somewhere else, I'll call you on your cell phone. Here."

"What's this?" Arnaldo said, taking the paper that Silva was offering him.

"The de Castros' address."

Arnaldo glanced at it and let out a low whistle. "Avenida da Boa Viagem," he said. "Looks like they're well off."

"They might have been," Silva said, "but not any more."

Avenida da Boa Viagem is the toniest address in all of Recife. One side of the broad thoroughfare is lined with expensive high-rise condos and hotels. Across the street, beyond the beach, white foam breaks over a *recife*, a reef that gave the city its name.

The de Castros' ample terrace, where they received Arnaldo, was high up and had a view of the beach.

"I thought we'd sit out here," Otávio de Castro said, coming forward and offering a hand. "I don't know if you're a smoker. . . ."

He was in his midfifties, with brown eyes set into deep sockets of grayish skin. He looked like he hadn't slept for a week.

"I gave it up," Arnaldo said.

"Me too," de Castro said, forcing a smile. "Four times. I'm Otávio. This is my wife, Raquel."

Raquel looked younger than he did. She was too thin, almost gaunt.

"Why don't you take that one?" She pointed to one of four metal chairs encircling a table with a glass top. "Can I offer you some refreshment, Agente? Nunes, isn't it?"

Arnaldo sat. "Yes," he said, "Nunes. No, nothing, thanks. I'm fine."

"You're sure?"

"Well, maybe a glass of lemonade."

She must have had some prepared. She returned with a sweating glass and perched on a chair opposite Arnaldo. Her husband, on his feet until then, took one of the remaining two places, pulled it against his wife's and settled so close to her that their thighs touched.

"How can we help?" she asked, coming abruptly to the point. It wasn't strictly polite by Brazilian standards, but Arnaldo forgave her for it.

"Why don't we start," he said, watching her carefully to see how she'd react, "by talking about Andrea's relationship with Marta Malan? You're aware of the fact that she, too, is missing?"

"Yes."

She glanced at her husband then back to Arnaldo. "What do you want to know?" she said.

"Marta's grandfather, the deputado, told us they're lovers."

Raquel didn't flinch, didn't seem taken aback, simply nodded.

"The deputado doesn't approve," Arnaldo said.

"Neither do we," Otávio said.

"But not for the reasons you might expect," his wife added hastily. "It's not that we don't accept Andrea's sexual preference, it's just we . . . well . . . it was a bit of a disappointment, at first, knowing she'd never give us grandchildren. She's our only child, you see." She crossed her arms and hugged herself, as if she was fighting a chill. Her husband put an arm around her. She rested her head on his shoulder.

Arnaldo made silence his ally. Down below, a wave broke and surf hissed over the sand. After an interval, she went on. "All we want, Agente, is for our daughter to be happy. Almost—let me see, how long has it been?—six years ago, when she started having doubts about her sexuality, she came to me right away. I reassured her, told her it was nothing to be ashamed of. Some people are just born that way."

She sought Arnaldo's eyes, looking for a sign of disapproval. She didn't find one.

"We've always been honest with each other," she said. "I wanted to keep it that way. Oh, I suppose she must have her little secrets, but she's open with us about the big things in her life."

Arnaldo thought of his sons, how secretive they'd become since entering adolescence. He almost told Raquel de Castro she was lucky, but the words stuck in his throat. He took a sip of his lemonade. It was delicious, just the right combination of tart and sweet, but he found he had to force it down.

"You knew about, and accepted, her . . . sexual preference, and yet you disapproved of her relationship with Marta Malan?"

"Because of Marta's age, Agente. Marta is three years younger than Andrea, sometimes four, depending on the month. The Malan family may have concluded that our daughter led Marta astray, but it wasn't like that at all. Marta made the first approach, not Andrea. I told Marta's father that, but he didn't believe me. Then *his* father called me, and he—"

"*His* father, the deputado?"

"Yes. The deputado. He accused me of . . . pandering for my daughter."

"If I lived in Recife," Arnaldo said, "the deputado wouldn't get my vote."

"He never got ours," Otávio said. "Not even before that telephone call."

"Have they known each other long?" Arnaldo asked. "Andrea and Marta?"

"More than a year."

"So Marta must have been fourteen when they met?"

"Exactly. That's the reason we disapproved. Otherwise, they're well suited to each other, similar interests in every way. Marta is very mature for her age."

"What did you do when your daughter told you she was . . . seeing a younger girl?"

"I talked with both of them, told them they weren't going to share a bed in this house, told them that if they really loved each other they were going to have to wait."

"And they wouldn't agree?"

"Teenagers are teenagers, Agente. Do you have any children?"

"Two. Both boys, both teenagers."

Raquel lifted her hands, palms upward. "Then you know what I'm talking about," she said.

Arnaldo was a first-class interrogator, good at reading his subjects. He liked what he saw and heard from Raquel and Otávio de Castro. They were being honest with him, holding nothing back.

But he was. And the burden weighed on him.

Raquel noticed.

"Are you all right, Agente?"

"Just . . . tired," he said. Then, before she could ask him anything else, he inquired, "When was the last time you heard from your daughter?"

"That would have been the message she left on the answering machine," Raquel said promptly.

"Message?"

She frowned at him, surprised.

"I told the officers about it. I'm sure they wrote it down. Didn't they put it in their report?"

"In a case like this," Arnaldo said, "we don't start by reading other people's reports. We get to them eventually, but we find it works better when we begin by collecting information first-hand."

"Maybe I'd better tell you the whole thing then," she said.

"I think that would be best."

She took time to gather her thoughts. Below the transparent surface of the table, Arnaldo could see Otávio squeezing his wife's hand.

"Marta's father came home and found the two of them in bed," Raquel said. "They were . . . in a compromising position. He pulled Andrea off the mattress by her ankles. Marta screamed. Andrea started gathering her clothes, but he didn't give her time to find her shoes. He grabbed her by the wrist, dragged her to the front door and threw her out. Then he took a belt to his daughter. When he finished beating her, he locked her in her room, but Marta had a toolbox under her bed. She waited until her parents were asleep and took the door off its hinges. She came straight here and rang our doorbell. By that time it was a little before four in the morning. She and Andrea started talking about running away together. We—"

Raquel looked at her husband and bit her lip. He took up the tale.

"—discouraged it," he said. "I'm a lawyer. I explained to Marta that she's still under the custody of her parents. She had no *right* to run away, and if she did, they'd have every right to bring her back, forcibly if necessary. I told her she'd have to go home and face the music.

"They asked for time to discuss it. They went into Andrea's room and came out about fifteen minutes later. They said they understood. Andrea was dressed by that time, and the sun was already up. She said she was going to walk Marta home. That was the last time we saw her."

"Weren't you suspicious?"

Otávio shook his head.

"We're not accustomed to having our daughter lie to us. Discretion is one thing, an out-and-out lie is another. I didn't think Andrea would ever do that."

"You mentioned a message on your answering machine."

"Yes," Raquel said. "That was later. She left it at a time when she knew Otávio would be at work, and I'd be out shopping."

"How could she know you'd be out shopping?"

"On Wednesdays, there's a *feira*, on the Rua Santa Rita. It's where I go to buy fresh vegetables and fruits. Andrea could have called me on my cell phone, but she didn't. She called here, when she knew I'd be at the feira."

"Did you save the message?"

"I meant to. I erased it by mistake."

"We both heard it, though," Otávio said hastily. "We listened to it several times. Even if we'd kept it, it wouldn't have added anything to what we know."

Otávio was wrong. Sometimes the electronics guys could pull amazing things out of the background noise of a recording, but Arnaldo decided not to mention that. The couple was already suffering, and there would be a great deal more suffering still to come.

"She said she was with Marta," Raquel said. "She said Marta didn't want to go home. They'd taken a nap on the beach. A woman had come along and started talking to them. She told them she was a talent scout. Our Andrea is a pretty girl. So is Marta Malan. The woman offered them jobs as models. They thought it was a godsend. Literally, as if it was a sign from God that He was blessing their relationship."

Arnaldo looked at each of Andrea's parents in turn. They

didn't give any more credence to that story than he did. He wondered if the girls had always been that naïve, or if they'd simply grasped at a straw.

"I suppose Marta must have lied about her age," Otávio said.

"If the woman ever asked," Arnaldo said, "which I'll bet she didn't."

"Andrea said I wasn't to worry," Raquel said. "Imagine that. What was she thinking? How could I *not* worry?"

"I don't suppose she said where they were going?" Arnaldo said.

"Oh, but she did," Raquel de Castro said. "She said they were going to Manaus."

Merda, Arnaldo thought.

But he didn't say it.

Chapter Twelve

RECIFE/BRASILIA/MANAUS

Arnaldo Nunes arrived at Recife's delegacia central at 11:55 the following morning. The corporal on the reception desk was a slim fellow with a wispy beard who looked more like a clerk than a cop. Before Arnaldo had a chance to say anything, the corporal asked, "You that federal guy, Nunes?"

"Do I look that much like a cop?"

"Frankly, yeah," the corporal said. He picked up the phone. "You're expected. Have a seat over there."

Two minutes later, a tough-looking brunette with a shoulder bag came into the reception area and stuck out a hand.

"Vilma Santos," she said. "I'm your lunch date."

Vilma had dark brown eyes and used little makeup. She had broad shoulders and stood erect. Her grip was as strong as a man's.

"Come on," she said. "My car is out front."

When they were seated in her beat-up Fiat, she said, "I'm a delegada. You call me Vilma. I'll call you Arnaldo. You know Olinda? You like *pitu*?"

As a delegada, Vilma was a senior cop. Olinda was the ancient colonial city bordering on modern Recife. Pitu, a freshwater crayfish, was a specialty of the region.

"Yes and yes," Arnaldo said. "We gonna meet the chief?"

"Nope," she said. "I'm all you get. You work with Silva?"

"Uh-huh."

"Cool. I wish I did."

"How come I don't get to see Venantius?"

"You're not important enough."

"Huh?"

"You're just an agente, so you get me."

Arnaldo looked her up and down. "I'm not complaining," he said.

The drive to Olinda took twenty minutes. It was a city long past its prime, many of the historic buildings in near ruin. Century-old palm trees and stately churches spoke of former grandeur. She took him to a restaurant fronting the sea. They chose the terrace, shaded by an awning.

"Actually," she said, "you're better off with me than you'd be with the chief."

"I told you, I'm not complaining."

She leaned closer. Arnaldo could smell her perfume, something citric, like sweet lime juice laced with orange blossoms.

"You know who Norberto Venantius's big brother is?" she asked.

"The mayor?"

"Bingo. Norberto doesn't know shit about law enforcement. He went from running the family's sugar mill to chief of police in one easy step. The mayor figures to move on soon. He's gonna be the governor, and Norberto's gonna be the candidate for his old job. He'll win."

"Like that, is it?"

"Yeah, it's like that. The old families still run this town. But don't be hurt that he won't see you. The chief doesn't spend time with anyone who knows anything at all about police work. They're liable to embarrass him by asking him questions about which he knows less than nothing."

"Like catching felons?"

"Exactly. And he's too pompous to want to be embarrassed. Something else too: he hates dealing with anybody who isn't important."

"Like me?"

"Like you." She looked him up and down. "But I'm not complaining." She flashed him a grin. "I see you wear a wedding ring. You play around on the side?"

"No," Arnaldo said.

"Good for you," she said.

They drank beer with the pitu, peeling them as they went. During the meal, she rehashed the situation, then added, "It's a political hot potato. The mayor is big buddies with Deputado Malan."

"Yeah, I heard. So what's your conclusion? What happened to the girls?"

"At first, I assumed they were runaways."

"But you don't any more?"

"No."

The waiter intervened, bringing them little bowls of warm water, slices of fresh lime floating on top, and linen napkins with which to clean their hands. When he'd gone away, Arnaldo asked, "What made you change your mind?"

"A girl who calls her parents within a few hours of leaving home, you think a girl like that's going to let a couple of months go by before she calls again?"

"I guess not. Coffee?"

"Yes, please."

Arnaldo signaled the waiter. He arrived with two cups and left with the plate of pitu shells.

"Something happened to her in Manaus," Vilma said, "or on her way to Manaus, or maybe some sicko killed her right here in Recife and hid her body."

Arnaldo took a sip of his coffee. It was first-rate, and he said so, then added, "And you figure whatever happened to Andrea happened to Marta as well?"

"Marta's father is a drunk and a womanizer. Her mother is just a drunk. They've got money and influence, but they're not happy people. It must have been a relief for Marta to get away. But she and Andrea were more than just good friends. They'd stick together. Whatever happened to Andrea happened to Marta as well. I'd bet on it."

Arnaldo was itching to tell Vilma what he knew, but he didn't.

"So I guess you asked the cops in Manaus to keep an eye out for her," he said.

She sat back in her chair and expelled air through her mouth. "You know Manaus?"

Arnaldo nodded. "Unfortunately," he said.

They exchanged a look.

"The cops are worse than the town itself," she said.

"Nothing's worse than the town itself," Arnaldo said.

"The cops are worse," she repeated. "They're lazy and crooked, and every request we make for help falls into a black hole. We never got answers. I told Norberto I wanted to go up there and have a look around."

"You must love your job."

"It's my substitute for not being able to find a good man."

Arnaldo didn't want to go there.

"And what did Venantius say?" he asked.

"He said he wasn't going to send me off on vacation, that he had better things to do with his budget."

"Vacation? I guess he's never been to Manaus."

"I guess not. Anyway, I don't think it had anything to do with the money. I think he did it to get off the hook. If Marta and Andrea are in Manaus, they're out of our jurisdiction. That means it's no longer Norberto's problem."

"Yeah, but it's still mine. You figure the next step is for someone to go to Manaus?"

"That's what I figure."

"Uh-oh," Arnaldo said.

"UH-OH," MARIO Silva said when Arnaldo told him.

Being young, female and without protection was bad any-where in Brazil, worse in the major cities, much worse the farther north and west you got. And no major city in the country was further north and west than Manaus.

"How about sending Babyface?" Arnaldo said.

The more than seventeen hundred kilometers of copper wire, microwave links and electrical disturbances between Recife and Brasilia made for a very bad connection, but didn't conceal the note of hope in his voice.

"Babyface is in Rio," Silva said. "He won't be back until the day after tomorrow."

"Oh," Arnaldo said, hope fading. "Hector then?"

"Hector's still recovering from jet lag."

Arnaldo, desperate, appealed to friendship.

"Come on, Mario. You know how much I hate Manaus."

"Everybody in their right mind hates Manaus," Silva said. "Stay at the Plaza. It's close to the center of town."

"Which is like being close to the center of a sewer," Arnaldo said, bowing to the inevitable. "I'll stay at the Tropical. It's outside of town, and it's got a swimming pool."

"The Plaza. It's cheaper, and you won't have time to use a pool."

Silence.

"Arnaldo? You there?"

"I can hardly hear you. It's a lousy connection."

"Don't give me that. You heard me. The Plaza."

"The Plaza is a dump."

"You're not going on vacation."

"You're telling me. Who the hell would be crazy enough to go to Manaus on vacation?"

"Lots of people. There's the river, the jungle, the duty-free zone, the old opera house—"

"Dengue, malaria, yellow fever, bad food—"

"I think it might help," Silva said, breaking in on this litany, "if you had photos of the killers in the other snuff films. I'll send them by courier to the Plaza."

"Tropical."

"Plaza. We already sent the cops in Manaus a photo of the guy who killed Andrea. First thing tomorrow morning, I'll light a fire under them."

"Speak up," Arnaldo said. "I can't hear you."

Silva spoke up, but it didn't do any good. The line was dead.

Later, but before Silva got around to any fire-lighting, he spotted an E-mail in his inbox:

Subject: Photo and request for information

Your photo matches Damião Rodrigues, RG 146324682, seven arrests, two convictions. No pending warrants in this city or State.
  Please advise if you want us to find and hold.

The E-mail was signed by Bento Rosário, a clerk in the Manaus Police Department. Immediately after reading it, Silva called Arnaldo. But cell phones in the north were even more unreliable than they were in Brasilia. He succeeded only in leaving a voicemail message.

THE FOLLOWING morning, Arnaldo called from Manaus, the self-styled Capital of the Amazon.

"You're not going to believe this," he said.

"What?"

"Bento Rosário, the guy you—"

"I remember who he is. What about him?"

"They're telling me he doesn't work there anymore."

"He doesn't—"

"They said he quit."

"*Who* said he quit?"

"I just got off the phone with his supervisor. I also asked him about that felon, Damião Whats-his-name's rap sheet."

"Rodrigues. Damião Rodrigues. And?"

"There isn't any rap sheet."

"I don't believe it," Silva said.

"I told you you wouldn't," Arnaldo said. "When I . . . uh, expressed a similar sentiment, the *filho da puta* hung up on me."

"Are you thinking what I'm thinking?" Silva said.

"Probably. Try me."

"Soon after Bento shoots us his E-mail," Silva said, "someone above him in the hierarchy gets wind of what he's done. This someone has reason, probably financial, to keep the law off of Damião's back. This someone hides, or destroys, Damião's rap sheet, sees that Bento goes off on a little vacation, and puts out the word that he's moved on to greener pastures."

"That's how I figure it," Arnaldo said.

"Did those photos arrive?"

"Yeah, but you sent them to the Plaza by mistake. I had to go over there and pick them up."

"Because you're staying at the Tropical?"

"Sure," Arnaldo said, innocently. "Isn't that what we agreed?"

This time the silence lasted longer. Finally, Silva said,

"Here's what we're going to do: give me two hours, then go to the headquarters of the Manaus PD. By that time, the chief should be expecting you. I'm going to have the director call the governor of the state of Amazonas, or the mayor of the city of Manaus, or whoever it takes to shake those people up. You go in there and demand personal access to their archives. If they don't cooperate, call me immediately."

"Who are you going to tell what?"

"The director gets the truth about the clerk and Rodrigues's file. That will be enough to convince him we can't trust the people at the Manaus PD. I'll suggest he tells whoever he calls that it's a confidential matter of national security. He doesn't tell them about snuff videos, he doesn't tell them about Andrea, or Marta, he doesn't tell them squat."

"You think people are gonna buy into that national security stuff?"

"Who cares? They don't have to believe it. They just have to act as if they do."

"I love it when you're angry."

"Flattery will get you nowhere. And don't think for a minute you've heard the last of this business about the Hotel Tropical."

Chapter Thirteen

THE CHIEF OF MANAUS'S Civil Police was a florid man of slightly above average height and greatly above average weight. When Arnaldo was ushered into his office, his gray uniform jacket hung over the back of his chair, and he was sitting in his shirtsleeves.

"Damned air-conditioning is on the fritz again," he said with an accent that marked him as a *carioca*, a native of Rio de Janeiro. Rings of sweat stained the area under his arms. He was using a handkerchief to blot his forehead. He stopped blotting long enough to stand up, extend a sweaty palm across his desk and offer his hand.

"Ivan Pinto," he said.

"Arnaldo Nunes."

"I used to think Rio was hot, but it's got nothing on this place. I've been here almost five years, and I'm still not used to it. I ran a delegacia back home, and this was a step up, but I sometimes ask myself what I'm doing here."

Arnaldo studied the cop's ample waistline, watching the lethargic way he was patting his forehead. *Probably as little as possible*, Arnaldo thought. Cariocas were not famous for their industry.

"Have a seat," Pinto said, sinking back into a chair that protested under the strain.

The chief's gun belt was draped over one of the chairs in front of his desk. Arnaldo took the other one.

"Thanks for seeing me on such short notice," he said.

"You come well recommended," Pinto said, but there was

an underlying tone of resentment in his voice. "So, what can I do for you?"

"Bento Rosário."

"Who?"

"Bento Rosário, a clerk who works in your archives. I want to talk to him."

The chief seemed to think about it for a moment, then shook his head.

"Never heard of him," he said. "I seldom go down there myself. Too much dust. It makes my eyes water and my nose run. If you want, I'll get Alberto Coimbra in here. Alberto's the man in charge of the archives."

Arnaldo wanted.

They made small talk about the town and the river while they waited for Coimbra, who showed up shortly. He was stoop-shouldered, wore wire-rim glasses with thick lenses, and reminded Arnaldo of a ferret.

The chief made the introductions and asked about Rosário.

"Doesn't work here anymore," Coimbra said.

He sounded like a mouse might have sounded if a mouse could talk. Squeak. Squeak. Squeak. Arnaldo recognized the voice.

"You're the guy I talked to on the telephone," he said.

"Yes, I am," Coimbra squeaked, "and I told you the same thing then I'm telling you now. Rosário doesn't work here any more."

"Yeah," Arnaldo said, "and you didn't hang up on me, either."

"I *didn't* hang up on you. We were cut off."

Arnaldo paused long enough to let Coimbra know that he wasn't buying it. Then he said, "How about you go get me Rosário's *ficha?*"

Coimbra looked at his boss, then back at Arnaldo.

"I looked for it after you called," he said.

"And?"

"And I couldn't find it."

"Let me get this straight," Arnaldo said. "You lost his personnel file?"

"I didn't say we lost it," Coimbra said. "I said I couldn't find it. I'm sure it's around here somewhere. Leave your number. I'll call you when we locate it."

Which will be about the time the river freezes over, Arnaldo thought.

"How about the rap sheet on Damião Rodrigues?" he said.

"There is no rap sheet on Damião Rodrigues. There never was a rap sheet on anybody named Damião Rodrigues."

"How can you be sure? You have a personal acquaintance with every bad guy in this town?"

Coimbra's glasses had slipped down over his nose. He pushed them back, magnifying the size of his pale eyes.

Face like a ferret, Arnaldo thought, *but eyes like a Weimaraner.*

"I've been working in archives for twenty-two years," Coimbra said. "The name Damião is unusual. I would have remembered it if I heard it, and I assure you I never did."

"So how come we got this E-mail from Rosário?"

"I have no idea. You'll have to talk to him about that."

"Which is what I'm trying to do. Are you now going to tell me that no one in this building knows Rosário well enough to tell me where he lives?"

"Of course not," Coimbra said, adding a sniff to his squeak. "After we spoke, and in the spirit of interagency cooperation, I went over there myself and tried to find him for you. I just got back. He moved. No forwarding address."

"The E-mail is from yesterday, goddamn it!"

"I can't help that. He moved. That's all I can tell you, and that's what his neighbors will tell you, too. Go over there if you don't believe me. I'll give you the address."

"I might just do that."

Coimbra gave him a ferrety little smile.

Which is when Arnaldo knew for certain that going over there wouldn't do a damned bit of good.

After Coimbra left, Pinto raised both palms in a gesture of helplessness.

"Well, then," he said, as if that was the end of it. "Anything else I can do for you?"

Whatever was going on, the chief was a part of it. Arnaldo was sure of that.

"Maybe you can tell me a little bit about the trafficking of women here in Manaus?"

"Looking to get laid?" Pinto asked with a leer.

"Business," Arnaldo said.

"Business?" the chief said. "Prostitution is a local matter, and there's no law against it. It's no business of the federal police."

"I didn't say prostitution," Arnaldo said, "I said trafficking. That's illegal. And when it's happening across state lines, it *is* our business, especially when the girls being trafficked are minors."

The chief stopped smiling. "You been talking to that fucking priest?"

"What fucking priest?"

"Barone. That Salesian."

"No. I haven't. Should I?"

The chief swatted the air with his hand as if he was brushing away an annoying insect. The hand was still holding his handkerchief, and little droplets of moisture flew off and flecked the wall next to his desk. He brought the drenched handkerchief back to his forehead and resumed patting.

"I want to have a look at your archives," Arnaldo said.

The chief shot him an indignant look.

"What?" he said.

"Your archives. I want to go there and have a look around."

"Why?"

"I've got photographs. I'm gonna try to match them with names."

The chief's smile returned. "Coimbra can do that for you," he said. "Just give me the photographs. I'll make it a priority, have an answer for you in a day or two."

And I already know what that answer would be, Arnaldo thought. "I have to do it myself," he said.

The chief frowned, and his eyes turned cold. "Are you suggesting my people are untrustworthy?"

"Not at all," Arnaldo said blandly.

"Then what are you suggesting?"

"I'm not suggesting anything, Chief. The matter is confidential, a question of national security. I'm not supposed to delegate any part of it. If you want more information, you gotta talk to my boss."

"The governor called me," the chief said. "The governor *and* the mayor. They both got calls from the director of the federal police in Brasilia. He made them promise to cooperate, but he wouldn't tell them anything either."

Arnaldo raised both palms in the same gesture of helplessness the chief had used just minutes before.

"Well, then," he said. "If my boss won't tell the mayor and the governor, how can you expect me to tell you?"

***

THE ARCHIVES, LOCATED IN the basement of the delegacia, were a warren of ceiling-to-floor shelves, dusty, deprived of daylight, and lit only by fluorescent lamps. The stuffy atmosphere was entirely disagreeable and so was Arnaldo's reception. Coimbra showed his displeasure at the invasion of his lair. He and the chief exchanged what they probably thought were surreptitious glances.

"I want you and your people to extend Agente Nunes every consideration," Chief Pinto said.

"*As ordens*, Senhor. Every consideration."

The only things missing were a wink and a nudge.

"What, exactly, are you looking for?" Coimbra said.

"That's confidential," Arnaldo said. "Just show me your system."

"I don't like people digging around in my files," Coimbra said. "They get things out of order. All you have to do is tell me what you want, and I'll fetch it for you."

"I'd rather do it myself," Arnaldo said.

"And I'd rather you didn't," Coimbra said.

They glared at each other.

"I've got an idea," Chief Pinto said, as if it had just occurred to him. "Alberto here can help you. You can do it together."

Arnaldo shook his head.

"I'm gonna do it alone," he said.

ARNALDO WAS a believer in the adage "The enemy of my enemy is my friend."

After an unsuccessful morning in the archives, and an equally unsuccessful attempt to get a decent lunch in the *padaria* across the street, he was ready for a break. He decided to use it to locate the man the chief had called "that fucking priest." A Salesian, Pinto had said. By inquiring at the first church he came to, Arnaldo discovered there was only one Salesian in Manaus: Father Vitorio Barone, who ran a school in the São Lázaro district. The parish priest was even able to furnish him with an address: number fourteen Rua de Caxias.

The Rua do Caxias turned out to be a narrow lane bisected by a filthy canal, more of an open drain than a waterway. A smell of raw sewage assailed Arnaldo's nose. A mangy brown dog with visible ribs was tearing into a plastic sack of garbage in front of number twelve, a shack built of scrap lumber.

The neighboring building, number fourteen, was a mansion by comparison. Anywhere else it would have been categorized as a dump. Two stories tall, and twice as wide as any other house on the street, it was a haphazard pile of gray cinder block. An ancient pickup truck, painted yellow, but flaking in places to reveal the original blue, was parked in front. Arnaldo could hear children's voices, getting louder, as he approached.

The door was open. He stood on the threshold, waiting for his eyes to adjust from sunlight to shade. A gang of kids became visible. They were seated on the cement floor, singing the alphabet. One of them caught sight of the figure in the doorway and whispered something to the child next to him. That one whispered to another and soon seventeen pairs of brown eyes and one pair of blue were turned in Arnaldo's direction.

The blue eyes belonged to a priest in a black cassock. The singing faltered. The priest frowned. One of the kids saw the frown and elbowed his neighbor. The singing swelled. The priest stopped frowning.

They sang the alphabet through to the end. Then they sang it over again. When they finished for the second time, the priest clapped his hands.

"Dismissed," he said.

The kids streamed out, walking past Arnaldo, giving him the once-over. The priest came forward.

Something about him, perhaps his long legs, perhaps the way he kept his neck erect when he walked, reminded Arnaldo of a flamingo. A shock of unruly black hair capped his high forehead. The hair was cut as a man might cut it himself if he didn't care how looked.

"Father Barone?" Arnaldo asked.

He got a curt nod, then a question. "And you are?"

"Agente Arnaldo Nunes, federal police."

Father Vitorio's expression shifted from neutral to hostile.

"What do you want?"

"Your name came up at the police station," Arnaldo said. "The chief referred to you as 'that fucking priest,' or words to that effect."

The priest didn't blanch. "So?" he said.

"So right now they're probably referring to me as 'that fucking federal cop.' I figured we two fuckers should get acquainted."

"The chief," Father Vitorio said, "thinks I'm a pain in the ass."

"And the feeling is mutual, eh?"

"I didn't say that," the priest snapped.

"No, *Padre*, you didn't."

Arnaldo looked around the room, seeking something to defuse the tension. His eye fell on some children's drawings that were spiked onto nails driven into the unpainted wall.

"What's this?" he said, walking over to have a closer look.

"My art class."

The priest followed Arnaldo and stood at his shoulder.

"I get discarded computer paper from an office in the duty-free zone," he said. "The children make their drawings on the back. For the crayons . . . I accept contributions."

Arnaldo could take a hint when he heard one. He reached for his wallet.

The priest performed a vanishing trick with Arnaldo's ten-Real note. Then he gestured at the drawings.

"As you can see," he said, "there's a definite preference for gray, brown, and black. I offer them all the colors of the rainbow, but they choose gray, brown, and black."

Arnaldo studied the kids' pictures: stick figures holding guns, stick figures lying on the ground, houses with bullet holes in the walls. None of the kids showed any talent, and Father Vitorio, whatever else his abilities might have been, didn't seem to have a vocation for teaching technique.

"They don't draw bogeymen or monsters," the priest said. "The things that frighten them are real. Take this one, for example."

He put his finger on the drawing of a truck. Armed figures were leaning out of the windows. The figures were drawn in gray, the same gray as the uniforms worn by Chief Pinto and his men.

"Cops?" Arnaldo asked.

"Cops," the priest confirmed. "Some say they're trying to take over the city's drug trade. Until a year or so ago, they were fighting for it with pistols. These days, they use assault rifles. The bullets go through the walls of the houses and kill innocent people. That, Agente, is the children's experience of the men who are supposed to be protecting them. And it's mine, too. So I ask you again, what do you want?"

Arnaldo reached into his breast pocket and took out two enhanced blowups cropped as head shots. One was of Andrea de Castro, the other of the man he believed to be Damião Rodrigues. Both had been lifted from the DVD Hector brought back from Amsterdam.

"You know these people?" he asked.

The priest studied the photos. "Why are you interested?"

"You know what a snuff video is?"

"I'm not altogether ignorant, Agente. But snuff videos don't exist. They're an urban legend."

"You're wrong, Padre."

"I don't think so. But what do these people have to do with these so-called snuff videos?"

"The girl was snuffed. The man did it."

"Special effects," the priest said. "These days, anything's possible."

"All right, Padre, have it your way. Do you know them? Have you ever seen either one of them?"

"No," the priest said. "And, now, if you'll excuse me . . ."

"Wait."

Arnaldo took a card out of his wallet, clicked his ballpoint, and scrawled some numbers.

"This is my cell phone," he said. "I'm at the Hotel Tropical. If you hear, see, or remember something that might help me, please call."

The priest hesitated for a moment, then performed the same vanishing trick with the card as he had with the ten-Real note.

Chapter Fourteen

IT DIDN'T MATTER WHAT the girls said. They could talk until they were blue in the face. It wouldn't change a thing.

And they *did* talk. They talked all through the long afternoon. They badgered, they cajoled, and one even threatened her.

But it didn't do them a damned bit of good. How could it? She wasn't like them. They were poor, she was rich. They were frightened of The Goat, she wasn't—well, not as much as they were, obviously. They were nobodies, she was somebody. She was Marta Malan, of the Pernambuco Malans, granddaughter to one of the most influential men in the republic. She'd always had fine clothes, lived in a big house, had enough food to eat, had people to wait on her.

But a lifetime of privilege hadn't made her weak. If The Goat thought that, he had another think coming. She'd resist even if he starved her, beat her, kept her locked up. She'd show him she was made of better, stronger stuff than the lower-class riffraff he was accustomed to dealing with, girls who'd never even *heard* of the perfumes she wore, didn't know the proper forks to use at a formal dinner, and wouldn't be able to name a single brand of designer jeans.

She, Marta Malan, had *not* been born to work in a brothel.

Finally, just before dark, that filthy pig with the broken nose, Osvaldo, came to fetch her. After the pressures of the afternoon, she was almost relieved at the thought of going back to her cell. But she remained resolved never to give in. She told Osvaldo that, just as he was slamming the door.

She could hear him laughing as he strolled away.

***

WHEN HER door opened on the following morning, it wasn't Osvaldo, it was Rosélia. She came in and closed the door behind her.

"We need to talk," she said.

"About what?" Marta didn't try to keep the insolence out of her voice.

Rosélia took a seat on the bed. She wasn't carrying her club, but there was something threatening about her all the same.

"About your attitude," she said. "We're fed up with it. It has to stop. You're setting a poor example for the other girls. You're giving them ideas."

"Really?" Marta felt a glow of satisfaction.

"Last night, after you spent the afternoon shooting your mouth off, Jociane told a customer she wasn't going to let him have her. There was never a single problem with her, but, now, all of a sudden, she's telling us what she will and won't do. She said he stank, and he was too old. We can't have that, querida. How can we run a business if we let the girls decide who can have them and who can't?"

"I don't care about your business," Marta said, raising her voice, hoping that at least one of the other girls would hear that she wasn't afraid to talk back. "It has nothing to do with me. It's your problem, not mine."

Rosélia didn't get red in the face, or show any other sign of losing her temper.

"No, querida," she said. "It isn't just my problem. Now it's your problem too."

She stood up, walked to the door, and opened it. The Goat was waiting on the other side.

And in his hand there was a length of rubber hose.

***

"I THINK we should get together and talk," Father Vitorio said.

Arnaldo moved his cell phone to his other ear, shoved aside his breakfast and leaned back in his chair.

"Why the change of heart, Padre?"

"The Church, Agente, has informal links in virtually every field of endeavor. I took the trouble to make a few inquiries."

"You checked up on me?"

"I did."

"Hell, Padre, I could have made it easy for you. All you had to do was—"

"Do you want to meet, or not?"

"When and where?"

"It wouldn't be wise for us to be seen together. I suggest this evening at my home, sometime after dark, say nine o'clock? I live above the classroom. Knock on the front door. I'll come down and let you in."

THE PRIEST'S apartment consisted of a single room. A shower and a toilet shared one corner, a sink and a tiny refrigerator another. There was no closet. His clothing and other personal effects were stuffed into stacked wooden crates. The remaining space was just large enough for a bed, a small table, and two wooden chairs.

A bulb, unfrosted and dim, was suspended from the ceiling, the cord looped to allow it to hang just above the table. Every now and then a moth would blunder into it. Sometimes they'd drop making a soft *pat* as they hit the table. Sometimes they'd fly away. Those that did soon came back.

Outside, someone was frying fish. The odor drifted through the shutters, as did the voices of some kids having an argument about whether Ronaldo *Fenômeno* played better *futebol* than Ronaldo *Gaúcho*.

"How about a drink?" Father Vitorio offered.

"I wouldn't mind," Arnaldo said.

The heat was damned near unbearable. While the priest fetched a half-empty bottle of *cachaça* from the top of the refrigerator, Arnaldo stood up, removed his jacket, and hung it over the back of his chair.

The priest brushed a couple of dead moths aside and poured straw-colored liquid.

"*Saude*," he said, to your health, and downed his glass in one gulp.

Arnaldo took a cautious sip. The cachaça was mellow, probably five or six years old. He nodded in approval.

"Back home in Italy," the priest said, "I was brought up on wine. My father used to make his own. *Vino nero*, he used to call it. Black wine. Not *rosso*, red, but nero, black, it was that dark, almost like ink. Strong too. More than fourteen percent. I really miss it. Not just my father's wine, any kind of wine. But it's too expensive here, even the Chilean and the Argentinean varieties. Every Real I spend on myself is a Real less to spend on the children, so I make do with this. More?"

Arnaldo held a hand over his glass.

"Not just yet," he said.

The priest poured for himself.

"All right, Agente, let's start all over again. I have nothing to offer you at the moment, no answers to the questions you posed, but I want to apologize for having been so abrupt the first time we met. I didn't know you. You arrived without references. I have to be careful."

"Careful of what?"

"Not pushing Chief Pinto and his associates too far."

"You think they're out to get you?"

"I think they've considered it. I'm not paranoid, if that's what you're thinking."

"That's not what I'm thinking. What have you done to get on the bad side of the chief?"

"I've been very vocal about the exploitation of minors for sexual purposes. It's made me . . . unpopular, not only with the chief, but also with the mayor and the governor."

"The governor? Hell, Padre, you don't fool around, do you? How did you get to him?"

The priest smiled a sardonic smile. "He didn't want to talk to me at first. The mayor or Chief Pinto must have complained about me. But I was insistent. I asked my bishop to intercede. The bishop is . . . a realist. He told me it was a waste of my time, but he was willing to let me try. He called the governor on my behalf and set up an appointment."

Another moth fell, this time onto Father Vitorio's cassock. He brushed it aside with a practiced gesture.

"The bishop was right, of course. It *was* a waste of time. I think I knew that going in, but I felt I had to try."

"Let me get this straight. You tried to talk to the governor about the sexual exploitation of minors, and he brushed you off?"

"He did."

"It's a crime, for Christ's sake!"

The priest took another swallow of cachaça, only half the glass this time.

"You want to know what he told me? He said that not everyone has the strength to lead a life of celibacy, or even to maintain a monogamous relationship. He said I had to understand that the brothels contributed to a lowering in the indices of sex crimes and that they're perfectly legal."

"As long as the girls are eighteen or older."

The priest took a deep breath and another gulp of cachaça.

"I conceded the point. I told him I wasn't there to talk

about brothels or prostitution per se, but rather to call his attention to the exploitation of children."

"And what did he say to that?"

"He said that Amazonas is a poor state, that we can't afford to turn tourists away, that having sexual congress with minors—that's not the way he put it, but that's what he meant—was something that brought in the foreigners. You must have seen them, Agente, planeloads of them, Germans, Dutch, French, Americans. . . ."

"I've seen them," Arnaldo said. "It's not the first time I've passed through this town's shitty airport." He took another sip. The fiery liquid was making him sweat even more.

"They say they come here to see the river and the jungle," the priest went on. "Sometimes that's true. Mostly, it's just sex tourism, pure and simple. But it isn't only the foreigners. They're just the tip of the iceberg. A man like The Goat doesn't earn his money from the foreigners. His customers are all locals. I told the governor that, and he just smiled. It made me furious. I lost my temper. I told him what was happening was against the laws of God and man, told him economic gains couldn't be allowed to cloud the moral issue, told him that, by the time most of those girls are twenty, they're burned out and sick with every venereal disease there is. I begged him to help me put a stop to it. I told him God would surely punish him if he didn't."

The priest's face was flushed, and not just from anger and heat. He upended his glass, swallowed, uncorked the bottle, and poured another.

"And then?" Arnaldo asked.

Father Vitorio took another gulp of cachaça and looked down at his shabby tennis shoes. "And then," he said, "the governor called in two of his security people. They threw me out."

Arnaldo shared the priest's outrage, but he had no help to offer. The Brazilian Federal Police was a smaller organization than the police departments of many major cities. He and his colleagues couldn't be expected to right all of the wrongs in a country larger than the continental United States. Besides, the Ministry of Justice had long ago determined that the federal police's limited resources were not to be expended on helping girls whose families mostly didn't give a damn about them and who weren't old enough to vote. The politicians in Brasilia *claimed* they were engaged in a major effort to curb the sexual exploitation of children, but in practice they weren't doing anything. So he didn't attempt to respond to the priest's remarks. Instead, he retrieved the cropped photo of Marta Malan from the breast pocket of his jacket.

"I'd like you to have a look at this," he said.

"Another photo?" Father Vitorio said.

"Yes. A different girl. Recognize her?"

The priest leaned over for a better look and shook his head.

"Who is she?"

"Sorry, Padre, I can't tell you that."

The priest picked up the photo and held it closer to the light.

"Would I be correct in assuming she's a person of some importance?"

"Can't tell you that either."

"I'll take that as a yes."

Father Vitorio went back to studying the photo. Arnaldo could smell the pungent cane spirit on his breath.

"Nice clothes," the priest said. "Pearl earrings. The chain on her crucifix looks like gold. She's from a wealthy family."

Arnaldo remained silent.

"Can I keep this? I'd like to show it to someone."

Arnaldo nodded and took another sip of his cachaça. "You mentioned The Goat," he said. "Who's he?"

"Surely you've heard of The Goat?"

"I wouldn't be asking if I had."

"He's a whoremaster of the worst type. He runs a house specialized in offering adolescent girls."

"And the police know about this?"

"He's a former policeman himself. Many of the younger ones on the force take him as a role model."

"A role model?"

"They want to grow up to be just like him. He makes a lot of money, they don't. The base salary for a policeman in Manaus, Agente, is less than five hundred Reais a month."

"Don't ever mention that to my boss. I keep telling him *I'm* badly paid."

The priest didn't crack a smile.

"Obviously," he said, "you can't support a family on five hundred Reais a month. All cops look for ways to supplement their income. The Goat is their ultimate success story."

Arnaldo took another sip of his cachaça. The stuff was making his tongue feel thick.

"He works alone?"

"He has an associate, a woman by the name of Rosélia Fagundes."

"A whore?"

"You'd expect that, wouldn't you? But, no. She studied to be a nun. She worked as a schoolteacher."

"A nun, and a schoolteacher, and now she works with a pimp? What happened?"

Father Vitorio shook his head.

"I can't say. I don't know that anyone can, perhaps not even Rosélia. Some girls, some women, are attracted to evil.

The Goat seduced her, I know that much. Why she stays with him"—he threw up his hands—"who can tell?"

"What's her part in the deal? What does she do for him?"

"Recruitment, mostly. She also helps manage the girls."

"Recruitment?"

Father Vitorio uncorked the bottle and waved it in Arnaldo's direction. Arnaldo shook his head. The priest poured himself another hefty dose. This time he drank half of it down like water.

"She travels," he said. "She goes to towns like Belém and Santarém, seeks out girls from the poorer classes. She makes promises, offers them jobs in *bistros*, shops, restaurants, that sort of thing."

"And they believe her?"

"They believe her, and they come back with her. I told you, Agente, she's not a whore. She dresses well, speaks well. They take her for a businesswoman, and I suppose she is, in a way."

"Then, when the girls get here, it's the old story? They're told they owe money for their passage and for their food along the way?"

The priest nodded glumly. "I see you've heard it all before," he said, and drained his glass.

"Yeah," Arnaldo said. "No bistros, no shop, no restaurant, just a *puteiro*."

"Sometimes," Father Vitorio said, "the girls go to the police. Sometimes they try to run away. But The Goat and others like him pay for protection. If a girl files a complaint, the authorities tear it up and tell the owner of the brothel. If a girl tries to run away, Chief Pinto and his men track her down. Once she's back, the whoremaster beats her. He does it in front of the other girls to set an example, to send a message: there is no escape, so it's healthier not to try."

"Tell me more about this woman, Rosélia. You say she recruits girls from all over. How about Recife?"

"Why are you interested in Recife?"

"Sorry. I can't tell you that."

Father Vitorio reached for the bottle and uncorked it. "Last chance," he said.

Arnaldo nodded. The priest divided what remained in the bottle, doing the Christian thing by giving Arnaldo a few extra drops.

"Recife?" Arnaldo prompted.

"Maybe," Father Vitorio said.

"You think this Goat might be capable of making a snuff video?"

The priest brushed the air. It might have been an impatient gesture, or he might have been swatting at one of the moths.

"I've already told you, Agente, snuff videos don't exist. They're—"

"An urban legend. Yes, you told me. Let me put it another way: do you think The Goat would be capable of killing someone in cold blood?"

The priest didn't hesitate. He shook his head.

"No, Agente, I don't. He's bad, but he's not that bad. He wouldn't kill anyone unless he was severely provoked."

"You seem to know quite a bit about him. And that's why you wanted to keep the photo. You've got a source. Who feeds you information?"

The priest's eyes sparkled. "Now, I'm the one," he said, "who can't tell you that."

ARNALDO RETURNED to his hotel to find the bedside lamp switched on and the window wide open. *To air out the room*, the note from the chambermaid said.

By the time he'd closed the window and turned on the air-conditioning, he was covered with mosquito bites. He called housekeeping and got no answer. He went down to the lobby, and they directed him to the hotel's shop.

In the shop was an entire shelf of outrageously priced spray with which to kill mosquitoes and another of an even more outrageously priced cream to treat the bites.

Even if Arnaldo had had a less-suspicious nature, he would have spotted the connection: somebody was making money out of "airing out" the guests' rooms.

While she was processing his credit card, the smiling sales clerk asked him if he was enjoying his visit to Manaus.

When he left the shop, she was no longer smiling.

THE FOLLOWING morning at breakfast Arnaldo, once burned, refused the bread and the rancid butter. The fruit plate came with a number of exotic fruits he couldn't identify and a few that he could.

So far, so good.

But then he made the mistake of adding some thin, bluish milk to his coffee. The milk tasted like fish.

After a futile attempt to remove the taste by strenuous brushing of his teeth, he went back to the archives. His none-too-cheerful greeting was met by sullen silence. The other clerks were taking a lead from their boss, Coimbra.

Arnaldo grabbed an armful of files, propped a chair under the doorknob of the little room they'd set aside for him, and got back to work. Less than an hour later, he got his first hit. Eighty-five minutes after that, another. He took both rap sheets, put them into his briefcase, and went back to his hotel.

In the restaurant, already the scene of several culinary disappointments, he thought he'd be safe with a salad. His first bite suggested that the lettuce had been in close contact with less-than-fresh fish. He dropped his fork and went back to the hotel's shop. When the salesclerk from the previous evening saw him coming, she sent a teenager to wait on him and ran into the back.

He bought a candy bar and some bottled water. Then he wandered around the hotel until he got a good signal for his cell phone.

"OUR CUP runneth over," he said when he had Silva on the line. "I got two hits."

"Cup runneth over, eh? Sounds like you've been spending time with that priest, Father Vitorio."

"How come you know about him? What are you? Psychic?"

"He had someone checking on you," Silva said. "It got back to me, so I decided to check on *him*. Other than being—and here I'm quoting the head of the Salesian Order in Brazil—'a little too sure of being right, even if the rest of the world thinks he's wrong,' Vitorio has a good rep. Was he of any help?"

"Not yet."

Arnaldo told Silva about his two conversations with the priest.

"How come he's being secretive?" Silva said when Arnaldo was done.

"Could be he's just playing games. He wanted to have a name to go along with Marta Malan's photo. I wouldn't give him one. He wanted to know why I asked about Recife. I wouldn't tell him. He wanted to know if she was somebody important. I wouldn't tell him that either."

"Tit for tat, huh?"

"Maybe. Or maybe he made a promise to his contact to

keep his or her name out of it, or maybe he's just being cautious."

"When are you seeing him again?"

"He'll call me if he comes up with anything."

"How about that archives clerk, the guy who sent us the E-mail?"

"Bento Rosário. Still missing."

"Speaking of missing, how are you going to make sure those rap sheets don't disappear like Damião's did?"

"No chance. They're in a safe place."

"Don't tell me you stole records from their archives?"

"Okay, I won't tell you."

"But you did, didn't you?"

"You told me not to tell you. By the way, this town is the worst—"

"You're not going to start that again, are you?"

"Seriously, Mario. Listen. All the food in this town tastes like fish. The salads, the meat, the butter, the cheese, the milk: it all tastes like fish."

"You hate fish."

"Exactly. I'm starving to death."

"Wouldn't hurt you to lose a few kilos."

"A few kilos? Hell, by the time I get out of here, I'm gonna be so thin my wife isn't going to recognize me."

"Should be a treat for her. She'll probably ask me to send you back twice a year. What about those rap sheets?"

"I'll fax them."

"From the hotel? Probably not a good idea."

"I'll do it myself, tell them I want to be left alone while I'm at it."

"Names?"

"Carlos Queiroz and Nestor Porto, both *pistoleiros*, both natives of this hellhole."

"You add Damião Rodrigues, and we've got three from the same hellhole."

"Not likely to be a coincidence, huh?"

"No. Sounds like you localized the infection. It jibes with what the Dutch cops told us. The woman phoned Amsterdam from Manaus."

"How about some help tracking her down? We could try to find that clerk, Rosário, while we're at it."

Silva was silent for a moment, thinking.

"I don't want to open this up any further," he said; "not yet, anyway. I'll come myself, and I'll bring Hector. It'll take a day or two to clear my schedule. I'll E-mail you with my travel plans. Meanwhile, watch your back."

Chapter Fifteen

THE NAME ON HIS birth certificate was José Luis Ignácio Braga, but nobody called him that. The people who'd known him as a child nicknamed him Lula, and that's what they still called him. The whores who worked for him called him Senhor, and sometimes Senhor Braga; but most people called him The Goat, or simply Goat.

He'd grown up in a little shack on stilts, wedged in among several hundred other shacks on stilts, all of them lining the banks of the Rio Negro, and sometimes, during the rainy season, *in* the Rio Negro.

The rainy season was both a curse and a blessing.

It was a curse, because you couldn't get out of your shack unless you had a boat. And if you did, there was always someone trying to steal it. It was a curse, too, because the river could kill you, creep up on you at night like some stealthy beast and knock the stilts away, and carry you and your whole family out into midstream, where the current was swift, and the water a hundred meters deep.

But the rainy season was also a blessing, because it was then that the water covered the garbage-strewn, human-waste-littered mud that held up the stilts and supported the shacks. The noxious odors arising from that mud changed so often you could never get used to the smells. They got into your hair and your pores, and wherever you went people wrinkled their noses and knew exactly where you came from.

Only the poorest people smelled like little Lula. Anyone who had a bit of money to spare built his home well above the high-water line. It was still a slum, but it was a cut above the houses on stilts.

There were places, farther upstream and down, where higher ground made it possible to live *on* the river without occasionally having to live *in* the river, but those places were prime real estate. There were big houses there, and docks for boats, and gardeners tending lawns of grass. But in little Lula's neighborhood, there was no high ground, only gently shelving flats of black mud, even blacker than the water itself. The mud got its color from raw sewage. The water got it from tannins leached out of leaves farther upstream. The mud was filthy, but the water wasn't. You could put an oar into it and still see the tip, even if you held it upright.

Little Lula's family consisted of his mother, three older sisters, and himself. The mother and the sisters were whores, but they doted on him, and that, for little Lula, had been the greatest blessing of all. They'd worked to send him to school, recognizing that education was the key to financial success, hoping he'd support them in their old age, when they got to be forty or forty-five and could no longer attract even the poorest customers. So The Goat had gotten his start in life from prostitution. Now, more than forty years on, he still drew sustenance from it.

His education lasted through eight grades of primary school. That had been enough to get him into the municipal police. He'd never had a shot at being a delegado, of course. But he'd attained the respectable rank of sergeant before leaving the force and dedicating himself to running a string of girls full-time. There had only been three of them in the beginning, friends of his sisters in need of protection.

Protection was a concern of all the girls. If you worked the streets, you had to have a strong man to watch your back, to assure you didn't get stiffed for your fees, to assure that, if you got beat up, it was only a little. It was a job cut out for The Goat. He was a head taller than most of the men he had to deal with, and he was adept at wielding a truncheon, something his police training had taught him. He was adept at wielding something else too. Back in those days, he was sexually insatiable. One of his whoring buddies, a reprobate carioca with a serious drinking problem and a classical education, once remarked that there was only one difference between Lula and a satyr: a satyr, being only half-goat, wouldn't fuck just anything, but a goat would. And so would Lula. Thus was his new nickname born.

The Goat had mellowed down through the years. These days, girls in his house were seldom summoned to service the boss. And he seldom mistreated them, which is to say he was never more violent than he had to be. Occasionally, it was true, he beat one of them with a rubber hose. But he only did it because he felt they deserved it, not because he enjoyed it. He was generally even-tempered. He had friends. He had money. He had a stable business. It was a business that most women in town didn't approve of, but the vast majority of men did. He was, therefore, not stigmatized, but rather enjoyed a limited degree of celebrity. He had a nice house, and a fishing boat, and a loyal subordinate in Rosélia. He should have been a happy man, and he was, in every respect but one: he could never shake free from a morbid fear that some day he was going to wake up and find himself back in that shack on stilts. He was deathly afraid of being propelled back into the poverty and misery of his youth. He wouldn't be able to tolerate that. Not anymore. He'd do anything to prevent it. Anything.

"WHEN ARE you leaving?" The Goat asked. He was in his office, tucked in behind the boate, gazing through the window at the Rio Negro.

His boat was down there, not fifty meters away, moored to the dock. Beyond it, in midriver, a large ship was making a turn. The ship moved slowly at first, but then the current caught the bow, swung it over and started to sweep the vessel downstream. Intent on watching it pick up speed, The Goat hadn't bothered to turn around when he'd asked the question.

Instead of responding, Rosélia posed a question of her own. "How's your hand?"

He'd been holding Marta with his left hand while he beat her with the right. She'd twisted under the blows, and he'd inadvertently struck his own knuckles. He flexed them, studied the discolored flesh, and grunted.

"When are you leaving?" he repeated.

"I don't think I should go at all," she said. "Not while a federal cop is sniffing around."

She'd been planning a trip downriver to Santarém to troll for new girls.

"Pinto says all the guy's doing is hanging around the delegacia and looking at rap sheets," The Goat said.

Pinto had just left, having traded the information for the services of a girl who was eleven years old and a bottle of Scotch that was twelve. He'd sampled the Scotch on the spot and taken the rest of the bottle away with him.

The Goat didn't care about the girl, a renewable resource, but he *did* care about the whiskey. He'd bought it from a *contrabandista*, but it had still set him back almost eighty dollars, American, and gone was gone.

"Maybe it has nothing to do with us," Rosélia said.

The Goat had a feeling that it did, but he wasn't ready to admit it.

"Maybe it has something to do with Carla Antunes," she said. "She's sending girls to European brothels. That's international trafficking, a federal rap. And most of those girls used to be *our* girls. What if they nail her, and she talks?"

The Goat thought for a moment. "I could have a talk with her," he said. "Make it clear it would be . . . unhealthy if *her* business fucked up *our* business."

"Why don't you?"

"Okay. I was planning on talking to her anyway."

"About what?"

"About this Marta Malan."

"What about her?"

"I'm ready to give up."

"You? Give up?"

"Christ, Rosélia, I've gone about as far as I can go. I don't want to kill her."

"Of course not. But are you really ready to give up? It'd be the first time."

"You know what she did this morning after I gave her the treatment with the hose?"

"What?"

"She spit in my face. There she was, with bruises all over her, and a broken tooth, and she spits in my face. Starving her didn't make any difference. Giving her the solitary treatment didn't make any difference. Letting her talk to the other girls didn't make any difference. We let her loose on a customer, she's gonna bite him and scratch him. Either he's gonna run out of the room and create a scene, or he's gonna kill her. Either way, it's bad for business."

"So you're going to sell her?"

"To Carla. It's the best way. At least we get some money out of it. Then she's not around to talk to the other girls, she's not in the country to talk to the federal cops, and she's somebody else's problem."

"Seems like a nice, clean solution," Rosélia said.

***

THE HOUSE was in the old colonial style with a red-tiled roof, whitewashed walls and blue trim. The São Paulo industrialist who'd built it told his wife it was a fishing lodge.

His wife told him he was full of shit. She knew it was underage whores, not fish, that drew this *paulistano* to Manaus. But she could never prove it.

On those rare occasions when she tried to stage a surprise visit (the paulistano always knew when one was coming because his pilot had strict instructions to advise him if she commandeered the plane), he'd board the seventeen-meter motor yacht he kept tied up at the bottom of the garden and come back late in the evening, surrounded by his so-called fishing buddies, ostensibly delighted to discover her there.

The Goat, as Manaus's premier supplier of underage whores, had been a frequent visitor to the lodge, but he'd only been there on three occasions since the death of the man who'd built it.

The first of those occasions was in response to a telephone call from a fourteen-year-old whore named Geralda Mendes. Geralda had been leaning over an armchair, letting the paulistano fuck her doggy fashion, when the magnate suffered a massive coronary and collapsed on Geralda's back. As soon as she realized he wasn't simply gathering energy for a final assault, she wriggled out from under him and grabbed the telephone next to the bed. Fifteen minutes later, The Goat showed up to give advice. After a quick evaluation of the situation, he suggested that the paulistano's fishing buddies wash his genitals, clothe his naked body, and haul it onto the yacht before calling the police.

They'd agreed, except for the washing part. They made Geralda do that.

The true circumstances of her husband's death never became

known to the widow in São Paulo, but the story was told and retold in the bars and boates of Manaus.

One of the people who got considerable mileage out of it was a well-known raconteur named Miguel Marcus. It was Marcus who started calling Geralda "The Kiss of Death." The nickname stuck, and for some months thereafter The Kiss's services were in great demand. Some people said it was bravado on the part of the older customers, others that any girl who could bring on a heart attack in an otherwise healthy man of fifty-seven must be very hot stuff indeed and had to be tried. But the novelty didn't last. After six months of constant attention, the first four by reservation only, The Kiss's popularity began to decline. The Goat, ever attentive to the needs of his customers, promptly sold her to Hercules, a friend of his who owned a boate in Santarém.

Within a week of his demise, the paulistano's widow put his house and yacht up for sale. The yacht wasn't a problem. It was bought within a week. The house remained empty for almost six months, and six months is a long time to weather in the Amazon: paint peels; termites and other insects bore into wood; bats take up residence under rafters; snakes and rats creep into drains.

The widow was getting fed up with the cost and aggravation of maintaining the property by the time a woman who styled herself Carla Antunes came along.

SELVA MACIEIRA, the real estate agent who handled the transaction, was more than a little surprised when Carla declared an intention to make her home in Manaus.

Selva, an *Amazonense* herself, knew as well as anyone that Manaus was a cesspool of filth, that it suffered from a dreadful climate, that the inhabitants were mostly limited in their intellectual capacity and that they were overwhelmingly lethargic.

Intelligent people, if they could afford to do so, moved *out* of Manaus. They didn't move *in*. Not unless they had a compelling reason to do so. Carla Antunes was obviously intelligent, so she must have had one. Selva, one of the nosier women in the city, was anxious to find out what it was.

"You have relatives here?"

"I want a place on the river," Carla said.

"Ah. The river. We have quite a few people who come for the river. Scientists mostly. Are you a scientist?"

"Preferably with four bedrooms," Carla said, "and preferably with a dock at the back."

Except for the fact that there were five bedrooms instead of four, Carla could have been describing the paulistano's place. Selva lost interest in the woman's background and concentrated on the sale. In the end, she managed to dump the place for a little less than half of what it had cost the paulistano to build it, which was pretty good considering the fact that there had been no previous offer.

The widow wasn't overjoyed with the deal, but her husband had been worth millions, and the fishing lodge was only a minor issue in the brewing legal battle between her and the paulistano's kids from his former marriage.

THE GOAT'S second post-heart-attack visit to the house was when the new owner invited him to discuss what she'd called "a business deal."

She'd received him with two thugs who apparently lived with her, both of whom she treated like servants, not lovers.

"I understand you run a stable of girls," she'd said.

"What's that to you?"

"The European market. I have contacts."

"You want me to get you whores?"

"Yes."

The Goat drained the whiskey she'd offered him, put the glass on the table, and got to his feet.

"Forget it," he said. "Why should I sell you any of mine? Go get your own."

One of the two thugs, a guy with bags under his eyes, took a step forward, but the woman held up her hand.

"I want the ones you're finished with," she said.

"I already got people I sell them to," The Goat said.

The guy with the bags under his eyes let out a low growl, like a watchdog, but The Goat ignored him.

"You don't understand," the woman said. "I want the ones you can't sell."

The Goat shook his head. "You don't want them," he said. "They're too old."

"Not for Europeans," the woman said.

"Oh, yeah?" The Goat said. He sat down again and held up his empty glass.

THE GOAT'S next visit to the lodge was when he finally gave up on Marta. By that time, Carla had already purchased thirteen of his girls and had, he believed, shipped them all off to Europe.

She received him on the terrace overlooking her floating dock. The whiskey she offered him was brought by a *capanga*—tough guy—with bags under his eyes.

"Thanks," The Goat said.

The capanga grunted like a pig and made himself scarce.

While The Goat was making his proposition, the mayor's yacht went by. The old buzzard was sitting there in the stern with one of The Goat's girls. They were being served drinks by a guy in a white coat who The Goat knew for a fact was on the city payroll.

The Goat waved and the mayor waved back.

"How come you're being so generous?" Carla said, when The Goat was finished with his sales pitch.

"What do you mean?" The Goat said innocently.

"Come off it," she said. "I get your rejects. I know that. It's fine. It suits my clientele. But now you come along and tell me you want to sell one of your young ones. What's wrong with her?"

The Goat looked pained. "She's trouble," he admitted.

"Trouble?"

"I couldn't break her. I tried everything, but I couldn't break her."

The tip of Carla's tongue came out. She licked her upper lip.

"She's still a virgin?" she said.

"Yeah, a virgin."

"Why don't you fuck her yourself? That should bring her around."

"It won't. She's like a wildcat. She'd bite off my ear or something."

"Tape her mouth shut. Tie her spread-eagled so she can't move."

The Goat sighed and shook his head. "You don't have to teach me my business," he said. "If I thought it would help, I'd do it. But it wouldn't. I could never trust her with a customer."

"So what you're basically asking is if I'll take her off your hands?"

The Goat took a pensive sip of his whiskey.

"Maybe in Europe she'd act differently, being so far away and all. Maybe she'd even like being over there. It's a different life. I met a girl once, friend of my middle sister. She worked in Switzerland, later in Holland. Got enough money to come back here and buy a house. Except she didn't come back here. She went to Bahia."

"What kind of shape is she in?"

"Over the hill. She admits to being thirty-seven, but I think she's at least—"

"Not your sister's friend. The girl."

"Split lip, chipped tooth, some bruises. Look at this." He displayed his discolored hand. "I hit myself while I was taking a hose to her. It made me mad, and I kind of got carried away. Beat her like I never beat anybody, and when I was finished she spit in my face."

"Messed her up, did you?"

The Goat shook his head.

"I know how to hit a girl. She's not too bad. Give her a couple of weeks, and she'll be as good as new—except for the tooth."

"So I'd have to keep her until her looks improve?"

"Her looks aren't that bad now. Anyway, we could do a deal. You pay me up front, and I'll keep her for you."

"How much?"

"Five hundred a week."

"Don't make me laugh. At those prices, I'd keep her myself."

"So you're interested," The Goat said.

She made him wait for an answer.

"Maybe I could use her," she said.

The Goat started to smile.

"However," she continued, "if I took a chance on somebody like that, there's no way I'd pay you full price."

The Goat's smile became a scowl.

"You mean full price for a chick."

In the parlance of the trade, a chick was a girl under eighteen. Hens, girls who looked older, were cheaper.

"No, not the full price for a chick," she said. "And not even the full price for a hen. Tell you what: I'll give you two thousand American dollars."

"Two thousand? You've got to be kidding. She's worth more than that."

"To whom? You think you can get a better deal? Two thousand and that's it. Take it or leave it."

"I'll take it," The Goat said.

Carla went inside to get the money. The Goat sat there, watching the river, remembering the day The Kiss had called him, remembering the dead paulistano's flabby body, the way he looked when he'd seen him last, his organ still partially distended.

Unpleasant thoughts.

Like his conversation with Chief Pinto about the federal cop.

Carla came outside again with a glass of beer in one hand and a wad of banknotes in the other.

She sat down, put the beer on the table and started counting the money. When she finished he scooped it up, folded it, and put it in his pocket.

"When do you want to pick her up?" he said.

"Tomorrow. Around noon."

She took a sip of her beer.

"Suits me," The Goat said. "There's something else I gotta talk to you about."

She didn't say anything, just sat waiting for him to tell her.

"There's a federal cop snooping around town," he said.

She suddenly got very still. Her eyes locked on his.

"How do you know that?" she said.

"Chief Pinto. He tells me things."

"And what did he tell you about this federal cop?"

"It's like this: a while back a request came in from Brasilia, asking about Damião Rodrigues. Remember him?"

"Sure I remember him," she said. "That pistoleiro. Friend of Chief Pinto's."

"'Friend' is a stretch. More like a business associate. By the way, have you seen him around lately?"

"No."

"Me neither. Funny. He hardly ever missed a Friday night. Anyway, the federals had a picture of him. They asked the Manaus PD to match it with a name."

"And?"

"And they did, and it was Damião. The clerk who handled it, some rookie, shot off a reply before checking with his boss. Asshole. Trying to show how efficient he was."

"And then?"

"Chief Pinto heard about it. He knew Damião did me the occasional favor, knew I wouldn't appreciate having the federal police mucking around."

Carla sipped her beer. She feigned unconcern, but he didn't buy it. She was definitely acting.

"Pinto called in the clerk and reamed him," he said, "told him to make himself scarce. Then he trashed the file, told the feds it had gone missing and the clerk had quit."

Carla put down her glass so violently that it was a wonder it didn't break.

"It sounds to me," she said, "like there are at least *two* assholes in the Manaus PD, and one of them is Chief Pinto. Didn't it occur to him that acting like that would bring the feds down on him like a swarm of hornets?"

"Apparently not. Anyway, the swarm turned out to be just one guy. He started asking questions about the exploitation of minors and all that kind of crap. He had authorizations from the mayor and the governor, and he wanted personal access to the archives. The chief said he'd be happy to help. The Fed said no, he'd do it himself, and he didn't want any company. One of the chief's guys peeped through a crack in the door while the fed was working. The fed had a bunch of photos, and he was comparing them to rap sheets from the archive."

Carla's pupils seemed to dilate. Her eyes hadn't left his. Her mouth was slightly open.

"This federal cop," she said, "what's his name?"

The Goat rubbed his forehead.

"Armando something . . . or maybe Arlando something."

"Not Costa," she said. "Not Hector Costa."

The Goat shook his head.

"The chief told me, but I really don't—"

"Silva?" she said. "Mario Silva?"

"Silva?"

Now, she'd surprised him.

"Silva?" he repeated. "Hell, no. Not him. Him, I woulda remembered. What makes you think a big shot like Silva would be interested in people like us? Unless, maybe, there's something you're not telling me."

"Nonsense."

"Is there?"

"What is this?" she said. "An inquisition?"

The Goat sat back in his chair and took another sip of whiskey.

"All right, Carla," he said. "I don't tell you my business, why should you tell me yours? But you'd better make god-damned sure that yours doesn't interfere with mine. And if the feds pick you up, you'd better keep your mouth shut. You don't say a word about me. Not a goddamned word, understand?"

Her eyes narrowed.

"Are you threatening me?" she asked.

The Goat drained his glass and stood up.

"Yeah," he said. "I am."

Chapter Sixteen

When The Goat left, she summoned Hans and Otto.

Hans Hauser and Otto Weil were descendants of Bavarian immigrants who'd settled in the southern state of Santa Catarina. Their ancestors' reluctance to mix their blood with that of inferior races like the Portuguese, Spanish, and Italians who'd also populated the region resulted in inbreeding. Physically, the effect had been minimal. Both were splendid specimens of Teutonic manhood. Mentally, though, it was a different story. They were, moreover, as mean-spirited as they were stupid. They'd been the kind of children who'd beat up smaller kids on the playground, drowned stray cats, and pulled the wings off butterflies. Then they'd grown up and graduated to theft, rape, and murder.

Hans, being slightly more intelligent, was the leader of the pair. He had long blond hair and a moustache that made him look like a Viking. The hair and moustache turned heads on the street, even back home in Santa Catarina and especially in Manaus, where blond hair was rare.

Otto's salient features (apart from the tattoos on his upper arms, one of which was a dagger dripping blood and the other a girl who'd wiggle her hips if he'd tighten his bicep in a certain way) were the bags under his eyes.

Claudia had never seen him without those dark circles. She wasn't sure if they were there because Otto never got enough sleep, or whether they were simply part of his physiognomy. Distressed at having to stare into those dark pits every time she looked at him, she'd taken to buying him sunglasses. He kept losing them, one pair after the other.

They sat in front of her like a couple of Rottweilers expecting dinner while Claudia told them about the federal cop who was poking around in the police archives.

"I want you to follow him," she said. "Make damned sure he doesn't notice you."

"He won't," Hans said. "We're good at that."

"What do you want us to do with him?" Otto said.

"I just told you."

"I mean after we follow him," he said.

"Take a camera," she said. "Take photos. I want to know what that federal cop looks like."

"You think he's after us?" Hans said.

"Maybe."

"Why maybe?"

She considered how much to tell them. After a long moment, she said, "Arie Schubski, my distributor in Amsterdam. The police got him."

"Merda," Hans said. "Somebody should go over there and shut that bastard up before he spills his guts."

The implication was that the "somebody" should be Hans himself. Mostly, it was Otto who got to do the bag work, carrying tapes to the Netherlands and bringing the money back. Hans had been angling to be chosen for the next delivery, but a murder would do just as well. Claudia knew how his mind worked. He was already thinking about getting high in one of those coffeehouses and fucking a blond girl.

She shook her head.

"What Arie had to tell," she said, "he's already told. Besides, he didn't know a hell of a lot. Not even my real name."

"So what brought the federals to Manaus?"

"That's what we've got to find out," she said.

Apparently, it didn't occur to Hans that she might be lying to him as well.

"I dunno," Otto said. "Maybe we should just keep out of his way. Maybe lay low for a while." Otto was the dumber one of the duo. He'd been caught more often. It had made him cautious.

"Let me do the thinking," she said. "You just do what you're told: follow the federal, make sure he doesn't know he's being followed, take photos."

"You're the boss," Hans said.

"You're goddamned right I am," she said.

WHEN HANS and Otto left, she sat down and contemplated her next move.

Now that she'd struck a deal for the girl, she was anxious to get started. It had been too long between videos, and she was beginning to feel restless. Restless wasn't perhaps the right word, but it had been the word her uncle Ugo always used when he came to her in the night.

"I'm feeling restless," he'd say. Then he'd ruffle up her nightgown. He always cried afterwards. She was only eleven at the time, and often she'd cried with him. Then he'd wipe away his tears, and hers, and tell her that she mustn't ever tell anyone what they'd been doing, "because then they wouldn't let us do it anymore."

As if she cared. She didn't care about sex then; she didn't care about it now. And she didn't cry anymore either. About anything.

The Goat's description of her latest acquisition had intrigued her. She rather liked the idea of a girl who was a virgin and would fight to stay that way. Her customers were accustomed to seeing girls willingly submit to the sex, sometimes even get actively involved in it, before being surprised by the sudden turn of events. Now, she'd be able to offer them something different: a girl who struggled from the very beginning, a girl who'd be beaten bloody before she was penetrated.

She began thinking about a protagonist, the man who'd do the raping and the killing. One thing Arie Schubski had taught her, and he'd taught her a great deal in that single meeting of theirs, was that anyone shown on camera couldn't be left alive.

"It's bad for me," Arie had said, "and bad for you too. They get nabbed, sure as hell they're going to squeal. They're the only ones who don't have deniability. What they've done is right there for all to see, and they'll be looking for a deal with the prosecutors. You have to prevent that. You have to kill 'em all, or we don't do business."

He'd been right, of course. Just as he'd been right about covering the snuff in one continuous shot, without intercuts; right about the trick of opening up the aperture on the lens so the blood wouldn't be underexposed and register as black, rather than a rich, full red; right about the value added of leaving the volume control on the microphone open to capture the victim's dying gasp.

Arie was a man who knew his business, knew all the ins and outs, knew the technical side, knew what his clients liked. But she wouldn't miss him. She could trust The Surinamer to come up with another distributor. The Surinamer could always get you anything you wanted, drugs, false papers, anything. He could have people killed, even Dutch cops. All you needed was the money to pay him. She could have used a man like The Surinamer right now, but he was far away, in Amsterdam. She'd have to make do with what she had.

She looked at her watch. It was still early enough to call

Chief Pinto and invite him to lunch. Some good whiskey, a wad of banknotes handed across the table in a white envelope, and he'd get cracking, probably suggest someone suitable for testing within a day or two.

Her story to the chief was always the same: some friends of hers, friends in Europe, needed someone for a job, someone who could get tough, someone who could get very tough if the situation warranted it.

All the people the chief suggested wound up disappearing for good. He wasn't stupid. He'd noted that. He'd even mentioned it once.

"Maybe they like it over there," she'd said. "Maybe they finished the job and decided to stay."

"All of them? Every last one of them?"

"You know how many illegal Brazilian immigrants there are in Europe?"

The chief had told her he had no idea and that he, frankly, didn't give a shit.

"Good riddance," he'd said. "They were all punks anyway."

But since that conversation he'd never again fed her people whose services he might be able to use in future.

SÃO PAULO
Decades earlier

THE FUNERAL Claudia Andrade's parents planned to attend was that of a great-aunt, but they never made it. On the way, their car was broadsided by a truck. Both were killed instantly. It drew newspaper headlines at the time due to the irony of their being on the way to a funeral and winding up at their own.

But Claudia's parents, owners of six fast-food franchises, were really nothing more than glorified shopkeepers. Nothing other than wealth distinguished them. Their case was soon forgotten.

Claudia had been seven, her brother, Omar, two years younger. He'd been a momma's boy, deemed too young to attend the double burial, so Claudia, the one who'd always avoided her mother's embraces, was the one who got lifted up over the coffin.

"Kiss your mother good-bye," her uncle Leonardo told her.

Claudia did as she was told, dutifully pressing her lips against the dead woman's cheek. Her mother's flesh was cold. Claudia reacted by making spitting noises and rubbing her mouth. Everybody knew Claudia was a strange little girl. They didn't blame her for making a scene. They blamed Leonardo. He shouldn't have done what he did. The Andrade family hated scenes. They remembered the incident, but Claudia promptly forgot all about it. She hadn't been particularly fond of either one of her parents. She hadn't been particularly fond of anyone.

It was another five years before it occurred to her that death was worth thinking about. Then, two weeks before her thirteenth birthday, she had an epiphany. She was living, then, with her Aunt Tamara, her mother's spinster sister. School was over for the day. She and her brother were walking home. Omar was running on ahead, holding his books in one arm and squeezing his crotch with the other. He was desperate to get to a bathroom before he peed in his pants.

He crossed the street in front of the house, flung open the gate, and ran up the steps, ignoring the family dog, a miniature dachshund named Gretel. Claudia had never once scratched Gretel behind her ears, never once given her food, and yet the animal lavished her with unrequited affection. The dachshund dashed out through the open gate and started to run across the street.

Her happy barks were cut off with a loud *thump* and a wail of pain. The car, a black Ford LTD with tinted windows, never slowed down. Whether the driver was a man or a woman would remain a mystery. The cops weren't about to waste their time trying to hunt down someone who'd done a hit-and-run on a dog.

Gretel rolled over and over and came to rest in the gutter at Claudia's feet. She was still alive—barely—but she was bleeding from the mouth and panting for breath. Claudia put a hand on the soft, reddish-brown fur. She could feel Gretel's heart, fluttering, fluttering. Then, suddenly, it stopped.

Claudia shuddered. Her head began to spin. She sensed a shortness of breath, a sharpening of her senses, a wetness between her thighs.

It was . . . wonderful.

They buried Gretel in a corner of the back yard. Omar cried at the funeral and planted a cross of two sticks bound together with kite string.

Claudia squeezed out a tear or two, but more to make Omar feel guilty than from any sense of loss. Head down, hands over her eyes, she found herself thinking . . . thinking. *Would they catch me if I killed the parakeet? How about our cat? How would it be to be present at the death of a human being, instead of a mere dog?*

It was then and there, standing over that little mound of earth, that Claudia Andrade decided what she was going to do with her life.

She was going to preside over deaths.

Last moments, for thirteen-year-old Claudia Andrade, were profoundly exciting, more so than boys, toys, parties, pretty clothes, more so than anything.

She'd never, ever, be able to get enough of them.

***

MANAUS
Present Day

THE DOOR of the aircraft opened to suffocating heat, a strong smell of rotting vegetation, and a weaker one of decomposing fish.

Arnaldo was waiting in the shadow of the terminal building.

The three of them shook hands and started walking.

"It's Hector's first visit to Manaus," Silva said.

"Lucky bastard," Arnaldo said. "This is my fifth."

Just ahead, facing them, was a tourist, snapping photographs. When the guy lowered the camera Silva caught a glimpse of deep bags under heavy-lidded eyes.

On the way to the hotel, Arnaldo reviewed his conversations with Father Vitorio. Then he handed them the original rap sheets of Carlos Queiroz and Nestor Porto, the ones he'd lifted from the archives of the Manaus PD.

The photographs were much more legible than on the faxes received in Brasilia. There was no mistake. They were the same men who'd been seen performing on two of the snuff videos.

Queiroz and Porto shared two common features: protuberant lower jaws and piglike eyes. They looked like members of some primitive tribe.

"You take Queiroz," Silva said to Hector. "I'll take Porto."

"How about me?" Arnaldo said.

"You hate those archives, don't you?" Silva said. "The reception you got from Coimbra and his people, the dust, the heat?"

"Yeah, so what?"

"So stick with it. See what else you can come up with."

Arnaldo let out a sigh. "This is penance for that Hotel Plaza business, isn't it?" he said.

NUMBER TWENTY-SEVEN Rua da Independencia, Queiroz's last known address, was five stories of mildewed brick with a shop window on the ground floor. Beyond the glass, which looked like it hadn't been cleaned in Hector's lifetime, were religious articles: bibles of all sizes, hymnals, plastic statues of saints, icons of the Virgin Mary, rosaries, portraits of the Pope.

And, if God couldn't help, you had only to climb a flight of stairs where you could visit a fortune teller, a homeopathic physician, or a lawyer. The remaining floors in the building were given over to apartments, four opening off each landing.

Queiroz's place was listed as 3C, but the name next to the bell said Cintra. The girl who answered the door wore a red dress with a neckline that plunged to her navel and a hem that ended just below her crotch. She didn't look to be more than twenty, but it was a hard-lived twenty. The smile on her face faded when Hector asked about Carlos Queiroz and disappeared completely when he made it clear he had no interest in her services.

"Abilio," she said, raising her voice just a little.

A door opened somewhere behind her. Seconds later a mean-looking guy with a single earring pushed her aside and intruded himself into the doorway.

"What do you want?"

"I just told your girlfriend. I'm looking for Carlos Queiroz."

"Never heard of him," the guy with the earring said. He started to close the door, but Hector inserted his foot.

"What the hell. . . ?" the guy said, blustering.

Hector waved his credentials in the guy's face. "Let's start all over again," he said. "This is who I am. Who are you?"

"I don't want any trouble," the guy said, backing down.

"Me neither. Answer the question."

"Abilio."

"Abilio who?"

The guy paused for a moment then said, "Sarmento."

Hector figured it was probably true. He also figured it wasn't a name that Abilio normally answered to. Most people in Abilio's business didn't use their real names, hence the "Cintra" on the mailbox.

"Prove it," Hector said.

Abilio nodded as if he'd expected that and stepped back from the door. "You can come in," he said, as if he had a choice.

Like most places in Manaus, the place stank of fish. And it was hot, hotter even than down on the street. A sweat-stained couch, a folding aluminum table, and a TV set were the only furniture in the living room.

Abilio was wearing a pair of faded bathing trunks, plastic sandals, and nothing else. The sandals made little flopping sounds as Hector followed him down the hallway into the kitchen. The girl, barefoot, sloped along behind them. A pair of men's trousers had been tossed in a heap in the corner. Abilio bent over to retrieve them. As he rose a wallet fell out of one of the pockets.

The sink was piled high with dirty dishes, the stove with unwashed pots. Another girl, who could have been a younger sister of the first, was squatting on the floor, smoking a hand-rolled cigarette. She looked at Hector, then down at her bare toes, her brow furrowing as she tapped ash on the floor.

She's not just using marijuana, Hector thought. *She's on something stronger. Crack, or maybe heroin.*

Abilio rifled the contents of the wallet and came up with a dog-eared identity card. He handed it to Hector.

Abilio Sarmento, aged twenty-four, looked ten years older.

"Who else lives here?" Hector said.

Abilio said nobody did, said they'd been renting the apartment for the last three months, and that hell, yes, the girls were over eighteen.

Again, Hector told him to prove it.

Abilio left the kitchen and returned with both girls' identity cards. Like him, they were named Sarmento: Aparecida Maria and Maria Aparecida, nineteen and eighteen years old respectively.

"My sisters," Abilio said, before Hector could ask.

"Your parents didn't have much imagination, did they?"

"Huh?"

"Never mind. Anyone got a record?"

All three of them did: the young women for lewd conduct, Abilio for stealing a car and possession of cocaine. He'd pleaded guilty, done thirteen months, and claimed he'd been clean ever since.

None of them knew Carlos Queiroz. Aparecida Maria, the sister who wasn't stoned, said the building superintendent probably did. He lived down in 2D.

Hector told Abilio to show him around the apartment.

There were two bedrooms and three mattresses, two in one bedroom, one in the other. Clothes and personal effects overflowed cardboard boxes being used in lieu of furniture.

In the bathroom, shampoos, conditioners, and lotions surrounded the bathtub. Creams and cheap perfumes crowded the glass shelf above the sink. There was no shower curtain. The floor was wet from someone's recent bath. Nothing suggested that anyone else lived in the apartment.

Hector said he was going down to talk to the building superintendent, but he might be back.

Abilio didn't seem overjoyed by the prospect.

THE SUPERINTENDENT was a full-blooded Indian, not an unusual situation in a city where there were more natives than on any single reservation. From the way he spoke Portuguese, Hector figured he'd been educated by missionaries in his youth. That youth was gone, but he didn't have a single gray hair. He could have been anywhere between fifty and seventy, and was dressed in a clean blue shirt and a pair of khaki shorts. His living room was well furnished and a good deal cleaner than the one occupied by the Sarmentos.

"Carlos Queiroz?" he said. "Yes, I remember him. Good riddance."

"How long ago did he move out?" Hector asked.

"I'm not sure."

Hector frowned.

The Indian shook his head.

"It's not what you're thinking," he said.

"What am I thinking?"

"That I don't want to help. You're wrong. I'm happy to help, but we have a high turnover. It's easy to lose track."

"I don't need a specific date, just an approximation."

The Indian pulled his lower lip. "Look," he said, "it's this way: I collect the rent. It's due on Mondays. I go from door to door, pick up the cash, and take it down to the bank, where I deposit it in Senhor Aquino's account. Senhor Aquino owns the building, but he only drops by about once a year."

"So?"

"So on a Monday, about nine weeks ago—or it could have been eight or ten—I knocked on Queiroz's door, expecting to collect, as usual. He didn't answer, which I thought was funny, because it was about eleven A.M., which is the time he usually got up. I went back the next day and the next. I tried him in the early morning. I tried him late at night. It was always the same. For the whole two weeks he never answered, and I never saw him again."

"Two weeks? Why two weeks?"

"When they move in, everyone pays three weeks in advance. Two of those weeks are the security deposit. Tenants are supposed to pay every Monday after that."

"For an additional week, in advance?"

"Exactly."

"So, when he missed his payment, Queiroz had a right to stay for an additional two weeks?"

"Either that, or give us notice, tell us he's moving out. Somebody does that, we return what's left of their deposit."

"But Queiroz never did?"

"Give us notice? Never."

"Okay. And when the two weeks were up?"

"I did what I always do. Used my passkey. He'd left dishes in the sink. There were cockroaches all over the place. Big as *that*," he said, showing how big *that* was by distancing the tips of his thumb and forefinger.

"Queiroz left a light on," the superintendant continued, "as if he'd gone out at night and never come back. Very inconsiderate of him. Electricity is included in the rent, but Senhor Aquino doesn't count on people leaving lights on twenty-four hours a day. Queiroz's sweaty and dirty sheets were still on the bed. I didn't even want to touch them. The man lived like a pig."

"What else did you find in there?"

"His clothes. Everything I ever saw him wear. Some furniture, not much. Just a mattress, a kitchen table, a couple of chairs, and an old sofa."

"What did you do?"

"Left the furniture. Put a sign in the window. It didn't take long to find another tenant. These places are cheap, and they're close to the center of town."

"What about his personal effects?"

"I put them in boxes and stored them down in the basement. This Queiroz, he's . . ."

"He's what?"

"Well, for want of a better word, mean. Mean and a bully. I didn't want him coming back here and getting mad because I threw his stuff away."

"Can I have a look in those boxes?"

"Sure."

The boxes were of no help. Clothes, some condoms, a few pornographic magazines, toiletries, two bottles of cachaça, one of them full. There was nothing that gave Hector an insight into Carlos Queiroz or suggested where he might have gone.

"What do you think?" the Indian asked, gesturing toward the little pile of boxes. "Do I have to keep holding on to this stuff?"

"I wouldn't bother if I were you," Hector said. "I can pretty much assure you Senhor Queiroz won't be coming back."

"NESTOR PORTO lived with his mother and grandparents," Silva said.

"And wouldn't hurt a fly, sang in the church choir, and helped little old ladies cross the street," Arnaldo said.

The three federal cops were back at the Hotel Tropical, having a drink at the bar.

"Not quite," Silva said. "The grandfather seems like a hard-working guy, an electrician. Nestor was born when his mother was fifteen. Nestor's father took off when he found out she was pregnant. Nobody's seen him since. The grandmother was supposed to be taking care of Nestor while his mother finished school, but the grandmother contracted lung cancer and died within a year. The kid got into a bad crowd, dropped out of school, started using drugs, built up a habit, got caught robbing a house."

"Same old, same old," Arnaldo said.

"They put him away for fourteen months. Third day he was back, he smashed all the dishes in the house and beat the shit out of his grandfather."

"The grandfather file a complaint?"

"No. Nestor apologized, said he was on crack, swore he'd never do it again. After that, they pretty much left him alone, never knowing what might set him off. He started going out at night, coming back at all hours, sometimes not coming back for two or three days. Then he was arrested again. Armed robbery. He got five years, three of which he served with the big boys."

"I remember reading that part on his rap sheet," Arnaldo said. "The three years, I mean. They must have wiped the juvenile charges."

"Now, here's the thing," Silva said. "Last November, about two months after he got sprung for the second time, he joined his mother and grandfather for breakfast. They were surprised to see him at that hour of the morning. Normally, he didn't climb out of bed before noon. They asked him what he was doing at the breakfast table. He told them to mind their own business. When he left, he said he'd be home for dinner, but he never came back."

"So he disappeared," Hector said, "just like Carlos Queiroz."

"Indeed," Silva said. "Just like Carlos Queiroz."

Chapter Seventeen

EARLY ON, BEFORE SHE started testing prospects, Claudia had a disagreeable experience. A guy by the name of Pedro Soares told her that if she paid him enough he'd let her photograph him fucking anything on two legs and several things on four. But when it came time for him to perform, he'd proven to be a disappointment. The female lead was deft with both her mouth and her fingers, but her ministrations hadn't helped a bit. She couldn't tease an erection out of him. By that time, though, Pedro already knew too much to be allowed to live. Claudia sent him out on the river with Hans and Otto and sent the still unsuspecting girl back to her room.

A second mishap had been worse. The sex part went off without a hitch, but when it came to the snuff the subject balked.

"I'm not gonna do it," he said. "And I'm not gonna let you guys hurt her."

He was a big man, bigger than Otto, and accustomed to getting his way. He was already out of the bed and halfway toward Otto when Hans shot him, *pam, pam, pam*, three times in the chest, then, when he was down, *pam*, once more in the head. By then, of course, the cat was out of the bag. The girl knew what was going to happen to her, and she was already screaming. Claudia had to tell Hans to put a bullet in her head.

The camera captured it all, but Arie Schubski refused to distribute it. He said his customers didn't want quick kills with anonymous bullets coming in from out of frame. They wanted to savor the act. They wanted to see life slowly being forced out of a woman by a man who'd just had sex with her, not a quick execution carried out by an anonymous perpetrator.

So Claudia had been out the cost of the girl, a set of satin sheets and the time and effort that it took to clean things up. From then on, she preselected people who'd already proven their contempt for human life. That's where Chief Pinto came in. For a price, he helped her with recruitment. Sometimes the people he proposed were freelance pistoleiros like Carlos Queiroz and Nestor Porto. Other times, the chief might suggest a full-time employee of one of the great land-owners. Every large ranch had a few such men. Their job was to keep the other employees in line, making sure they didn't start bitching about the pittance they earned, making sure they didn't run off and, when they did, making sure they came back, alive if possible, dead when it became necessary to set an example.

The man Hans shot had been one of those, a fellow who'd probably killed a dozen people in his lifetime, but who'd inexplicably shied away from strangling a used-up whore. His action demonstrated to Claudia that she could never be absolutely certain how a man might comport himself at the critical moment, so she made every attempt to make the pre-selection as rigid as possible.

First, a candidate had to demonstrate that he was capable of getting an erection while in the presence of a bank of lights, a woman with a camera, and two other men. The way Claudia did it was to tell their prospective recruit that she had a paying customer, a European in Manaus on holiday, who liked to watch the recording of live sex, and who was willing to pay for the privilege.

If the recruit was interested, his next question was usually, "How much?"

Claudia made sure her answer always exceeded his expectations.

The deal struck, the prospect would soon find himself on a bed with one of The Goat's girls, surrounded by Hans playing the European, Otto playing Claudia's assistant, and Claudia herself operating the camera. The lights would be switched on and the couple would be told to begin.

Claudia hardly ever bothered to roll the camera during her so-called screen tests. She wasn't in the business of making simple pornos. And she never did the test and the shoot on the same day because she could never be sure of the man's ability to turn in a repeat performance.

Test or shoot, it didn't matter, she always had the whore service Hans and Otto first, so they'd be sated and keep their minds on business. That, however, required a willing female. It wasn't going to work with a fifteen-year-old recalcitrant virgin. And there was another good reason for not carrying out the screen test with Marta herself: when the protagonist discovered he was in for a fight he might refuse to get near her the second time around.

She resolved both problems by arranging to rent a whore from The Goat. The whore would service Hans and Otto, then apply herself to the "talent." On the day of the shoot, she'd rent another whore, or maybe the same one all over again. She'd be for Hans's and Otto's use, to be returned prior to rolling the camera. Marta would be kept for the killer. The rentals would add to expenses, but not by much. The Goat's girls were among the most expensive in the city, but Manaus was Manaus. She could get two of them for the price of a decent bottle of wine.

CHIEF PINTO came through, as he always did. Forty-eight hours later, Claudia was conducting the test.

The room smelled of sweat and testosterone. Little motes of dust had been kicked up by all the lunging and plunging on the mattress, and they danced in the glare of the lights. The candidate, a certain Delfin Figueiredo, gave a final thrust and groan and collapsed on top of the whore. The whore, looking over his shoulder, had a bored expression on her face. She rolled her eyes at Claudia as if to say, *What are you waiting for? He's finished*, but Claudia gave Figueiredo another ten seconds or so before she switched off the lights.

Figueiredo had performed more than adequately, and the girl had done her job. Otto was tasked with taking her back to The Goat's. She slipped into a dress, no underwear, put her feet into a pair of plastic sandals, and was out the door sixty seconds after Delfin rolled off of her.

Hans, playing the European, signified he was satisfied. He hadn't said a word during the entire process, and he didn't now. He simply handed over the wad Claudia had given him and left. Hans's silence had been an absolute necessity. He was no actor, and Figueiredo would have pegged him for a Brazilian the minute he'd opened his mouth.

Claudia promptly counted off the agreed-upon sum from the wad and handed it to Figueiredo. He counted it again, folded it, and reached for his underpants.

"You got any more work like this," he said, putting the underwear on, "I'm your man. Easiest money I ever made."

"What you earned today is a trifle," she said. "You could be earning a lot more if you've got the balls to go for it."

Claudia had questioned Delfin's manhood. Delfin reacted like she knew he would.

"What the fuck you mean 'If I got the balls'?"

"Just what I said."

"I got the balls for anything," he said. "Anything," he repeated.

"Then I've got a proposition for you," she said.

Thought lines creased what was normally a smooth brow. Delfin gave her a suspicious look, stuffed the money into a pocket of his jeans, and lifted one foot in order to pull them on.

"What have you got in mind?" he said, his foot still in the air.

"I hear you kill people."

He put his foot back on the floor.

"Who the fuck told you that?"

"Just something I heard," she said.

He lifted his right foot again, slid it into the jeans, and did the same with the left. Then he pulled the pants up to his hips, closed the top button and zipped the fly.

"Someone's got a big mouth," he said. "And why should you care?"

"Because," she said, "I've got a proposal that a man with your background won't be able to refuse, as long as he's got balls, that is."

Behind the door, Hans, who hadn't left, was listening to every word.

Carla was at the point where she was telling the dumb bastard there was only one thing her "European" liked better than watching people fuck.

Hans waited for a reaction. There wasn't any, at least none he could hear.

Carla went on for a minute or two more, then stopped.

There was a moment of silence.

"How much?" Figueiredo's voice.

Hans smiled, put his Glock back into the holster on his belt, and strolled into the kitchen to get a beer.

WHEN MARTA HEARD THE rattle of keys, she sat bolt upright and set her back against the wall behind her.

But when the door opened, it wasn't The Goat. It was a woman, and she was carrying a tray.

Marta hadn't eaten in almost twenty-four hours. Even her pitcher of water was long since empty. She smelled coffee, and milk, and, yes, *pão de queijo*, the little round cheese breads she'd always loved, especially when they were dripping with butter.

"Hungry?" the woman said.

Marta nodded, her throat too dry to speak.

The woman knelt, put the tray on the floor, and slid it forward with her foot.

"Well, then," she said, "eat."

Marta stretched out a hand, watching the woman all the while, and felt around until her fingers touched one of the little yellow balls. It was still warm from the oven. She grabbed it, stuffed it in her mouth, and almost choked. Her throat was that dry.

"Take your time," the woman said. "Drink some coffee."

Marta dropped her eyes long enough to make sure she got a good grip on the mug, expecting it to be hot.

It wasn't. It was lukewarm. She meant to take only a sip or two, but the *café com leite* had been sweetened, and once she got going she couldn't stop. She drained more than half in one go.

"I'm Carla Antunes," the woman said.

Marta didn't care what the woman's name was, but she very much cared about the remaining cheese breads. She took another one, savoring the chewy consistency, wishing the woman had brought butter.

"I'm going to get you out of here," Carla Antunes said.

Marta stopped chewing.

"Let me see your face," Carla said. Then, leaning in closer, "Oh, my. You poor thing."

That did it. A memory struck Marta with the force of a

blow. She and Andrea had been on the beach together, Marta had stepped on a shard of glass from a broken bottle, and Andrea, as she was examining the wound, had used exactly those words: *Oh, my. You poor thing.*

Marta started to cry.

Carla was ready with a paper handkerchief, then another and another. When the sobs subsided, she let Marta finish her meal, not hurrying her at all, even telling her to slow down so she wouldn't make herself sick.

"Who are you?" Marta asked her when she'd eaten the last of the bread and drained the last drop from the mug.

"I told you. I'm Carla Antunes."

"But why are you—"

"All in good time, Marta. Shall we go?"

The woman took her by the arm, gently, and they stepped through the doorway into the corridor.

They walked through the boate and approached the main entrance, a double door that Marta had only seen when it was chained and padlocked. But now the padlock was gone, the chain was hanging in a loop, and the doors were ajar. Daylight was streaming through the crack. She hadn't seen that much daylight in over two months.

She turned her head to look behind her. Topaz stuck her head around the doorjamb that led to the bedrooms and quickly withdrew it, but she saw no one else, not The Goat, not Rosélia. Outside, the sun was near its zenith. She blinked in the dazzling light. A man was waiting there, a big man with long blond hair and a moustache that made him look like a Viking.

Momentarily, it occurred to Marta to run. But she rejected the idea almost as quickly as she thought of it. The man looked to be in good shape, and his legs were much longer than hers. She wouldn't have gotten very far.

The Viking led them to a car and ushered them into the back seat. Then he climbed behind the wheel and started the engine, all without saying a word. They took her to a house with a tiled roof and whitewashed walls. Beyond it, a cabin cruiser, not unlike the one her grandfather kept in Brasilia, was floating at a dock on the river.

As they got out of the car, Carla took her arm again. The big man with the mustache moved in front, took out a key, and unlocked the front door.

The house looked old on the outside, but inside it was modern. The floors and window frames were light-colored wood, varnished to a high gloss; the light fixtures were brushed aluminum; the walls were painted in pastels. Through a doorway, she caught a glimpse of a large room with tripods, cables, and what looked like photographer's lights. A king-sized bed occupied the center of the space.

On the opposite side, ten steps further down the corridor, was a bedroom.

"Here's where you'll sleep," Carla said.

The space was a considerable improvement on her accommodations at The Goat's. There was a coverlet on the bed, an air-conditioner hummed away in the wall, and a bedside table supported a lamp. There was a bookshelf, piled high with paperbacks and magazines, all well thumbed. There was an armchair, a wardrobe cupboard, even a window. The window looked over a green lawn to a distant stand of trees. But there were bars set into the masonry.

"I'm going to be straight with you," Carla said. "I'm not Mother Teresa. I'm a businesswoman. I send girls to Europe."

"Prostitutes?"

"I prefer to call them escorts. They're working girls, yes, but they don't have to work anywhere near as hard as the girls work at The Goat's place. They wear beautiful clothes and go to good restaurants. Sometimes they stay with a man for as much as a week, sometimes only for a night, but they never have to make love to more than one man a day."

"You call that making love? It's not making love, it's fucking for money. I won't do it."

Carla smiled. "We're going to have to let those bruises heal," she said. "There's a bathroom through that door. Soap, towels, shampoo, conditioner, everything you need."

"I told you I'm not going to do it. Do you have any idea who I am? Do you have any idea what kind of risk you're running here?"

"Risk? No, frankly I don't. Enlighten me."

"I'm the granddaughter of Deputado Malan."

"Really?" She could see the woman didn't believe her. "Let's talk more about it when you're rested, shall we? Are you still hungry?"

Marta nodded.

"There's bottled water in the cupboard. Hans will bring you some food."

Carla turned to leave.

"I have a friend," Marta blurted out.

Carla had almost reached the door. She turned around.

"I know," she said. "Andrea."

Marta's mouth opened in surprise.

"You know Andrea?"

Carla nodded.

Marta took a deep breath.

"You know where she is?"

Another nod.

"Would you like to join her?" Carla inquired.

"Oh, yes! Yes!" Marta said.

"I think that could be arranged."

* * *

HANS WAS WAITING IN the corridor. Claudia led him down the hall, out of earshot.

"Get her some food," she said. "What have we got?"

"Pacu."

Claudia made a face. Pacu was one of the most common fish in the river, no less prized by Amazonenses for all of that.

"It's all we got," Hans said, "that, and rice, and beans, and corn meal."

"Okay," Claudia said, "Give it to her. She's probably hungry enough to eat anything."

"How about the shoot?" Hans said.

The shoot. Talking like he belonged to a film crew.

"Soon," she said. "Now that we've recruited the talent, there's no sense putting it off."

"Right," Hans said; then, as she turned away, "Where are you off to?"

"Out to find something better to eat than pacu."

INSIDE HER room, Marta was exploring. She slid up the window sash—it moved easily in its tracks—and wrapped her fingers around one of the white-painted bars. It was warm to the touch, probably steel. She shook it, but it didn't budge. She tried all of the bars, one by one. None of them budged. When she drew her hand back, some flecks of paint came along with it. Her efforts had done no more than expose bare metal. The space between the bars was narrow, so narrow she couldn't get her head between them, much less her shoulders. Above and below, the bars were solidly set into the thick concrete wall. Without tools, there wasn't a chance she'd be able to get out through the window. And even *with* tools, removing them would make far too much noise.

She checked the closet and the bathroom, the walls and the ceiling. No vents, not a single one. She managed to get the front cover off the air-conditioner and examined the mounting screws. That, too, was a dead end. The screws were deeply embedded in the masonry. She left the door of the room for last. The one at The Goat's had been sheathed with metal. This was solid wood, hung to open inward. The hinges drew her particular attention. She leaned forward for a closer look.

Like the hinges in her room at home these were made out of brass with little decorative spheres drilled and threaded to hold the hinge pins in place. The night she'd escaped and fled to Andrea's, she'd had to take a pair of pliers to the spheres because they'd been frozen in place by a coat of paint. But these were different. They were larger, fluted on the outside, and had never been painted. Gingerly, she reached out a hand, grasped the topmost sphere as tightly as she could and tried to turn it.

It didn't budge. She tried the one at the bottom of the same hinge, felt it give, then give some more and finally begin to turn. If she could remove just one sphere on each of the three hinges, she could pull out all of the pins. And once the pins were out, she'd be able to remove the door. She screwed the sphere she'd been working on back into place and attacked another one.

WHEN CLAUDIA got back from lunch, Otto was waiting.

"I got the photos," he said.

"Finally. What took you so damned long?"

"The guy at the photo shop said they were going to be ready by nine this morning. They weren't."

"You ever hear of a digital camera?"

"I don't understand those things. They got too many buttons."

"Give me those," she said, and snatched the envelope.

The first photo was of an athletic-looking man crossing a parking lot. Arnaldo Nunes. She recognized him immediately. The second shot showed him entering the main entrance to the airport. Both shots were in profile, the background out of focus, obviously shot with a long lens.

She shuffled to the third photo in the stack and froze.

Otto came around to look over her shoulder.

"Those are the two guys he met at the airport," he said.

When she didn't say anything, he prompted her. "You recognize them?"

"That one," she said, "is Mario Silva."

Otto leaned forward for a better look. "No shit?" he said. "That's Silva, huh? You sure? He looks different from when you see him on the news and stuff."

"It's the outfit," she said. "The bush shirt. Every damned photo you ever see of the man, every time he's on television, he's wearing a gray suit."

"He'd have to be crazy to wear a suit in Manaus. A suit would kill him in this climate."

"Then I wish he'd wear one and save us the trouble," she said.

Otto looked at her nervously.

"Hey, Carla," he said, "you're not thinking of offing a federal cop, are you?"

"Why not?"

"Uh . . . well, if you are, we gotta talk about it."

"What's to talk about?"

"That's heavy stuff, killing a federal. What are you worried about? What makes you think he's after us?"

"He's after *me*," Claudia said.

Otto looked at her, waited for her to tell him more. When she didn't, he said, "What makes you so sure?"

She didn't reply.

"What?" he insisted.

Again, no reply.

"You're sure it's him? Really sure?"

She stabbed the photo with her forefinger.

"*That's* Silva, and *that's* his fucking nephew, Hector Costa. And the guy who met them, the guy who was already here in Manaus, is an old-time sidekick of both, an agente named Arnaldo Nunes."

"But how can you—"

"Shut up, Otto. I know what I'm talking about."

She wasn't about to tell him *why* she was so sure, or *why* she knew he was after her. That, and her real name, were none of his damned business.

Chapter Eighteen

IRENE WAS SITTING UNDER a beach umbrella, reading a book, just the trace of a smile on her face. Silva was stretched out on blinding white sand, soaking up the sun, his head on his arms. He had one eye open and was studying her.

He heard his son call him.

"Look, Papa, look!"

He turned his head toward the voice, toward the clear, green sea. Little Mario, his ankles bathed in receding foam, was pointing at three dolphins swimming in the shallows, their dorsal fins skimming along the surface like the sails of tiny boats.

And little Mario wasn't so little anymore. He looked to be about twelve. His olive skin had been darkened by the summer sun, and his smile showed teeth like pearls.

Silva got up and walked down to the water. They plunged in together. The dolphins came to meet them. Silva reached out to touch one—and the telephone rang, summoning him away from another experience he'd never had and now never would.

Long accustomed to calls in the night, he was alert by the time the receiver was against his ear.

"*Alô*," he said.

"Mario?"

Arnaldo's voice. Silva threw the covers aside, managed to get a hand on his wristwatch, but couldn't find his glasses.

"What time is it?"

"Almost six," Arnaldo said. "I just got a call from Father Vitorio."

"At this time of the morning?"

"The man has no sense of propriety. Or maybe he's just an insomniac. Anyway, he wants to meet."

Silva walked to the window.

"What's so important? Couldn't he have waited a few hours?"

"Apparently not. But at least he didn't ask us to go over to that slum he lives in. He's coming to us. The restaurant. Half an hour."

"Call Hector," Silva said.

Arnaldo agreed and hung up.

Silva parted the curtains. The rising sun painted a golden stripe across the black water of the river, but there was a line of black clouds on the horizon. And they appeared to be moving directly toward him.

FATHER VITORIO was punctual to the minute.

"Six thirty on the dot," Arnaldo muttered when he saw him in the doorway. "Must have been waiting outside so he could make a grand entrance."

There were no other guests at that hour. The restaurant was quiet, so quiet they could hear the priest's cassock rustling as he approached the table. He stood there, waiting for Arnaldo to complete the introductions before he took a seat.

"Coffee," he said tersely to the hovering waiter.

Silva didn't think the priest needed it. He looked wired enough already.

The waiter departed in the direction of the kitchen. Father Vitorio leaned across the table and lowered his voice.

"You're Silva, aren't you?"

"I am."

"I thought so. I've seen you on television."

"I have news about the young lady."

"Which one?" Silva said.

"The pearl earrings and the gold crucifix. I've asked this before, but your man"—the priest cocked a thumb at Arnaldo—"wouldn't tell me. So now I'm asking you: Who is she?"

He's going to find out anyway, Silva thought. *There might be some benefit in letting the news come from me.*

"She's the fifteen-year-old granddaughter of Roberto Malan," he said.

Father Vitorio responded in a hoarse whisper. "Malan? The deputado? *That* Malan?"

Silva took a sip of coffee and nodded. "Him."

The priest ran a hand over the stubble on his cheek. "The old story," he said.

"What old story?"

"The rich and famous get priority treatment. How many of the thousands of fifteen-year-old girls in this country could have brought three federal policemen to Manaus?"

"It's not just the girl, Padre. This case is far more complex than you think," Silva said.

"Is it? Tell me."

"I can't do that, not at the moment. But I promise to brief you thoroughly before we leave this city. Now, what have you got?"

"The deputado's granddaughter is here in Manaus."

Silva put down his cup and sat upright in his chair. "You're certain?"

"Yes."

"Where?"

"I don't know."

"But you just said—"

"I know where she *was*. From there, it should be possible for you to discover where she currently *is*."

"I hope to God you're right. Where was she?"

"In a brothel."

"Goddamnit," Arnaldo said. He sounded as if he'd been expecting it all along.

The priest turned on him. "No need to take the Lord's name in vain, Agente. He's taken good care of her up to now, and I'm confident He'll continue to protect her. She entered that brothel a virgin and she left a virgin. She—"

"Which brothel?" Silva's voice was a whip.

"All in good time. First, I want—"

"Padre, please," Silva said. "Time is critical."

"She's been in Manaus, Chief Inspector, for more than two months. I don't see that an extra few minutes—"

"If what you're going to say is that an extra few minutes won't make any difference, you're dead wrong. They could make every difference. Who's your source?"

"I insist on discretion."

"You'll have complete discretion. Who's your source?"

"His name is Lauro Tadesco. He's one of my ex-students. His ambition is to become a priest."

"How did he—"

"He's my own undercover investigator, my inside man. He gathers information we'll be able to use in a future legal action against those whoremongers. He does it by visiting brothels."

Both of Arnaldo's eyebrows went up. "He does *what?*"

"You heard me, Agente. But you can wipe that expression off your face. Lauro has made a vow of chastity. Once he gets the girls alone, he makes it clear he doesn't want sexual congress, only information. He always takes the precaution of asking them to keep his inquiries confidential."

"Let me tell you something about whores," Arnaldo said. "Somebody starts asking a whore questions, she knows her pimp is going to want to know all about it. Whores will shop your boy for a flask of cheap perfume, or a bottle of cachaça. They probably already have. It's *their* discretion you should have been worrying about, not ours."

The priest frowned.

Silva intervened.

"I doubt that Lauro is in any immediate danger, but I'm very much afraid that Marta is. Come on, Padre, out with it. Tell us everything you know, and tell us right now."

THE GIRL'S name was Topaz, at least that's what she'd said. She'd claimed to be sixteen, but looked younger, and she worked at a brothel owned by an ex–police sergeant whom everyone called The Goat.

According to Topaz, The Goat had been holding Marta for two months. He'd applied a lot of pressure, but she'd always refused to cooperate, kept saying there was no way she was going to let him turn her into a whore. On the afternoon of the previous day, she'd been taken from the boate by an older woman, a brunette. "This brunette," Silva asked, "did Topaz see her personally?"

"Only for a moment and only from the rear," Father Vitorio said. "She was unable to give Lauro an adequate description."

"Merda," Silva said.

"Merda, indeed," the priest agreed, "and it's partly my fault. The Goat specializes in underage girls. I knew that. Perhaps I should have sent Lauro as soon as I spoke to Agente Nunes here, but it didn't immediately occur to me. Our investigation is far more extensive, you see. We're not concerned with only one girl."

"I appreciate that, Padre. You've been a big help. Now, if you'll excuse us—"

Silva started to get up, but the priest put a hand on his shoulder to restrain him.

"You're going there, aren't you?" he said. "To The Goat's?"

"Immediately," Silva said.

"I want to go with you."

"You *what?*"

Silva was totally surprised and made no attempt to hide it.

Father Vitorio plunged on: "I want to be there when you question The Goat. I want to look into that man's eyes when you confront him."

Silva shook his head. "Out of the question."

The priest leaned forward. "This is important to me. I can't tell you how important."

"You're not a cop. I couldn't answer for your safety."

"You don't have to answer for my safety. God takes care of my safety."

"The answer is no."

The priest flushed. "I helped you. I gave you a lead. You have an obligation to me."

"Right on all three counts, Padre. But you're not going with us, and that's final. Don't waste your breath trying to get me to change my mind, because I won't."

Father Vitorio clenched his jaw. Then, without another word, he stood and made for the door.

THE GOAT's *boate*—his "nightclub" brothel—was a sorry sight in daylight. The weathered wood of the façade was badly in need of paint. Beer cans and empty cachaça bottles littered the parking lot. The three cops had to sidestep a pool of vomit to get to the front door.

Silva lifted his fist and pounded on the wood.

There was no response.

"Wake them up," he said.

The house was isolated. Arnaldo got the message. He looked around him, then took out his Glock and pulled back the slide. Silva and Hector covered their ears. Arnaldo pointed the muzzle in the air and pulled the trigger. The sharp report came echoing back from the hill across the road.

"That should do it," Silva said.

He was right. Seconds later, they heard stirring inside.

"Go away, you crazy bastard," a woman's voice said. "We're closed. Go sleep it off. Come back tonight."

"Police," Arnaldo said.

"I told you to beat it."

"You hear what I said? Police."

"Yeah, I heard what you said. Go home and jerk off. Or maybe you want me to call Chief Pinto?"

"*Federal* Police," Arnaldo said, "and you're the one who's jerking me off. Open the fucking door before I shoot off the lock."

That produced some nearly inaudible muttering. Two voices now. One of them could have been male.

Arnaldo hit the door with the butt of his Glock, leaving a visible dent in the wood.

"You hear me?"

"Yeah, yeah, I heard you," the woman said. "Wait a minute. I gotta get the key."

Time passed, enough of it and more to fetch a key from the remotest corner of the building.

"They're stalling," Silva said.

But then they heard the rattle of a chain. A moment later, one of the double doors opened to reveal a woman wearing no makeup, a nightgown, and a suspicious expression.

"Show me some ID," she said.

Arnaldo flashed his badge.

"Anybody can buy a badge," she said. "Something with a photo."

He produced his federal police ID and held it up for her inspection.

"Okay," she said. "And now the other gentlemen."

"Jesus Christ," Arnaldo said.

"Let's see your own ID," Silva said.

He was hoping she'd step away from the door to fetch it. But she didn't. She'd been holding it ready, behind her back.

Arnaldo took it and scrutinized it.

"Rosélia Fagundes, huh?"

"I've shown you mine, Agente, now I want your friends to show me theirs."Silva and his nephew pulled out their credentials. She took her time studying them, particularly Silva's. Then she addressed him.

"What do you want?"

"A look around."

"You have a warrant?"

"Not yet."

"What are you looking for?"

"Minors. One minor in particular."

"You've come to the wrong place. All our girls are over eighteen. We operate strictly within the law."

"Not the way I hear it."

"Then you hear wrong. We've got competitors. They're jealous. They like to spread rumors about us. Who's the minor?"

Wordlessly, Silva pulled out a photo of Marta Malan.

She took it, studied it and didn't bat an eye.

"Never seen her before," she said. "What's she done?"

"You've got it backward," Silva said. "She didn't do a damned thing. People are doing something to her. And we think you're one of those people."

"Me? That's absurd."

"The way we hear it, you've been holding her prisoner for more than two months."

"You hear it wrong. She's not here."

"We know that."

"And she's never been here."

"And that's bullshit. How come you won't let us in?"

"I never said you couldn't come in. Come ahead. Come in. Look around all you like. Then get the hell out of here and let us go back to sleep."

She swung the door open, went to a neighboring wall and toggled a switch. The room filled with light. They were in a bar: no windows, tables of rude wood, folding metal chairs, an area in the middle raised and cleared for dancing. The place smelled of beer, cachaça, sweat, and, faintly, of perfume.

"This is the social area," she said, kicking off the tour. "Cops drink for free at The Goat's. You're guests of the house while you're in Manaus. Cachaça and beer only. Whiskey is extra."

Silva ignored the invitation.

"What's behind that door?"

"A toilet. Males only."

"And that one?"

"A storeroom."

"And that one over there?"

"Leads to where the girls sleep and work."

"Then that's where we'll start."

There were twenty-two bedrooms, seven of them occupied. Every bed had been slept in, but there were only seven girls. They all had identity cards proving they were eighteen or older. None of them looked it. None of them admitted to knowing a girl who called herself Topaz.

"Where are the others?" Silva said.

The Fagundes woman looked him straight in the eye.

"There are no others."

"Why so many bedrooms for so few girls?"

She shrugged.

"Girls come, girls go. Sometimes we have a full house, sometimes we don't."

"How come the other beds are unmade?"

"We haven't cleaned up from last night," she said. "We alternate rooms. That way the sheets get a chance to dry out. It's hot in here, in case you hadn't noticed."

"I noticed. Where's The Goat?"

"He doesn't sleep here."

"He doesn't, eh?"

"Only sometimes."

"And you?"

"Sometimes."

"How many entrances to the building?"

"The one you came in and one more. It's around in back, leads to the annex."

"Annex?"

"For the staff." She held out five fingers, used her other hand to fold them one by one as she enumerated. "One bartender, one cleaning girl, one bouncer, one cook, one laundress."

"Point out the way," Arnaldo said.

The door was unlocked and ajar. It opened on a narrow alleyway between the main building and the annex.

Arnaldo pulled out his pistol and turned left, creeping on the balls of his feet. Unlike many big men, he could move quietly when he wanted to. There were no windows in the main building, but there was one in the annex. Arnaldo stood next to it for a moment, his back to the wall. Then he wheeled around and forward, dropping to a crouch and extending his Glock in a two-handed grip.

He found himself pointing it at the forehead of a woman who wasn't more than a foot away. She gave a yelp and dropped the pipe she'd been smoking onto the window sill. Ashes and sparks exploded from the bowl.

Arnaldo lowered his gun.

"*Calma*, Senhora," he said. "I'm a cop."

The woman only had eyes for his pistol. She licked her lips and followed the Glock all the way back to the holster on his belt. Then, and only then, she said, "A cop, huh? What happened? You fall asleep? Spend the night? You better get your ass outta here. The Goat doesn't like anyone inside after closing time. The girls know that. The Goat finds out which one of them you were with, he's gonna whip her for sure."

She had black skin and gray hair, and she wore a dress with short sleeves. She looked to be at least seventy. And now that she was over her fear, she was starting to get angry.

"I'm not a customer," he said. "I'm a federal, and I just arrived."

"A federal? You after The Goat?"

"Why would you think that?"

"I can think any damned thing I want, doesn't mean I have to tell you. You scared me half to death."

"For which I'm truly sorry. How long have you been sitting there?"

The woman retrieved her pipe and stared sadly at the empty bowl.

"Maybe ten minutes. I like to have a pipe before I get my hands in the suds. I just lit this one."

"You see anybody go by?"

"Nobody special. The Goat, Osvaldo, some girls."

"How many girls?"

"Hell, you think I'm gonna count 'em as they go by?" She

stabbed at the air with her finger, did it three times. "One . . . two . . . three."

"I don't need an exact number, just an estimate."

"Well, you're not gonna get one."

"A dozen?"

"Maybe a dozen."

"Young ones?"

"All young ones."

"Which way did they go?"

She pointed toward the end of the alley, curved her wrist to indicate they'd taken a turn to the right, toward the river.

"Merda," Arnaldo said and went back to fetch his companions.

Chapter Nineteen

THE GOAT TOOK THE binoculars from their case on the console, looped the strap over his neck and looked back at his floating dock. The men on it were standing in a compact group, shading their eyes and looking out at the water.

He was at least a kilometer away, and even with binoculars he couldn't see the cops' features. That made it damned near certain they couldn't see him at all.

And besides, there were at least two dozen boats within sight of that dock. There was no way they could know which one was his.

His heartbeat began to slow as he assessed his options.

Federals were bad news. It wasn't likely he'd be able to bribe them, and he couldn't expect any help from Chief Pinto. Pinto wouldn't want to do anything that might bring the wrath of the federal government down on his head. But without the girls, the federals didn't have a case. All he had to do was to send them off to somewhere safe and keep them there until the fucking federals went back to Brasilia, or wherever the hell else they had come from. In a flash of inspiration, it occurred to him that he was sitting on the solution: the boat. It would be a little cramped, but it was the dry season. Some of them could sleep on deck, or at worst, in shifts, some girls sleeping by day and the others by night. The Anavilhanas Archipelago was less than a hundred kilometers away. There were more islands there than days in a year, lots of beaches, too, where the girls could escape the cramped quarters, go ashore and lie around on the sand.

He had plenty of fuel. All he had to do was stop off at one of those floating shops, lay in a supply of food, cigarettes, and cachaça, then keep the bow pointing upriver. Once he'd found a hiding place amid the islands, he could drop anchor and sit there until things blew over. They'd never find him.

Him? Hang on! Why the hell should he go himself? Without the girls, what could they prove? Why didn't he just send Osvaldo?

He'd taken Osvaldo on the boat for two reasons: firstly, because the old bastard was a lousy liar and, secondly, because he knew far too much. It would be disastrous if the federals got a chance to grill him.

Osvaldo had been a fisherman. He knew the river. He'd jump at the chance. Who wouldn't? Jesus. What was better than being anchored off a sandy beach with no work to do, plenty of cachaça, and a boatload of underage whores? The dumb fuck should pay *him.*

The Goat disembarked at a place where he could catch a passenger boat going toward Manaus. Osvaldo couldn't wait to get away. When he was about fifty meters off, the motor going flat out, a broad smile creasing his face from ear to ear, he looked back over his shoulder and gave The Goat a happy wave.

IT TOOK him three hours to get home. He had to take a taxi from where the boat came in, the immense floating dock near the center of town. It had been built by the English nearly a century ago at the height of the rubber trade. The city fathers kept assuring everyone it was safe, but The Goat didn't trust them. He expected that dock to sink sometime soon, and he was never entirely comfortable when he was on it.

Rosélia started talking as soon as he came in the door. And the more she talked, the more worried The Goat became. When she'd finally spilled all of the details about the visit from the federal cops, The Goat promptly reached for the telephone and as promptly slammed it down again.

What am I thinking? The bastards might already be running a tap.

So he went outside, got into his truck, and drove around for a while, always with an eye on the rearview mirror. When he was absolutely certain that he wasn't being followed, he went to Carla's place.

The guy who answered his knock was one of Carla's thugs, the one who looked like a Viking. He raised his eyebrows when he found The Goat on the other side of the door.

"You here to see Carla?"

"I'm sure as hell not here to see you," The Goat snapped. "Get her."

"You better watch your mouth," the Viking said, but he stepped aside. Carla's other capanga, the guy with the bags under his eyes, was standing just behind the door, putting a big pistol back into his shoulder holster.

While the Viking went to get Carla, the guy with the bags made small talk about the weather, which was stupid because the weather in Manaus was always the same: rain during the rainy season, less rain during the dry season, hot and humid all year long. But guys from the south were like that. They got four seasons a year down there, all variable, and when they had nothing else to talk about, they talked about the weather.

When the Viking came back, Carla was with him.

She found The Goat pacing back and forth between the door and the window.

"What's wrong?" she said.

"Hello, Carla," The Goat said. "What makes you think something's wrong?" He was eyeing Hans and Otto.

"There's got to be something wrong, or you wouldn't have shown up here unannounced," she said. "And anything you've got to say you can say in front of them."

"Aren't you gonna offer me something?"

She led him to the kitchen. Hans and Otto trailed along behind. They'd been drinking coffee. Their cups were still on the table, still steaming.

"Coffee?" she said.

"You got something stronger?"

She took a bottle of cachaça out of a cupboard, a glass out of another, and put them both on the table.

"Take a seat," she said.

Claudia and her capangas sat down as well. The Goat poured himself a drink, polished it off in one gulp and immediately refilled his glass.

"Before you have any more of that," she said, tapping the bottle with the nail of her index finger, "maybe you should tell us why you're here."

So he did. He told them about waking up to the sound of a shot, the visit of the cops, how he'd sent Osvaldo upriver with the girls who were too young to practice their trade legally.

"Lucky bastard," Otto said.

Claudia ignored the interjection.

"Sounds like you're home free," she said. "What are you worried about?"

"When I got back," The Goat said, "Rosélia told me they showed her a photo of that girl I sold you, the young one."

"Marta?"

"Her. You have any idea who she is? She's the grand-daughter of that deputado Malan, that's who."

"Merda," Claudia said.

"Merda is right. She told Rosélia who her grandfather was,

but Rosélia didn't believe her. I wouldn't have either. What would the granddaughter of a deputado be doing sleeping on a beach, huh?"

So they're not here for me after all, Claudia thought.

She felt a surge of relief. It made sense that a big-shot deputado like Malan could bend the federal police to his will, even get them to assign Silva, the best man they had, to lead the search for his granddaughter.

"Where is she?" The Goat asked, drawing Claudia away from her thoughts and back into the conversation.

Claudia raised an eyebrow.

"I don't see that it's any of your business," she said. Then she added, as an afterthought, "You sure you weren't followed?"

"Aha," he said. "So she's still here in the house?"

He tossed off his drink and poured another.

"I'd go easy on that stuff if I were you," Claudia said.

"Yeah? Well, you're not me. So she's still here in the house?"

Claudia nodded. "Locked up in her room."

"Those cops told Rosélia they *knew* she'd been at my place, *knew* it."

"How?"

"God knows. What did you do with her girlfriend?"

"Andrea?"

"Yeah, Andrea. What did you do with her?"

"You already know what I did with her. I passed her on to some friends in Europe. Why?"

"Because your friends in Europe snuffed her, that's why."

"What?"

"Those federals had a picture of her, too. Said they have a video of her getting fucked and murdered." The Goat narrowed his eyes and leaned closer. "You didn't have any idea that your friends were going to do something like that, did you, Carla?"

"The cops are lying. They're just trying to pressure you."

The Goat stared at her for a moment. Then he moved on.

"You'll never be able to get that little bitch, Marta, on an airplane. Not now. They'll be watching the airports like hawks. Use your boat. Go upriver. Hook up with Osvaldo and leave her there."

Carla snorted.

"Excuse me," she said. "Are you telling me what to do with my property?" She looked at her Viking, who went into Rottweiler mode, lowering his eyebrows and making a growling sound.

The Goat ignored him.

"Do it," he said.

"No," Claudia said.

"Don't be stupid, Carla. Listen to what I'm telling you."

The Goat was getting red in the face.

"She's promised to someone," Claudia said. "It's a done deal. I'm not sending her upriver, I'm sending her to Europe."

"How the fuck do you think you can get her out of the country?"

"That's my problem, not yours."

The Goat's eyes went cold.

"If the federals get their hands on her," he said, "it's *our* problem, Rosélia's and mine. We're the ones who snatched her; we're the ones who held her for the longest time. She's seen both our faces. She's not afraid of anything, so threats don't work. If she squeals . . ."

"I'll take care of it," Claudia said, "but it won't be by sending her upriver."

The Goat poured himself another shot, drank it off in one draught, and stood up.

"All right," he said, "do it your way, but do it—and soon."

Claudia bristled.

"I'm getting tired of your threats," she said.

"I don't give a shit whether you're getting tired of them or not," he said, "but if you know what's good for you, you'll take them to heart. Don't fuck with me, Carla. Don't ever fuck with me. I'll make you sorry if you do."

When the door closed behind The Goat, Claudia picked up the bottle of cachaça, poured a hefty dose into her coffee cup and took a ladylike sip. If Hans and Otto hadn't been watching her, she would have gulped it down.

"We have to find out," she said, "how Silva and his pals knew Marta was at The Goat's place."

"Maybe they didn't know," Hans said. "Maybe they were bluffing. Maybe they told the same story to everybody."

Sometimes he surprised her.

"Good point," she said. "How many other people do you know who run brothels?"

"Hell, I don't know. I musta tried every one in town some time or another. Maybe a hundred?"

"Call around. See if the federals told anybody else the same story."

"And if not . . ."

"We're going to have another talk with The Goat."

"No way," The Goat said three hours later.

They were in his bar, sitting at one of the tables. The front door was open, allowing some light to spill in from the direction of the parking lot, but the room was otherwise dark. They would have been there sooner, but two of the three hours had been spent in making sure they weren't being followed and that The Goat's boate wasn't under surveillance.

"No way," he repeated, shaking his head.

"Had to be," she said. "No other explanation makes sense."

"I can't believe it. There's no way one of my own girls would talk to somebody about what happens in this house. And, even if she did, she'd come to me and tell me."

"You're acting like they're your daughters," Claudia said. "They're not. If you don't think they have their little secrets, you're a fool."

"Watch out who you're calling a fool."

"I take it back. Let's ask them a few questions."

"All right," he said, then raised his voice: "Rosélia, turn the lights on and bring the whole gang out here."

THE QUESTIONING went on for an hour, first communally, then one by one.

"Satisfied?" The Goat said when the last of them, tears running down her face, was allowed to go back to her room.

"With them, yes," Claudia said. "You said you're keeping the others on a boat. Where's the boat?"

"I don't know exactly," the Goat said. "Somewhere in the Anavilhanas."

"The what?"

"The Anavilhanas Archipelago. This time of the year, the water goes down and you get sandy beaches and canals. Some of the cruise ships go there, but they don't go very far in."

"How long would it take to find them?"

The Goat shrugged. "With luck, maybe a few hours; without it, a couple of days. Why?"

"Because," she said, "We're going to pay them a visit."

CLAUDIA'S BOAT wasn't as big as The Goat's, but it was faster and more comfortable: twin diesels, air-conditioning, two staterooms, a saloon, and a hot-water shower with an electric pump.

At first, The Goat was reluctant to go along, but when he saw how eager Hans and Otto were, he decided it might be a good idea. He didn't want the two thugs getting among his girls unsupervised.

Claudia had never been to the Anavilhanas Archipelago, but she'd been around boats since her childhood. And it wasn't as if the river posed any navigational problems. All she had to do was to keep the bow pointed upstream and stay close to the bank to minimize the effect of the current. She decided someone had to stay behind and keep an eye on Marta. Hans and Otto drew straws. Otto lost.

They planned their departure for two thirty in the morning. Any earlier, and they'd find themselves among the islands in the dark.

MARTA AWOKE to the ringing of an alarm clock. It was on the other side of the wall, and it wasn't very loud, but she'd always been a light sleeper. She threw off her sheet, got out of bed, and walked to the window. The moon was still high in the sky, almost full. With her cheek against the side of the glass she could see it sparkling on the river, a thin band of silver painted on the black water.

A light in the neighboring bedroom went on, illuminating the grass. She heard a toilet flush and footsteps in the corridor. She put an ear against the door.

"I don't know how long it's going to take to locate the damned boat." *Carla's voice.* "Don't expect us back before dark, and don't forget to feed the girl."

"Feed the girl. Feed the girl. Caralho, Carla, how many times you got to say it? You think I'm stupid or something?"

That was the one with the bags under his eyes. He sounded sleepy, maybe a little drunk.

"Don't be impudent with me, you imbecile."

Still sniping at each other, they moved off in the direction of the kitchen.

What they were saying became indistinct, but she could hear the rattle of cutlery. A little while later she smelled coffee. When the back door slammed, she returned to the window. Carla and the big man were walking toward the boat. Just before they vanished from her line of sight, she heard Carla say something about picking up The Goat at his dock. A minute or so later, the boat's engines came to life, loud at first, then fading, fading until they were gone. The house was silent again, the only sound the nightly chorus of insects in the nearby jungle.

It was the chance she'd been hoping for. She didn't think she'd get a better one. For a while, she sat on the edge of the bed, getting up her courage. All that time she could feel her heart pounding, feel the sweat on her palms. She tried controlled breathing, taking the air in through her nose, four seconds for every breath.

Finally, when the moon was down, and the darkness as deep as it was going to get, she stood up, put on her clothes and attacked the door. She left the middle pin for last, broke a nail getting it out. There was a squeak, then a *thump* when the door disengaged from the frame. She caught it on her shoulder, got a hand on either side, and lowered it gently to the floor. Once it was down, she paused to listen. The thug was still snoring.

Her instinct was to run, but she suppressed it. She stood there, breathing heavily, looking at the gaping black hole that led to the corridor and freedom. The snoring seemed much louder now, and it was coming from the left, the direction she'd have to go to get to the front door.

She crept down the corridor, wincing with each creak of floorboard. The snoring persisted, deep, steady, and getting louder. She eased her head around the corner and looked into the room it was coming from.

There were three windows along one wall, all hung with heavy curtains, but the curtains were pulled back. In the glow of dim starlight, she could see equipment strewn around the floor, the kind of stuff she'd once seen in a photographer's studio: tripods, small lights with little flaps mounted on the front, big lights that looked like scoops. In the center of the clutter was a single piece of furniture: a king-sized bed. The snoring man was stretched out on top of it, fully clothed, lying on his back with one arm across his eyes. His mouth was open.

Marta continued creeping toward the front door. She took a cautious step and listened, another cautious step and listened, forcing herself not to hurry.

The key was dangling from the lock. She turned it, stepped out into the night, and gently closed the door behind her.

Only then did she break into a run.

Chapter Twenty

THE WORLD'S LARGEST FRESHWATER archipelago, the Anavilhanas, begins some seventy kilometers upstream from Manaus. At that point, the Rio Negro is almost twenty kilometers wide.

During the rainy season, about two hundred of the islands lie submerged, but the vegetation covering them continues to protrude above the surface of the water. Clinging to the tops of the trees, seeking refuge from the flood, are monkeys half the size of a man and snakes as thick as telephone poles.

But it wasn't the rainy season. Beaches had appeared. Channels had opened between the islands. The snakes and monkeys were crawling around at ground level.

The low water demanded careful navigation and made the search for The Goat's boat all the more difficult. It took Claudia and her companions all morning and the better part of the afternoon to locate Osvaldo and his cargo.

Osvaldo had chosen his hiding place well, anchoring in a little cove, largely concealed behind a neighboring island. The boat was surrounded on three sides by dense rain forest.

Osvaldo wasn't pleased to see them arrive, but he was downright delighted when The Goat told him they weren't going to stay.

The Goat had him row the girls ashore and line them up on the beach. He addressed them as a group, holding a piece of rubber hose, slapping it against his thigh for emphasis.

"I know for a fact," he said, "that somebody was in the house asking about Marta." *Slap*. "I also know, for a fact, that some-one shot off her mouth and said we were keeping her." *Slap*.

Silence.

"I want to know who it was." *Slap*.

The girls started looking at each other.

"If whoever it was tells me all about it," *Slap* "nobody's gonna get hurt. But if she doesn't step forward right now," *Slap* "and I mean right now," *Slap Slap* "all of you are in for the beating of your lives."

Now they were looking at one girl in particular, Vileini Rabelo, the girl who called herself Topaz.

Vileini put her hands over her face and started to cry.

"IT'S THAT priest," The Goat said when they were on their way back to Manaus. "He's behind all this. Got to be him."

"What priest?" Claudia said.

"Vitorio Barone. He runs a school for slum kids in São Lazaro. When he's not in the school, or sleeping, Barone is shooting his mouth off. He's got a thing about young girls."

"He likes to fuck young girls?" Hans asked.

"Hell, no," The Goat said. "Just the opposite. Barone doesn't want *anybody* to fuck them."

"Fucking Nazi. What's it to him?"

"He's tried bitching to Chief Pinto, the mayor, and the governor. They all blew him off. Now, he musta gotten into bed with the federals."

"How do you figure?" Claudia said.

"This Lauro kid, what did Topaz say his last name was?"

"Tadesco."

"Tadesco. Yeah, that's it. Lauro Tadesco. He's too young to be a cop himself, right?"

"Right."

"And he's a local. He has the accent, knows the town.

Topaz said so. How could they recruit him? Tell me that. They couldn't start asking around for someone to take a risk like that without Chief Pinto hearing all about it. But Barone, the priest, he'd know a kid like that."

"Hmmm," Claudia said.

"Something else too," The Goat said. "Lauro didn't want to fuck, he only wanted to talk. He coulda done both, fucked and talked, but he only talked. And he let Topaz wrap him around her little finger. If that doesn't smell like priest, I don't know what does."

Claudia recalled Topaz's tearful confession.

The kid had asked Topaz if that was her real name. She'd told him it was. Then she'd asked him for his.

"Lauro," he'd said.

He wasn't bad-looking, she'd said, so she played the coquette, fished for a return visit, said she didn't believe his name was really Lauro, said that a lot of guys lied to the girls they met in boates.

And just like that, the kid pulled out his identity card.

Lauro Tadesco.

Topaz even remembered his last name, probably due to some kind of fantasy on her part, a fantasy of getting out of the life, seeing herself as Senhora Tadesco, set up in a house of her own with a couple of kids. Well, that was behind her now. She wouldn't be talking to Lauro Tadesco anymore.

The Goat shook his head at the gullibility of both of them; Lauro's even more than Topaz's.

"Who the hell needs to impress a whore? Who even cares what a whore thinks? This Lauro, he must be some kind of religious freak."

Claudia mulled it over. If Lauro was feeding information to Silva, there might be a way to use him to bait a trap. She thought about discussing her emerging plan with The Goat, then rejected the idea. He wasn't as threatened as she was, and he wouldn't be as likely to consider extreme measures.

MARTA MALAN had been talking for almost an hour, first to the couple who'd picked her up, now to the fat guy who wanted her to tell the whole story all over again. Everything she'd said was true, but she'd left a few things out. For one thing, she didn't feel obligated to explain the true nature of her relationship with Andrea. That was nobody's business but their own. She said that Andrea had been sold off because she was too old, but didn't mention that it was also because she was no longer a virgin. She *did* mention her grandfather. That had impressed the first two, and it seemed to impress the man who was interrogating her now. His eyebrows had gone up when she said it.

She took another sip of her third café com leite. He didn't press her, just sat there, silently, waiting for her to go on.

"I turned left on the main road," she said. "There wasn't much traffic at that time of the morning. The first set of headlights I saw, I panicked. They were coming from behind me, and I thought it might be that brute I'd left back at the house. I crawled into the brush to hide."

She looked down at the old-fashioned cassette recorder he was using to take her statement, felt her eyelids drooping. Now that the danger was over, adrenaline was no longer keeping her awake. Any moment now, she was liable to fall asleep right there at the table. Her throat was dry from talking. She took another sip of coffee and continued. "When daylight came, I went to look for a stretch of road where I could see the cars coming from a long way off. As soon as I was sure it wasn't that woman, or her capangas, or The Goat, or his girlfriend, I'd step out and try to flag them down. Nobody stopped. They must have thought I was a thief, or a prostitute, or something. I got so sick of it that when I saw that couple coming, I went out and stood in the center of the road. They had to either stop or drive over me. They stopped. And they brought me here."

The fat man pushed the button to stop the tape.

"They did the right thing," he said, "and so did you. Now, why don't you lie down in my office and get some rest while I get busy and do my job?"

Marta felt a glow of satisfaction. They were in trouble, all of them, and they were going to pay for what they did to her and to Andrea. She thought about asking the fat man if she could use his telephone.

But she was tired, so very tired, after her long ordeal. She'd have a short nap first. Then she'd call her mother.

OTTO WAS on the dock, waiting for them. While Hans was still tying off the mooring lines, he climbed on board and rushed up to Claudia.

"It's the little bitch," he said. "She's gone. Escaped. Took the fucking door right off the hinges."

"And where were you?!'"

"Sleeping."

"Sleeping it off is more like it! How long has she been gone?"

"Hell, I don't know. I told you, I was—"

She wanted to scratch his eyes out, tell him what a stupid, incompetent bastard he was, but there was no time to lose. She swallowed her anger and said, "Come along, both of you." She jumped onto the dock and started hurrying toward the house. They followed a few paces behind. "We'll take the boat," she said, without looking back. "You, Hans, take some plastic garbage bags and fill them with food from the kitchen. You, Otto, get the camera, lights, recording tape, anything else that looks incriminating. I'll get my papers and the cash I've got on hand. Hurry, both of you."

The telephone was ringing when they opened the back door. Hans stopped to pick it up. Claudia rushed toward Marta's room to see things for herself. She was standing there, cursing, when Hans handed her the wireless phone.

"Chief Pinto," he said. "Says it's urgent."

Claudia took the phone and put it to her ear.

The chief was in the best of moods. "Hello, Carla," he said, "I hear you lost something."

"You heard what?"

"Yeah," the chief said. "Listen to this."

She heard a *click* then Marta's voice: *"As soon as I was sure that it wasn't that woman, or her capangas, or The Goat, or his girlfriend, I'd step out and try to flag them down. Nobody stopped. They must have thought I was a thief, or a prostitute, or something. I got so sick of it that when I saw that couple coming, I went out and stood in the center of the road."*

There was another *click*.

"Where is she?" Claudia said.

"Sleeping in my office. She's gonna have, as they say, a rude awakening."

"THAT'S REALLY funny," Hans said.

He pushed aside the bag he'd half-filled with canned goods and reached for the bottle of cachaça. Otto shoved his glass forward for a refill.

"It's not funny at all," Claudia said. "It's sheer luck. What if the little bitch had run into the federals first? What if she'd made a telephone call before they dropped her off at the delegacia? Where would we all be then? Tell me that!"

"We'd be in deep shit," Hans said. "But she didn't, so we're all right."

"We're not all right. We'll only be all right when those federal cops are no longer a threat. I want them dead."

"If we kill them, the feds are gonna go ballistic. They'll send ten more."

"But it won't be Silva or Costa, because they'll be dead, and that's the way I want it."

Lines creased Hans's forehead. He rubbed his chin.

"It's something personal between you and them, isn't it?"

"That's none of your damned business."

"Killing a few whores is one thing," Hans said. "Killing a federal cop is heavy, really heavy. Why don't we just clear out and go somewhere else?"

"And have them on our trail forever? No, we're going to kill them. *Then* we'll clear out and go somewhere else."

Hans polished off his drink and cast a glance at Otto. Otto didn't open his mouth, didn't even move his eyes, but Hans nodded as if he'd voiced an opinion. He turned back to Claudia.

"We're not gonna do it," he said. "You can't kill three federal cops and get away with it. Those fuckers are re . . . rel . . ." He furrowed his brow. He couldn't think of the word, so he said it another way. "They don't give up. And when they catch up with you, they don't just slap the cuffs on you. They get payback. And then they kill you. Get somebody else to kill the federals. Then Otto and me will kill *them*. Make the trail a dead end."

Claudia taunted him. "Scare you, do they? The federals?"

Hans didn't bite. "You're goddamned right they do."

He would have said something else, but just then the doorbell rang.

"There they are," Claudia said.

* * *

THE CHIEF looked rumpled, as if he'd been awakened far too early, but there was a broad grin on his face.

Not so Marta. She was in handcuffs, her face pinched and pale, her eyes bloodshot.

"Welcome home," Claudia said.

"*Vai tomar no cú*," Marta snapped. Go fuck yourself.

Claudia would have slapped her for her insolence, but she didn't want to give the chief the satisfaction of seeing her lose her temper. Pinto rubbed a thumb against his forefinger, making the sign for money.

"I think you have something of mine," he said.

"I do," she said. She turned to Hans. "Take her back to her room. Cuff her to something. And fix the goddamned door."

Hans stood up and held out his hand. The chief dropped the key to the handcuffs into the center of his palm.

"Otto," she said, "fetch that twelve-year-old whiskey the chief likes, then go out and buy hasps and padlocks."

When she and the chief were alone, she said, "I need some people to do a job."

He thought about it for a moment. "Hell, Carla. I'm already taking a big risk here, what with those federals being in town and all. Tell you the truth, the only reason I brought the girl back is because I know I can trust you to take care of her."

"You can. And to make sure there's even less risk for the two of us, I need some people."

"How many?"

"Two should be enough."

The chief picked up his glass of whiskey, put it under his nose and sniffed at it before taking a sip.

"You're going after those federals, aren't you?"

"Do you really want to know?"

The chief didn't reply to that. He took another sip and looked at the ceiling, debating the wisdom of getting involved.

"Cost you," he said at last. "Cost you a bundle."

"How much?"

"Fifty."

He was just trying it on and Claudia knew it. Fifty thousand Reais was outrageous.

"Twenty-five," she said. "Reais, not dollars."

"You're busting my balls, Carla," he said and raised the glass to his lips. This time he swished the whiskey around in his mouth before swallowing it.

She didn't say anything, simply waited him out.

"It just so happens," he said, "that I got just the people: real nice guys, Joaquim and Luis Almeida. And when I say got, I mean it literally. They're in a cell down at the delegacia."

"What are they in for?"

"Killing an old couple by the name of Mainardi. The wife was eighty-four, the husband was eighty-six. There was a rumor the Mainardis were keeping their savings under a mattress. I don't know how that kind of shit gets started. You got to be an asshole to believe it. Anyway, the old guy told them it wasn't true, but the Almeida boys didn't believe him. Not at first, anyway. Not until they'd killed the old lady in front of him. *Then* they believed him, but by then it was too late. They figured they had to kill him too. And they might have gotten away with it, if they hadn't been drinkers. Joaquim shot his mouth off to someone in a bar."

"You think they could stay sober long enough to do this job?"

The chief nodded. "Here's the deal," he said. "You give me the twenty-five. I have a little talk with them. I tell them I'm gonna let them loose, but on one condition: they have to do a job for you."

"And they'll buy that?"

"In a heartbeat. I'll tell them I get a cut. Being greedy bastards, they'll relate to that."

"How much do I offer?"

"Not too much."

"How much?" she insisted.

The chief shrugged. "Best way to work it is this: You explain the situation and ask them to set a price. Don't agree right away. You're not going to pay them anyway."

"I'm not?"

"No, you're not. But you don't want them getting suspicious. Keep it simple. Plan it for them, otherwise they'll probably fuck it up."

"And afterward?"

"Afterward, you kill them. The Almeidas are scum. They're also broke, so there's no other way I'm gonna earn money off them. And there's no sense in letting them shoot their mouths off about this, or go back to being dangers to the good citizens of Manaus."

"What good citizens?" Claudia said.

WHEN THE chief left, he was carrying a substantial part of her ready cash, twenty-five thousand Reais for the Almeida brothers and an additional five thousand for returning Marta Malan.

Two hours later, he dropped the two felons off at Claudia's door. Joaquim was the elder of the two and the one who did all the talking. Luis sat and stared at Claudia out of a pair of thoroughly emotionless brown eyes. The eye color was about the only characteristic the two brothers shared, that and their willingness to kill people for money.

Joaquim was short, so short that he didn't quite come up to Claudia's chin. Luis, taller by a head, and with much broader shoulders, still had all his front teeth. Luis's face was elongated and shriveled by some kind of a disease. He obviously hadn't shaved in several days. The overall effect reminded Claudia of a jackfruit with hair.

Joaquim, in contrast, was clean-shaven and round-faced. The few front teeth he had left were stained with tobacco. He only showed them when he smiled, which wasn't often, but he was smiling now, even after hearing that three of the people they were being asked to kill were federal cops.

Or maybe because of it. It wasn't every day that somebody asked you to kill a federal cop. A "service" like that was worth a bundle.

"I'll give you a group rate," he said, "twelve thousand for all three of them."

"Four thousand each," Claudia said. "The cops might be worth that but a priest and a kid aren't."

"Wait a minute," Joaquim said. "The chief didn't say anything about a priest and a kid."

"I'm saying it now," she said. It had always been her intention to kill Father Vitorio and Lauro Tadesco as well, but Chief Pinto didn't have to know that. If he did, he'd ask for more money. "A priest and a kid. How much?"

Joaquim ran a hand over his chin. "Three thousand sounds about right for a priest," Joaquim said. "How old is the kid?"

"I don't know. Eighteen? Nineteen, maybe. But he isn't going to give you any trouble. I have the impression he's rather naïve."

"Okay. A thousand for him. How much is that altogether?"

"Sixteen thousand," Claudia said. "I'll give you thirteen."

"Make it fifteen and you got a deal," Joaquim said.

"Fourteen, or you can go back to jail."

Joaquim's eyes hardened.

"Chief Pinto wants half," he said. "So how much does that leave for us?"

"Seven," Claudia said, "but since he doesn't know about the priest and the kid, you can tell him I'm only paying you twelve. You give the chief six. That way you'll walk away with eight."

Joaquim might have been lousy at math, but the idea of screwing Chief Pinto obviously appealed to him.

"Done," he said. "How do you want to do it?"

"We have to get them away somewhere. Not too far from town, but isolated enough not to attract any attention while you're busy."

Joaquim smiled. "I got just the place," he said. "Little house off the main road. Dirt road to get to it. Brush and banana trees all around. Deserted."

"Deserted?"

"Used to be owned by a couple of old farts named Mainardi, but they're dead now."

"All right. Now, do you know the *favela* of São Lazaro?"

"Yeah. That slum? What's that got to do with the federals?"

"If you shut up and listen, I might tell you." She waited for him to look suitably chastened, but it didn't happen. He just kept staring at her out of those emotionless eyes of his.

"You go there," she said. "You ask around until you find a school run by a priest by the name of Vitorio Barone."

"Barone. That's the priest you want dead?"

"That's him. You want to write it down?"

"Uh . . . yeah. Maybe I'd better."

She pushed a pad and a pencil across the table. He licked the point of the pencil and made a careful note.

"Okay," he said. "Then what?"

"As soon as you find out where the school is, knock on some of the neighbors' doors. Tell people you're looking for a kid named Lauro Tadesco. And, before you ask, yeah, that's the kid I want dead."

"Wait."

He wrote that name down too, pursing his lips as he spelled it out. "Okay. So, we find this Tadesco guy. How do we get him, and the priest, and the federals out to the Mainardi's place?"

"You find a girl who works the streets, somebody who can tell a good story."

"Shouldn't be too difficult," he said. "Most whores are pretty good liars. What story?"

"Pay attention," Claudia said.

Chapter Twenty-one

ARNALDO'S CELL PHONE RANG while they were picking at their dinner, a fish stew larded with coconut milk and *dende* oil. Arnaldo put down his spoon to take the call, but he didn't pick it up again after he hung up. He shoved the half-empty plate aside, put the phone back into his pocket, and braced his elbows on the table.

"The Goat's back," he said.

Silva stopped chewing. "Who says so?"

"Father Vitorio."

"And how does he know?"

Arnaldo shrugged.

"He didn't say. I didn't ask."

"Cheeky bastard," Hector said, then added, "The Goat, I mean, not Father Vitorio. You want to go over there now?"

"Unless you gentlemen want to finish this first," Silva said, pointing to the bowl in the middle of the table.

The three of them stood up.

THE MUSIC in The Goat's boate was loud, too loud: a Daniela Mercury *axé* tune, distorted by high volume and cheap speakers. The light was dim, the smell of perfume stronger than on Silva's last visit. A tired-looking whore was shuffling around the dance floor with a customer. Three men were grouped together at a table. They were drinking beer and leering at the remaining merchandise, consisting of five brunettes, who'd probably been born that way, and one blonde, who definitely hadn't. The Goat had them displayed with their backs to the wall, one girl to a table. The whores recognized the federal cops, and each of them found somewhere else to look.

The Goat might have noticed if he hadn't been beaming at Silva and his companions, whom he took to be new customers. He continued beaming as they approached the bar. Silva took a seat in front of him.

"*Bem vindo*," The Goat said, raising his voice so Silva could hear him over the music.

"You the guy they call The Goat?" Silva asked.

"That's me," The Goat said, a gold incisor catching a pinpoint of light from the candle that stood between them.

Before Silva could produce his badge, something over his shoulder caught The Goat's attention. Silva turned around to see what it was.

Rosélia was standing in the doorway that led to the bedrooms making frantic signs to The Goat. She stopped when Silva caught sight of her, took a step backward and closed the door.

The Goat wasn't smiling anymore. "You're cops," he said accusingly, as if they'd intentionally deceived him.

"Yeah," Silva said, "cops. I'm Chief Inspector Silva, federal police. This is Agente Nunes, and this is Delegado Costa. You want to talk here, or you want to go someplace quiet?"

"Here," The Goat said. "I gotta take care of my customers."

"So turn down the music."

The Goat complied.

"Hey," one of the guys sitting at the table said. "Turn the fucking music back up."

Silva swiveled his barstool, leaned his elbows on the counter behind him, and fixed the man with a look.

"Shut up," he said.

The man narrowed his eyes and looked to his friends for

support. Both of them suddenly discovered something interesting in their beers. After a second or two, the music lover decided there might be something interesting in his beer too.

Silva turned back to The Goat.

"Your boat around back?" he asked, remembering his last visit.

The Goat shook his head sadly.

"Sunk."

"Sunk, huh?"

"I was going upriver," The Goat said, "running flat out, when I got hit by a tree trunk coming the other way. Big bastard, maybe twenty meters long, with the branches pointing the other way. Musta been almost as heavy as the water, because it was hardly floating at all. Went right through my hull. My boat went down in minutes. I was lucky to get to shore alive."

"Right," Silva said. "Lucky. And where did this unfortunate accident happen?"

The Goat pointed in the general direction of the river. "Upstream," he said, "maybe three or four kilometers that way, right in the middle. It's a damned good thing I was towing my dinghy, because the water there is eighty meters deep, maybe more, and the current is so fast it drags things along the bottom. The hulk could be anywhere by now. Not a chance of salvage. It's a bitch. I wasn't insured."

"Uh-huh. And you reported this disaster to the naval authorities, right?"

"Not yet. It only happened yesterday. I was pretty shook up. I'm gonna go down there tomorrow."

The guy who'd been dancing leaned across the bar, brushing shoulders with Silva and Arnaldo and enveloping them in a cloud of cachaça fumes. "Give me a ficha," he said, throwing a handful of notes on the bar.

The Goat counted the banknotes, nodded to himself, and put them in his pocket. Then he produced an old cigar box. He put the box on the bar. The contents rattled like coins.

"Just one?" The Goat asked. "For two fichas you get a whole hour."

"What do I need an hour for?" the man said. "Fifteen minutes is plenty. She's been rubbing my cock right out there on the dance floor."

The Goat shrugged and handed over a brass disk with a number on it.

"Give it to the girl when you're done," he said.

"I know how it works," the man said.

He took the girl by her arm and led her toward the bedrooms. She shuffled along next to him as if she were half asleep.

"What happened to the girls?" Silva said.

"What girls?"

"Your underage girls, the ones you had on the boat. What happened to them?"

"Nothing happened to them because there weren't any. I was alone."

"Alone, huh?"

"Yeah, all alone."

"Where's Marta Malan?"

"Marta who?"

"Malan."

The Goat shook his head.

"Never heard of her."

"Or her friend Andrea either, I suppose."

"You suppose right."

Silva leaned over the bar, getting into The Goat's face.

"You had a girl working here," he said, "who called herself Topaz."

The Goat recoiled slightly. "No," he said.

"Where is she?"

"I run a legitimate business here. I don't employ minors—"

"Who said Topaz was a minor?"

The Goat swallowed.

"You did," he said.

"No, I didn't," Silva said. "Listen to me, you piece of garbage. I know you're running a house with underage girls. I know you kidnap them and make them prostitute themselves, and I think that's disgusting, but I'm after an even bigger fish. You help me, and I might be inclined to overlook a few things."

"What do you mean by an even bigger fish?"

"I mean a psychopath. I mean somebody who makes videos of people being murdered."

"Yeah, Rosélia said you guys were looking for somebody like that. But I'm not him."

"I didn't say you were. Matter of fact, I just said you weren't. How about it? Are you going to help me or not?"

"I got no idea what you're talking about," The Goat said.

"Yes, you do," Silva said.

He took a card out of his pocket and put it on the bar. "I'm at the Hotel Tropical," he said. "If I get some cooperation, I'll see what I can do for you. If not, I'm going to make sure they throw the book at you. Think about it."

The Goat wet his lips. For a moment, Silva thought he was going to say something, but then he shook his head.

Silva gave it up for the moment.

The door to the boate had barely closed behind them when the music reverted to its original volume.

***

"Psychopath?" Claudia said.

The Goat nodded. Once again, they were in her kitchen. It was two o'clock in the morning. She'd been sleeping soundly when he'd pounded on the door, but now she was wide awake. The Goat took another belt of Claudia's cachaça.

"Or maybe it was sociopath. I don't remember. One or the other. Anyway, he said that anybody who makes videos like that has to be crazy. And you know what? I agree with him."

Claudia thought The Goat was sounding more and more like someone who was about to spill his guts to the federals. The temptation to call Hans and have him put a bullet in The Goat's head right then and there was strong. They could weight him down and throw him in the river, just as they'd done with Andrea, just as they'd done with so many others. Out near the end of the dock, the bottom was twenty meters down. They'd been feeding the fish there for more than a year. Dorsal fins converged on the spot whenever there was a splash.

But, no.

Rosélia knew as much as The Goat did, and if anything happened to him she'd be pissed. To keep her quiet, they'd have to kill her as well. And if she disappeared, there'd be no one to make sure the girls kept their mouths shut. There was no telling what they knew, so, to be safe, they'd all have to be killed as well. And there was no way she could get away with a massacre like that. It would attract far too much attention.

Claudia bit her lip. "So what are you going to do?" she asked.

"I'm going to make myself scarce for a while."

"Where are you going?"

"You don't have to know that. But Rosélia will. If you need to get in touch with me, send a message through her.

My suggestion is that you get out too, keep your head down until all this blows over."

"Maybe I will," she said.

"The Malan girl. You still got her?"

"Only for another day or two," Claudia said.

Chapter Twenty-two

NONE OF FATHER VITORIO'S neighbors had ever heard of a kid called Lauro Tadesco, and his name wasn't in the telephone book. No surprise there. Telephones were expensive. Most poor people didn't have them.

"How about I try the churches?" Joaquim said to the woman he knew as Carla.

"Are you crazy?" Claudia said. "It would get right back to that priest. Do this: go back to Pinto. Ask him to trace the kid through his national identity card."

"He's gonna ask me why I want to know. He's gonna want more money."

"We need him. I'll pay Pinto. It won't come out of your pocket."

So Joaquim contacted the chief, and the chief responded as predicted: "How come you want to know about this Tadesco guy?"

"That job of Carla's. She added a couple of people."

"How many is a couple?"

"A couple. Two."

"Gonna cost her more. You too."

"She's only paying me thirteen all up."

"Sure she is. You tell her to call me."

"Uh, maybe it was fourteen she said. Fourteen or thirteen. I can't remember."

"Just tell her to call me."

***

THE FIRST thing the chief said to Claudia when she got him on the phone was "You know who keeps those records? The federal cops, that's who."

"They get hundreds, maybe thousands, of requests like that every day," she said. "Why should they notice one inquiry?"

"You're not telling me anything I don't know already," he said, "but it's extra work for me. How much you agree to pay Joaquim?"

She told him.

"Lying *filho da puta*," he said. "Okay, you're not gonna pay him anyway. Me you're gonna pay an extra two thousand."

"Two thousand? For something that's gonna take one of your men no more than five minutes and isn't costing you a *centavo*?"

"Maybe you know some other place you can get the information? Two thousand."

Claudia sighed, but it wasn't as if she hadn't been expecting it. "I'll send it over," she said.

BY TEN o'clock the following morning, she knew that Lauro Alexandre Tadesco, age eighteen, son of Maria Lourdes Tadesco, father unknown, had listed his address as number thirteen, Rua Barbosa, in the *bairro* of São Conrado.

There was, of course, no guarantee that he still lived at the same address. But, according to one of the neighbors, he did. It turned out that Lauro was one of his mother's seven children, neither the oldest nor the youngest, and they *all* lived at number thirteen, Rua Barbosa, in the bairro of São Conrado.

According to the same neighbor, a talkative old crone with only a few teeth, the mother took in washing, and the kids did all sorts of odd jobs to keep the family afloat. They were poor, but they were decent churchgoing folks, and they never caused anyone any trouble.

But if Joaquim was to follow Carla's instructions to the letter, he still needed a visual of the kid. Fortunately for him, there was a bar just across the street. He settled in with a drink and watched the house.

About an hour later, when he was already feeling the effects of his sixth cachaça and was thinking of switching to Guaraná, a kid of about the right age came out of the front door of number thirteen and started walking purposefully toward a nearby bus stop. There was no one else in the bar, and the bartender and Joaquim had been having a spirited discussion about the national sport. If you wanted to bond with any male in Brazil, that's how you did it, talking about futebol. Joaquim touched his new buddy on the arm.

"That kid," he said, pointing. "You know him?"

The bartender turned around for a look.

"Yeah," he said. "Why?"

"Looks like a guy I used to know," Joaquim said, "name of João Catanga."

"Nah," the bartender said. "That's Lauro Tadesco. He lives there."

SILVA GAVE the whoremaster a decent interval, almost twenty-four hours, to ruminate upon what he'd said. Goat stew, Arnaldo dubbed the process. Then he went back to lean on him.

This time, Rosélia was behind the bar.

"Where is he?" Silva asked.

"Said he was going fishing."

"Fishing? Where?"

"Where else does one fish, Chief Inspector? On the river, of course."

"He told me his boat sank."

"It did. He went with a friend."

"What friend?"

"He didn't say."

"When's he due back?"

"He didn't say."

"Goddamn it, what *did* he say?"

"Just that he was going fishing."

"You're lying."

"No, I'm not."

"Yes, you are."

And so forth.

The investigation was going nowhere fast.

HER NAME was Socorro Lins, and she needed another abortion. The old lady who worked out of that shithole down by the municipal dock was going to charge her seventy Reais to do it, up from sixty for the last one.

She'd just paid her rent, had some rice and beans in the cupboard, and still had ten Reais sewn into a corner of her hammock. Coming up with the extra sixty meant she'd have to hustle, doing eight tricks for the next three days instead of knocking off after the usual seven. But she wasn't about to get uptight about it. Being pregnant was just another occupational hazard, like gonorrhea, and it was one Socorro had faced many times before. She'd been living the life for sixteen years now, and no longer remembered how many abortions she'd had, much less how many men. The wonder was that her body still kept trying to produce children. She thought it should have learned its lesson by now.

A few years ago, she would have said no to the creep with the round face, emotionless brown eyes, and tobacco-stained teeth. But now she was pushing thirty, and she hardly ever turned anyone down anymore. If they had the money, she'd deliver the goods. As soon as he'd met her price, she nodded and preceded him into an alley.

He did her standing up with her back against the wall of one of the buildings. There was no kissing, no stroking, none of that kind of crap. He just did a quick in and out. Fortunately, he was one of those guys who took precautions, and the condom he'd used was lubricated. It would have been a painful process without it.

She was using a tissue to wipe herself off, and he was zipping up his fly, when he came up with the proposition.

A few hours later, she found herself sitting in a car in São Lázaro, smoking another cigarette, a hundred and twenty Reais richer. And she was prepared to sit there all night if need be, because the deal was that she'd get another hundred when the job was done.

A dark-skinned kid, wearing eyeglasses, came out of a building in front of a bar and turned right, walking away from them.

"Merda," the guy with the stained teeth said. He started the engine.

"That's him?" she said.

"That's him. Sit tight, I'm gonna go around the block and get in front of him."

JOAQUIM WATCHED the whore wriggling her ass toward the kid and watched the kid cross the street to get out of her way. Then she crossed the street too and took up a position against a lamppost, right where the sidewalk narrowed.

Now the kid had three choices: he could turn back, he could cross the street again, or he could pass her at a distance of not more than a meter. He chose to pass her, but to do it with his head down, avoiding eye contact. He also picked up his pace.

But then she spoke, and he came to a sudden, almost comic, stop.

The whole drama didn't last long, no more than a minute or two. When she stopped talking, the kid reached for his wallet and handed her some money. She took it, smiled, and said something else. He listened, turned around, and went back in the direction from which he'd come, not once looking back. She let him get about a hundred meters away before she sashayed over to the car.

"Okay," she said, sliding into the front seat. "All done. You owe me another hundred."

Joaquim handed it over. She looked relieved, probably thought he was going to stiff her.

"You took money from him," he said.

She shrugged, unconcerned.

"You wanted him to believe me, didn't you?"

"So?"

"So what would a whore be doing out here on the street waiting for him, if it wasn't for money? You ever see a whore do anything for free?"

Joaquim gave that some consideration and came to the conclusion she was right. He thought about beating her up, or maybe even offing her and recovering his investment. But it was late, and he was tired, and two hundred and twenty Reais was peanuts.

"How about taking me back to where you found me?" she said.

"Fuck you," he said. "You got money. Call a taxi."

"SO THIS whore stops Lauro, on the street," Arnaldo said, spooning sugar into his café com leite, "tells him she's a friend of Topaz's, tells him she knows where they took Marta and for fifty Reais, she'll tell him." He sipped some of the froth, wiped his mouth with a paper napkin and looked first at Hector, then at Silva. "Come on, *amigos*, how likely is that?"

"Not very," Hector admitted. He took a dab of butter on the end of his knife.

"Watch out for that stuff," Arnaldo said.

Hector sniffed the near liquid. Rancid. He put down the knife, tore off a piece of the French bread and dipped it in his coffee.

They'd given up on the hotel's restaurant, opting for breakfast in the living room of Silva's suite. It was coming up to eight A.M., and the room service waiter had just left.

"How did she locate Lauro?" Arnaldo went on, driving his theory home. "What makes her think he's willing to pay? How did she find out where Marta is?"

"I think you made your point," Silva said. He glanced at his watch. "They should be here any minute."

Arnaldo took out his Glock, popped the magazine, removed a round, tested the spring with his thumb.

"It's a setup," he said.

TEN MINUTES later, Lauro Tadesco called from the lobby. Silva went into the corridor to wait. The elevator pinged. A dark-skinned kid with horn-rimmed glasses and a slight stoop got out.

"Where's Father Vitorio?" Silva said.

Lauro licked his lips.

"He went on ahead," he said.

"He what?"

"He knew you wouldn't want him to come, Chief Inspector. He couldn't accept that. He went on ahead."

The kid was deferential, but defiant.

"All by himself?"

"Yes."

"Goddamnit," Silva said.

FATHER VITORIO parked his ancient truck under the shade of a palm tree, climbed down from the cab and studied the house. There was a vegetable garden on one side and a banana grove on the other. A cloud, heavy with rain, moved in front of the sun. The whitewashed walls of the building seemed to dim and the surrounding vegetation to fade. What had been brilliant green only a second before was now dulled to a bluish gray.

The shutters were closed, the house silent. The people inside, if there were people inside, must have heard him arrive, but no one came to the door. Could it be that the woman had lied to Lauro? Father Vitorio remembered reading about the murder of the elderly couple who'd owned the place. Perhaps he should have waited for Silva.

No! This is what God wants me to do. He will protect me.

And yet there was something about the place that caused the gooseflesh to rise on his arms. He crossed himself before moving forward.

ARNALDO DROVE the rental car. Lauro leaned over Silva's shoulder to give directions.

"Turn right," he said, "when you come to the main road."

By the time they did, Silva had his temper under control.

"Father Vitorio," he said to the kid, "has no idea what he's getting himself into."

"Father Vitorio," the kid said, "is confident of God's protection. It's a question of faith, Chief Inspector. You either have it, or you don't."

He said it like he didn't believe Silva had it. Silva turned around in his seat.

"And it's no good looking at me like that," the kid said. "Father Vitorio warned me about you. He said you've got a childish belief in something called snuff videos and that while *we* work to save all the girls, *you're* only here because the girl you're looking for is the granddaughter of a prominent politician."

Silva pursed his lips and turned to stare through the windshield. The kid had hit a little too close to home with that one.

"Left at the next corner, then the first right," Lauro said. "The place is about two kilometers ahead. There's a sign with the name Mainardi. You can't see anything from the road, just a narrow driveway that snakes down toward the river."

"How come you know that?" Arnaldo said.

"Father Vitorio checked it out on the way to your hotel. Then he dropped me off and went back."

Silva ran a hand over his eyes.

"How come Father Vitorio wants to be in on the arrest?" Silva asked, this time without turning around. He found it easier to converse with the self-righteous little twit if he didn't have to look at him.

"God sent you here," Lauro said, speaking slowly, as if he was addressing someone of limited intelligence, "because He wants Father Vitorio to take advantage of the opportunity you present."

Silva couldn't help himself. He swung around again. "Opportunity? What opportunity?"

"The rescue of the deputado's granddaughter is going to be a big story, right? If Father Vitorio is present, the national press will want to interview him. That will give him a pulpit from which he can denounce what's happening to girls who are of equal worth in the sight of God, but don't have a deputado federal for a grandfather."

A headache had begun to form behind Silva's right eye.

He lifted a hand and started massaging his temple. "So he's already tipped the press?"

"Not yet. He wants to make sure you get the girl. Otherwise, there's no story, right?"

"What's the number of his cell phone?"

Lauro gave it to him, and Silva dialed it.

No one answered.

Arnaldo slowed to a crawl. Off to their left, they caught an occasional glimpse of the river through the foliage. On the right, the rainforest was a wall of green. The road was wide enough for two cars, but just barely.

"There," Lauro said, and pointed.

Arnaldo pulled over.

"You want to take the car in there?" he asked.

"Hell, no," Silva said. Then, to the kid, "You stay here."

"I think I have a right—"

"You don't," Silva said shortly. "Let's go."

The three federal cops got out and entered the access road on foot. The previous night, as on almost every night in the Amazon, there'd been rain. The surface under their feet was unpaved. Silva stayed in the middle, following the impression of tire tracks in the mud. Two sets of them appeared to be quite recent. One diverged toward the right margin and disappeared into heavy brush. While the others waited, Hector followed that one. Wordlessly, he picked up a *samambaia* leaf and showed them the stem. The leaf, almost as tall as a man, had been cut at the base. Hector gingerly removed another leaf, thereby exposing the front grille of a Fiat Palio.

The car had been artfully camouflaged and was positioned for a quick escape.

***

"You hear that?"

Luis's voice was little more than a whisper. Joaquim

cocked his head to listen. He heard birds, insects, the *thump-thump* of a diesel motor out on the river; nothing else.

"What," he said.

"I coulda swore . . . there it is again."

This time, Joaquim heard it too: rustling leaves. He disengaged the safety on his AK-47.

From their hiding place they had a clear view of both the front of the house and the last twenty meters of the approach road.

"They're not on the road," Luis whispered. "They're coming through the woods."

"Still gonna get a big fucking surprise," Joaquim said.

He checked the fire control on his assault rifle, making sure it was switched to full automatic. Luis worked the slide on his Glock, chambering a round, making what sounded to Joaquim like a hell of a racket. He shot his brother a look.

But, no, they were okay. The rustling hadn't stopped. It was just getting louder.

"Coming right at us," Luis said.

"Shut up, you moron," Joaquim hissed.

"Moron? Me, a moron? Watch your fucking mouth, Joaquim."

"Watch yours, asshole."

"Who you calling an asshole?"

THE COPS weren't far away. Lauro couldn't see them yet, but he could hear them, first doing something with one of their guns then arguing. One called another one a moron. Normally, Lauro didn't like arguments. In fact, he didn't like contention in any form. But he was pleased that the federal policemen were out of sorts with each other, because he was equally out of sorts with them.

Stay here, Silva had told him.

Stay and miss the climax of the operation that he, Lauro Tadesco, had brought about? Miss the liberation of the deputado's granddaughter? Miss the apprehension of the people who'd abducted her?"

Stay here, indeed!

He could see them now, just ahead.

But they weren't the federal agents. There were only two of them, not three, and one of them was pointing a—

Oh, God!

JOAQUIM, STARING over the sights of his AK-47, saw a flash of color moving among the leaves. He squeezed the trigger, felt the rifle kick into his shoulder and saw a red mist appear where his target's head used to be. The body below it slumped out of sight.

Gotcha, you fucker, Joaquim thought.

But he didn't release the trigger. He went on to blow through the whole magazine, hosing everything to the right and left of the man he'd just shot. Then he released the catch, changed clips, and was ready for another go.

SILVA THREW himself on the ground at the sound of the first shot. When the echo of the last round died he raised his head and looked at his comrades. Both were prone, both unhurt. He signaled them to stay where they were and to keep their heads down. The shooter had a weapon capable of full automatic fire. They had handguns. Their only option was to remain quiet and hope for an opportunity.

It wasn't long in coming. He could hear men crashing around in the brush, getting closer. A voice said, "Luis?"

"Yeah," a second voice replied.

"He's over here. He don't look like no cop," the first one said.

More crashing around in the brush.

"Lemme see here," the first voice said again. "Might be that kid."

"What kid?"

"The priest's little friend. Tadesco."

"Yeah?"

"Give me a minute. Yeah. It's him."

"Good. So that's one down, four to go."

Silva was sure now there were only two of them, still hidden by the leaves and only meters away. He rose to his feet, trusting that they were still distracted by the body of their victim. Silently, cautiously, Silva's companions followed his example.

"Merda," the man called Luis said. "His head's all fucked up. How can you be sure it's him?"

"I rolled him over. The other side of his face isn't blown out."

"Well, this side sure as hell is."

Silva could see them, now, standing with their backs toward him, looking down at Lauro's mangled body. Silently, he cursed himself. He should have handcuffed the boy to the steering wheel to keep him out of harm's way.

Hector stepped on a twig. It broke with a sharp *crack*.

The killers spun around. The taller one, a guy with a growth of beard and a face like a jackfruit, had a pistol in his hand and he raised it. Hector pumped three quick rounds into his chest. The man dropped like a stone.

The other guy, clean-shaven and round-faced, had an AK-47. Silva's single shot, aimed at his upper body, struck the breech of the assault rifle and slammed the stock into his ribs. Roundface squealed with pain, dropped the weapon and the game was over: cops two, killers zero.

Chapter Twenty-three

"FOR CHRIST'S SAKE," THE guy with the round face said, not for the first time, "get me to a hospital! My ribs are killing me!"

Arnaldo ignored the killer's complaint and continued going through his pockets. The rib thing was no revelation. In fact, he'd be surprised if the thug *wasn't* in pain. He'd given him a capoeira kick in the chest to bring him down, flipped him over, pressed a knee into his back, and leaned his full weight upon it while he was cuffing him.

The pockets contained a set of keys, some small change, a cell phone and a wallet. In the wallet were several hundred Reais in cash, a condom, a national identity card, credit cards in three different names, driver's licenses in two, and a dog-eared photo of a woman. The woman was smiling at the camera and wearing makeup that looked like it had been laid on with a trowel. She bore a strong resemblance to the guy who owned the wallet. Even punks like Joaquim had mothers.

The national identity card matched one of the credit cards and one of the driver's licenses.

"That your name?" Arnaldo said. "Joaquim Almeida?"

The punk stopped his litany long enough to tell Arnaldo to go fuck himself.

Arnaldo's response involved his right foot and elicited a howl of pain from the punk.

"This one was Luis Almeida," Hector said, reading from the sole identity card he'd found in the wallet of the guy who had a face like a jackfruit. "Brothers maybe."

Joaquim craned his neck and tried to look up.

"Was?" he said. "You mean he's dead?"

"Killed while resisting arrest," Silva said, "just like you."

"I ain't killed," Joaquim said.

Silva didn't respond to that, just looked at him.

For a few seconds, Joaquim didn't get it. And then he did. "Merda," he said. "Okay, okay, what do you want to know?"

"Who else is in the house?"

"Nobody."

Silva twirled a finger at Arnaldo. Arnaldo used a foot to roll Joaquim onto his back. Silva bent over him.

"Look me in the eyes, Joaquim."

"I'm looking."

"Who else is in the house?"

"I already told you. Nobody."

Arnaldo kicked him in the ribs.

Joaquim made a sound between a groan and a whimper. "There was just the two of us. I swear."

"And you were waiting for us? Us, specifically?"

"Yeah. She had a picture."

"Who had a picture?"

"The woman who hired us. She had a picture of you, that guy over there, and this gorilla here, all of you together."

"Watch your mouth," the gorilla said. "Otherwise I'll put a foot in it."

"She wanted you dead," Joaquim said, sounding like he thought having them dead was a good idea.

"How about the priest," Silva said. "Where's he?"

"Luis did him," Joaquim said.

FATHER VITORIO'S ancient yellow truck was parked near the front door. The priest was inside the house, lying on a carpet in the living room, his throat slit from ear to ear.

Arnaldo braced Joaquim against the wall.

"Luis, huh? Not you?"

"Luis. I swear."

"You'd swear to anything, you little prick."

"Go look at his shirt. Luis washed the blood off his hands, but he couldn't get it off his shirt."

"His shirt isn't going to tell us anything," Arnaldo said. "Luis managed to get his own blood all over it."

"Talk about killing the priest," Silva said, "How did it go down?"

"He pounded on the door like he was the fucking chief of police. Soon as we let him in, he started shooting his mouth off. Kept going on and on about exportation of little girls."

"Exportation? You mean exploitation?"

"Exploitation, exportation, whatever. He screamed until Luis took out his knife. Then he kept on screaming, only different."

"This woman who hired you, where is she?"

"I think that gorilla broke some of my ribs."

"Then you sure as hell don't want me to break any more, do you?" Arnaldo said.

Joaquim's Adam's apple bobbed up and down. "She's got a house on the river."

"She live alone?" Silva asked.

Joaquim shook his head.

"With two capangas. Big guys. Not from here. They talk funny. Must be from down south somewhere."

Silva looked at Arnaldo.

"Three of them," he said. "Looks like we're going need help from Pinto."

Joaquim's eyes went wide. "Chief Pinto?"

"And your point is . . ." Silva said.

"Keep him away from me," Joaquim said.

"Why?"

Joaquim spit it all out. He told the federal cops about the Mainardis, about the chief letting them out, about the deal with the woman.

"Pinto will kill me if he gets a chance," he said. "You take care of me, lock me up safe somewhere, and I'll sign anything you want."

"It won't be worth much," Silva said. "You're not exactly a pillar of the community."

"A what?"

"This woman? What's her name?"

"Carla."

"Carla what?"

"Merda, I don't know. Just Carla."

"Describe her."

"Classy. No dummy. Nice tits and ass. Black hair. Good-looking, except for a big nose."

The nose part brought Silva up short. He fished out his wallet, rifled through it, took out the photo he carried of Claudia Andrade, held it under Joaquim's nose.

"Is this her?" he asked. "Is this Carla?"

Joaquim squinted as if he needed glasses. Then he looked up at Silva.

"Yeah," he said.

DELFIN FIGUEIREDO didn't trust boats. One little hole, that's all it took. One little hole, and the damned thing would fill up with water and sink. Then where'd he be? At the bottom of the Rio Negro, that's where.

Somebody had once told him that this part of the river was a hundred meters deep. He didn't know if it was true, but he knew it didn't have to be more than two meters deep to drown him. Delfin wasn't a little guy, far from it. He stood exactly one meter ninety in his bare feet and weighed almost ninety-five kilograms, only a little of it fat. But the one meter ninety wouldn't do him a damned bit of good in a hundred meters of water, and the absence of fat would only make him sink faster.

Problem was, Delfin didn't know how to swim. He'd been raised on the river, but it had been farther downstream, below where the Rio Solimões flowed in, and where the water was as dark as chocolate. He'd seen the things with teeth that fisherman pulled out of that water, things longer than he was tall and with mouths that could engulf his head.

Just the thought of one of those creatures lying under the surface, waiting there in the dark, had always petrified him. Neither his family nor the kids he'd grown up with had ever been able to lure him, or to taunt him, into immersing himself in that water.

So, when the woman told him the video was going to be shot on a boat, he'd balked.

"Fuck her, okay," he'd said. "Kill her, okay. But no boat. There's no way I'm gonna do it on a boat."

"Why not?" the woman said. "What difference does it make?"

"It just does."

"Big guy like you, afraid of boats?"

"Afraid? Me, afraid? Hell, no. I just don't like them, that's all."

But then she'd offered him more money, and more money, and finally they were up to double the price he'd agreed upon in the first place. It was more than he'd ask if somebody wanted him to kill the mayor, or a senator. And how often did he get asked to kill the mayor or a senator? Never, that's how often. The truth was, Delfin Figueiredo had never been paid more than three thousand Reais to kill anyone in his entire life.

Delfin was a man of modest tastes. With what she was offering he could live for a year, screwing all the whores he wanted, drinking all the cachaça he wanted, only climbing out of a hammock to get another smoke, or another drink, or something to eat.

It was just too tempting.

It wasn't like she wanted him to get *into* the water. He didn't have to get his feet wet at all. All he had to do was get into a fucking boat. And the boat looked pretty solid, and there was another little boat she was going to tow behind, meaning they'd all have someplace to go if the big one sank, and the day, like most days in the dry season, was all sunshine and just a few fleecy clouds. There weren't going to be waves. There wasn't going to be wind. So Delfin had agreed, and he told her he wanted half the money in advance, and she'd said no problem, and he'd stuffed it into the trunk of his car near the spare tire, and here he was, out on the river in the cabin of a fucking boat.

Delfin looked across at the girl he was expected to kill. She had one ankle fastened to a brass ring. They were using a pair of handcuffs for that. The rest of her was trussed up like a tapir ready for roasting. She was gagged, too, which was a good thing, because she had a mouth on her like a sewer. Delfin had heard her spouting off before they left the house, before the guy with the bags under his eyes stuffed a handkerchief in her mouth and secured it in place with another one. Delfin wondered where a girl with a classy accent learned language like that. Maybe in one of those fancy schools, maybe all the girls talked like that when they were in the bathroom. Now *that* would be the beginning of a good porno movie, girls in a bathroom talking dirty. Not this, not being out on a fucking boat.

The girl didn't know about the killing, of course, but she

must have figured out the rest. Funny thing was, she didn't look scared. She looked angry. They'd warned him she was going to fight him. Well, as far he was concerned, that was fine. Delfin liked the rough stuff, but they wouldn't let him get away with it in the boates, so it'd been a while since he'd had a chance to beat a woman into submission. Not that this was a woman. She didn't look to be more than sixteen. She was a virgin, too, or so they said. Delfin found it hard to believe. Most of the girls he knew didn't carry their virginity beyond the age of eleven, twelve at the most.

He tried to concentrate on what was coming, not on the sloshing of the water outside.

And found himself getting hard.

WHILE SHE was setting up the lights, Claudia kept one eye on Delfin, studying him, as he studied Marta. He'd started out the trip nervous as a scalded cat, and she'd been worried about his ability to perform, but now he seemed to have adjusted to the situation. Claudia gave a little smile of satisfaction when she saw him open his legs and rub his crotch, displaying for the girl like the animal he was.

Marta turned her head aside in disgust.

"Getting close," Otto said, his voice coming through the companionway.

Claudia clambered on deck and looked over the bow. Hans was already up there, seated on the cabin roof, one hand on the anchor. The shoreline was about a hundred meters away. She relieved Otto at the wheel, took a ninety-degree turn and steered parallel to the bank. Over here on this side of the river there wasn't much to see, just the occasional fisherman's shack, surrounded by dense vegetation. Now and then, they heard the screech and saw the flash of a passing macaw. Occasionally they caught sight of a monkey leaping from branch to branch.

Claudia couldn't anchor in midriver. It was too deep, the current too swift. But she didn't need the middle of the river. Here, in the shallower water near the shore, they were thoroughly isolated and unlikely to be disturbed. It would have been a different matter if there'd been a bridge. Then the city would have spilled over to this side. But there was no bridge, not here, not for eight hundred kilometers upstream, not for more than sixteen hundred kilometers downstream all the way to the sea.

She motored along until she came to a little cove. The cove had a high bank shielding it on three sides and thick vegetation growing right down to the water. Above the scrub, above the high-water line of the rainy season, trees, some with trunks as high as thirty meters, towered upward and spread their branches to form a canopy. The land rose beyond that and the canopy seemed to go on forever.

Claudia threw the twin throttles into neutral, waited until the forward motion had stopped and told Hans to heave the anchor overboard. She put the boat into reverse, and he paid out line. Thirty meters from shore, she cut the engine and told him to snub the line on the cleat. The boat stopped with a gentle jerk, the nylon cord rising from the water like a long white snake as the hull adjusted to the wind and current. When she thought the process was complete, Claudia took a step forward, lined up a stanchion with a tree on shore, and verified that the anchor was holding. Then she went below and started to unpack her camera from its padded case.

Chapter Twenty-four

"Look who's here," Arnaldo said, pointing toward the driveway.

Silva turned his head. A uniformed man with a protruding stomach was strutting in their direction.

"The chief?" Silva asked.

"In the flesh," Arnaldo confirmed. "Kindly note how much of it there is. Is that guy fat, or what?"

Summoned by a telephone call from the federals, half a dozen local cops were already on the scene. The senior man, a sergeant, had attempted to assume jurisdiction and confiscate their weapons, but Silva had told him to go to hell. He figured him for the one who'd called the chief.

Pinto stopped in front of Arnaldo.

"What the fuck is going on?" he said.

"And good morning to you too, Chief," Arnaldo said.

"Who's this?" He pointed at Silva.

"My boss, Chief Inspector Mario Silva."

Pinto turned his back on Arnaldo.

"So maybe you're the one who can tell me what the fuck happened here?"

"A couple of thugs killed Father Vitorio Barone," Silva said, "and a young friend of his, name of Lauro Tadesco."

"What a shame," the chief said, without a trace of regret. "Who did it?"

"The Almeida brothers."

"Luis and Joaquim? They're scum. If both of them were dead, this town would be better off."

"Then it's half better off already," Arnaldo said.

Pinto blinked, but he didn't turn his head. "You killed one?"

"Luis," Silva said. "Shot while resisting arrest."

"Where's the other one?" Pinto said.

"Down the road a bit, in a car."

"Hand him over," the chief said. "He's mine."

"In your dreams," Silva said. "We're holding on to him."

"The hell you are. Murder is state, not federal. You can't hold him. I can."

"We're charging him with something else."

The chief's features drew together, as if he'd just tasted something nasty.

"What?"

"I can't tell you. It's confidential."

"Confidential? That's a load of crap."

"Is it?"

"You're gonna need a place to keep him."

"We have a place to keep him. The Tropical."

"You're gonna put a scumbag like Joaquim Almeida in the Hotel Tropical?"

"We're thinking of getting him the Presidential suite," Arnaldo said.

"Something else," Silva said. "According to Joaquim this was a contract hit. The woman who hired them calls herself Carla something, has a house down by the river, lives there with a couple of capangas, big guys from down south. Ring any bells?"

"Not a one," the chief said.

"We're going over there to arrest them, gonna need some of your men."

"Yeah? Well, you can't have any. Any arresting has to be done, we'll do it ourselves."

Arnaldo said, "You recall getting calls from the mayor and the governor? Something about full cooperation?"

The chief glared at him.

Arnaldo pulled out his cell phone.

"Maybe a call would help," he said. "Who do you want to hear it from? The governor, or the mayor?"

Pinto ignored Arnaldo, addressed Silva.

"How many men you need?"

"Ten should do it," Silva said. "Ten with automatic weapons and a forensic team. Have you got one?"

"Of course we've got one. This isn't the sticks, Silva."

"Could have fooled me," Arnaldo said.

IF LOOKS could kill, Joaquim would have been dead the minute the chief set eyes on him. He cringed to one side of the back seat, keeping Hector between himself and Pinto. The chief spoke to him through the open window.

"Where's this house, you little shit?"

Joaquim played along, just as the federals told him he should, acting as if he hadn't spilled his guts about the chief and as if the chief wasn't the prick who'd dropped him into all this shit in the first place.

LIKE EVERYTHING else in Manaus, the assault team took a while to assemble. But when they got there they turned out to be surprisingly well-equipped. They also looked like people who knew what they were about. Silva was impressed.

The house, too, impressed him. It was reminiscent of something built in colonial times: thick walls, small windows, a red tile roof. It stood in the middle of a clearing, providing a clear field of fire on all sides. If defended, it would be a hard nut to crack. The federal cops stood well back and let the team get on with it.

They hit the main door in a frontal assault, blowing it off the hinges with a small explosive charge and tossing in some flash-bangs before they went in themselves. It was all over in less than a minute.

The leader of the assault team appeared in the doorway and motioned the others forward.

"Clear," he said.

The federal cops crossed the threshold, dragging the surviving Almeida brother with them. It only took two minutes to confirm that the place was empty.

"Where did they go, Joaquim?" Silva said.

"How the fuck should I know? I told you, I only seen her once." Arnaldo was already balling his fists when the punk added, "But her boat's gone."

"Boat?"

"Yeah, she had a big fucking boat tied up to that dock behind the house."

"She might have taken her boat," Silva said to the chief. "Have one of your men check with the navy. Maybe they can get us the registration number and a description."

"If she isn't really stupid," the chief said, "she's gonna paint over the number, maybe even paint the whole goddamned boat."

"But maybe not yet," Silva said. "She doesn't know we've nailed Joaquim. She might just be out for a cruise on the river. Get your men out of sight in case she comes back."

The chief turned and gave some orders to a guy with a little moustache and sweat stains under the arms of his shirt. The guy ran off toward the house, shouting instructions, being self-important.

"Then too," Silva said, "maybe she didn't take the boat at all. There are only two roads out of this town, right?"

"Wrong," Pinto said. "There are three. You got one road that runs north, up to Roraima and on to Venezuela. You got another road on the other side of the river. That one runs from Careiro down to Porto Velho in Rondônia. The third one, the short one, is on this side of the river. It goes to Itacoatiara."

"Okay, three roads. That's it?"

"Christ, Silva, in case you hadn't noticed, that's the Amazon jungle out there." The chief threw out his hand like he was grabbing a piece of it. "Three is pretty impressive, if you ask me."

"The road to Itacoatiara, where's it go from there?"

"Nowhere. But it's a road. Anybody trying to get out of town could use it, then switch to a boat."

"And they'd also need a boat to get to Careiro and go south, right?"

"Right."

"So we have to cover the river."

"Forget the fucking river. We only got three boats. We'll never be able to stop everybody. You got any idea how much traffic there is, how many boats are out there?"

"A good reason not to try, right?"

"Don't put words in my mouth."

"I want people covering the airport as well."

"We can't go stopping every woman in a car, on a boat, or getting ready to board an airplane."

"You don't have to. You only have to stop one. I've got a picture of her. I'll let you copy it. I want it back."

"Where did you get a—"

Silva didn't let him finish.

"She might be traveling in the company of a fifteen-year-old girl. I've got a picture of her too. You gonna get on board with this, or you want to hear from the mayor and the governor?"

The chief gritted his teeth.

"Give me the goddamned pictures," he said.

* * *

MANAUS'S CHIEF crime-scene investigator was Caio Lefkowitz, but nobody called him Caio, only Lefkowitz. A *paulista*-resident of the state of São Paulo—from Campinas, he had curly black hair, ears that stuck out like a chimpanzee's, and thick eyeglasses. The glasses made him look like a studious monkey.

"Pleased to meet you, Chief Inspector."

Unlike almost everyone else Silva had met in Manaus, Lefkowitz sounded like he meant it. They were standing in the front yard, watching the assault team pack up their gear.

"Lefkowitz?" Silva said, rubbing his chin. "You have a brother who's a federal cop?"

"Uh huh. Jaime. Two years older than I am. Works out of Rio de Janeiro."

"I've heard good things about him," Silva said.

"And I about you. What brings you to Manaus?"

"I was about to ask you the same question."

"My wife," Lefkowitz said, glumly. "She's a biologist, loves poking around in the jungle, and I love her. Otherwise . . ."

"We get the picture," Arnaldo said, and stuck out a meaty paw. "Arnaldo Nunes. This here's Hector Costa. That punk over there is Joaquim Almeida, and he can go fuck himself."

"Hey," Joaquim said. "How about that doctor, huh?"

Everybody ignored him.

"The ladies and gentlemen of the press will be here any minute," Lefkowitz said.

"Merda," Silva said.

"Yeah. I thought I'd warn you. Pinto called them just now. That's why he's scribbling away over there, working out some kind of eloquent statement. He's a real hound for publicity, the chief is. Never misses an opportunity for an interview, and a murdered priest doesn't come along every day."

There was something about Lefkowitz that inspired Silva's confidence. He made a snap decision.

"How about we go inside the house?" he said. "Just the two of us."

"Sure."

He and Lefkowitz started walking.

"You asked me what I was doing here," Silva said, stopping when they were out of earshot, but still outside. He told Lefkowitz everything he hadn't told the chief: about the missing girl, about the woman who'd been calling herself Carla Antunes, about the snuff videos. By the time he'd finished, the eyes behind Lefkowitz's glasses were huge.

"So Carla Antunes is really Claudia Andrade," he said shaking his head. "The chief's gonna shit a brick."

"No, he isn't," Silva said, "because you're not going to tell him."

"You're going to keep Pinto in the dark?"

"You bet I am."

"How come you decided to come clean with me?"

"Because I trust you to keep your mouth shut, because I sense you're not a great fan of the chief—"

"You're right, I'm not."

"And because it will help you with your investigation. There are certain things you should look for."

They started walking again, climbed over the remains of the front door, and entered the house. When they came to a room with a king-sized bed in the middle of the floor, Silva let his eyes roam over the ceiling and the walls. Both were white, but the walls were a shade lighter.

"Fresh paint," Lefkowitz said.

"That's what I'm thinking."

"We'll find out for sure," Lefkowitz said, "and we'll also find out if there's anything under it. How long will it take you to get me Claudia Andrade's fingerprints?"

"A few hours, no more."

Lefkowitz looked around him. He'd been sweating in the heat outside, and his glasses were slipping down his nose. He pushed them back up with his forefinger, ran a forearm across his brow, and started to roll up his sleeves.

"Good," he said. "She must have left a few more around here somewhere. And, if she did, we're gonna find them. First, though, let's see if there's any blood."

LEFKOWITZ AND his two assistants mixed and sprayed Luminol, closed the heavy curtains, and turned on a blue light. The wall, and patches of the floor, lit up like Copacabana on a Saturday night.

"I did a job in a favela once," Lefkowitz said, looking at the glowing spots where blood had once splashed and pooled. "A whole family had been slaughtered: mother, father, and three kids. Drug thing. Father was a dealer, and he didn't pay his suppliers. They killed the lot of them, threw the bodies in the river and scrubbed the place with a liquid detergent." Lefkowitz turned toward him, his face eerie in the blue light. "This place is worse. There have been times when this room was swimming in blood."

"How many?" Silva asked. "How many did she kill here?"

Lefkowitz blinked behind his thick lenses. "I don't know if I'll be able to tell you that, but I'll try. First thing we'll do is to sort the blood residue by type."

"That the best you can do?"

"No. DNA testing is best I can do. But DNA analysis is expensive. The chief will never approve it."

"Fuck the chief," Silva said. "The federal government will pay."

"I like your style," Lefkowitz said, "especially the fuck-the-chief part."

Chapter Twenty-five

MARTA'S MOUTH WAS DRY, and it wasn't only because she was afraid. The handkerchief they'd stuffed into it was sucking up her saliva like a sponge.

It was obvious, now, what they were up to, as obvious as the tears streaming down her cheeks. Her captors would be thinking they were tears of fear, about which they'd be right, and tears of resignation, about which they'd be totally wrong. There was *no way* she was going to give in to rape that easily. She wasn't some simple country girl from the backwaters of the Amazon. She was a Malan. She'd resist them every centimeter of the way. She'd punch, and kick, and scratch. If they took out the handkerchief, she'd sink her teeth into the animal's ear. With luck, she'd get it clean off before he knocked her senseless.

CLAUDIA BECKONED to Delfin.

"Here," she said, and dropped a glittering thing into his palm.

"Put it in your mouth," she said. "Keep it in your cheek."

Delfin stared at the little brass key, bright against his skin. "What's it for?"

"The cuff on her ankle."

"What about the—"

He would have said *cord I use to strangle her with*, but Claudia cut him off. The girl was right next to them, listening.

"You're going use the one wrapped around her wrists," she said. "It's silk. Now, pay attention. I'm going to say 'action'—"

"What?"

"Action," she repeated. "I'm going to say the word 'action,' and when I do, you step into the shot—"

"What's that mean, step into the shot?"

"You go over to her," the woman said, "and you start cutting her clothes off."

"With what?"

"With this." The guy with the bags under his eyes handed him a knife. It was one of those commando things, sharp all the way down the front and halfway down the back.

"Last thing you do with it," she said, "you cut through the cord and free her hands. Just cut one loop. Unwind the rest. When you're done with the knife, drop it on the floor. Otto here"—she tilted her head toward the guy with the bags under his eyes—"will pick it up, so she doesn't get her hands on it. Can you remember all of this?"

"Sure," he said. "You think I'm stupid?"

She blinked her eyes at him and paused for a beat before she went on. "Once you free her hands, she'll probably try to scratch you. Don't worry about it. We cut her nails. Just make sure she doesn't poke out an eye."

"Okay."

"When her hands are free, hold her wrists, or sit on her, while you spit out the key and unlock the handcuffs. Make sure she never gets off that bunk. If she does, we have to start all over again."

"Can we do that?" he said.

"Of course we can, but try to get it right the first time. Once I turn those lights on, it's going to get very hot. None of us are going to enjoy being in here any longer than we have to."

"Okay. So once I get the handcuffs off her ankle, what's next?"

"You do what we discussed. Any questions?"

"No."

"Good. Otto, give me that camera."

The camera wasn't one of those little dinky things Delfin had seen the tourists use. It was almost as long as the woman's arm and had a pad on the bottom so she could rest it on her shoulder.

"Otto," she said, "lights."

Delfin was looking at the largest of them when it came to life. He looked away, but a blue spot persisted in his vision. It started to fade, but it was there when Claudia's European client came down the companionway and settled into the bunk opposite him. And it was still there when she said "action."

QUARTZ HALOGEN lamps are hot, and they seem hotter still when they're switched on in a confined space. Twenty-two minutes into the recording, and despite the air-conditioning working flat out, the ambient temperature in the cabin was up to a hundred and eighteen degrees Fahrenheit, fully five degrees hotter than in the blazing sun.

The smells made their discomfort worse. The acrid smell of sweat. The steely smell of blood. The smells of excrement and urine.

Claudia held on long enough to get a shot of Delfin disemboweling Marta with the same knife he'd used to cut her clothes off—proof for any viewer that the girl was really dead—then she made a sudden dash for the deck.

She found a place in the shade under the awning, put the camera on one of the seats, and took a deep breath of the muggy air. It was heavy with the odor of rotting vegetation, but a damned sight more agreeable than the aromas down below.

The next person out of the cabin was Delfin, nude, one eye turning black, holding Marta's panties against his ear to stanch the flow of blood.

"Bitch," he said and sat down.

Claudia wrinkled her nose. She didn't like having his sweating, filthy ass on her cushions. She made a mental note to have Otto scrub them clean after he'd flushed out the cabin.

Otto was already at it. Hans too. She could hear the splash of the hose, the trickle of water flowing into the bilge, the whir as the bilge pump kicked in. She leaned over the side and saw a pink stream gushing out of the hull.

Delfin was so dumb he still hadn't tipped to the fact a European customer wouldn't be down there in the cabin helping with the cleanup.

Hans came on deck, carrying Marta. He'd wrapped her corpse in a piece of black plastic sheeting.

"Still some pieces of her on the bunk," he said. "I'll have to shovel them into a bucket. Most are too big to wash into the bilge; they might clog the pump."

Delfin blinked. It was the first time he'd heard the guy speak. Claudia envisioned wheels churning in his head as he tried to figure out how some Euro freak came to speak Portuguese with a Gaúcho accent. He opened his mouth, maybe to ask, shut it, opened it again.

"Who woulda thought a little package like her could be so much trouble?" he finally said.

"You gonna just sit there and spout deep thoughts," Hans said, all pretense gone, "or you gonna help me get her into the river?"

"Help? Hell, no. I already did my part."

"Help him," Claudia said. The coaming around the cockpit was solid mahogany, and she didn't want bullet holes in it.

"Fuck," Delfin said, "Look what the bitch did to my ear."

He uncovered his ear and pointed to the place where Marta had mangled it with her teeth.

"It's stopped bleeding," Claudia said. "Just leave it alone."

He tried to assess the damage with his fingers.

"Leave it alone, I said."

"What are you, a fucking doctor?" he said, sarcastically.

"As a matter of fact," she said, "I am."

"Yeah, right."

By then, Hans had laid his burden on the foredeck and was grasping a length of chain.

"Go help him," she said again.

Delfin gave her an exasperated look and mumbled something, but he got up and moved forward.

Claudia watched the little drama play out on the foredeck: Hans telling Delfin to hold up her body so he could get the length of chain under it, Delfin doing it, Hans whipping out his pistol and putting two quick ones into Delfin's head. *Pam! Pam!*

Down below, the sound of the cleanup continued unabated. Otto must have heard the shots, but he didn't bother to stick his head out of the cabin.

Hans finished wrapping Marta and turned to Delfin. He'd already prepared a second length of chain, had it up there on the foredeck ready to use. He didn't bother to wrap Delfin in plastic. The deck was fiberglass, easy to clean, and Otto would hose it down when he finished in the cabin.

Claudia rewound the tape, and started reviewing it in the viewfinder: no dropouts, a little jumpy in some places, a few lapses of focus, but all in all, a good job, different from all of the others because the girl fought like a wildcat. It lent a degree of piquancy to the work.

She hadn't yet gotten to the point where Delfin was wrapping the silken cord around Marta's neck when she heard a splash up near the bow. She stopped the playback and took the viewfinder away from her eye just in time to see Hans push Delfin's body between two of the stanchions.

Another splash.

Hans came aft, toward the cockpit, discontent written on his face.

"I'm not gonna do this no more," he said, "not unless we get to do her first. You're a woman. You don't know how it is, having to stand there, and watch it, and not get any. I woulda had her when she was still warm," he said, "if you hadn't told that fuck to open her belly."

"Had to be done," she said. "That's what the customers want. Proof it isn't faked."

"Speaking of the fuck," he said. "How about the money you gave him? The fuck locked it in the trunk of his car. You want to go back and get it?"

Claudia nodded.

"But, first, let's make sure we haven't had any visitors while we've been away. Joaquim and Luis are probably back at the house by now."

Her cell phone was in a little compartment near the wheel. She pulled it out and dialed Joaquim's number. Someone picked up on the third ring.

But it wasn't Joaquim. Maybe a wrong number.

She hung up and tried again.

JOAQUIM ALMEIDA'S cell phone rang for the second time. Silva glanced at the screen.

"Same caller," he said to Joaquim and handed him the phone. "This time, you answer. If it's Carla, you tell her no one showed up for your little party. If she asks if it's safe to come back here, you say it is."

Another ring.

"We gotta talk," Joaquim said, "about what you're gonna do for me if I cooperate."

Another ring.

Arnaldo poked Joaquim's ribs with his forefinger.

"Take the fucking call," he said.

Joaquim winced and pushed the button.

"Yeah," he said.

Silva grabbed Joaquim's wrist and pulled the telephone a centimeter away from the thug's ear.

"Joaquim?"

Silva had heard the voice twice before: on the recording made by the Dutch police and on the video showing the death and dismemberment of Andrea. The hairs rose on the back of his neck.

"It's me," Joaquim said.

"Your voice sounds strange. Anything wrong?"

"No. Nothing."

"You wouldn't lie to me, would you, Joaquim?"

"Lie? Why would I lie?"

The woman had taken control of the conversation. Joaquim wasn't up to wresting it back.

"Where's that brother of yours?"

"He's around here someplace."

Silva and Arnaldo exchanged exasperated looks.

"Put him on," the woman said.

Only then did Joaquim recognize his mistake. He started to stammer.

"I . . . well . . . he's . . ."

Click.

She disconnected without even bothering to tell Joaquim he was a lying sonofabitch.

* * *

"SOME OF THEM COULD be broken. I'd need an X-ray to confirm it," the doctor said, slipping off his stethoscope and dropping it into his bag.

It was an hour later. They'd taken Joaquim Almeida back to the Hotel Tropical. The concierge had summoned a physician.

"See," Joaquim said, "I told you I needed a hospital."

"Shut up," Arnaldo said.

"On the other hand," the doctor said, looking at Joaquim like he was something he'd found sticking to the bottom of his shoe, "fractured or bruised, the treatment's the same. You can't splint ribs. I'll prescribe something for the pain."

"Something strong," Joaquim said. "Give me something really strong."

Silva cut in. "Will you certify he can travel?" he asked.

"You promise to get this piece of trash out of Manaus," the doctor said, "and I'll sign anything you want."

IN DEATH, Father Vitorio Barone achieved the notoriety he'd coveted in life. The next morning, *Rede Mundo* led its eight o'clock news with the story of his murder.

The news anchor, an attractive brunette with an overbite, dished up the details with a shiver of delight. And she didn't know the half of it. If the brunette had been aware that both a deputado's granddaughter and Claudia Andrade were involved, she would have had, as Arnaldo put it, a triple orgasm right there on camera.

But she wasn't aware, and Silva had no intention of enlightening her.

Chief Pinto, on the other hand, made a show of being totally forthcoming. He might not have known the whole story, but he knew how to make the best of what he had. His well-rehearsed sound bite went on for almost fifty seconds.

The chief described the priest's grisly demise in graphic detail, told how one of the murderers had been shot dead by the cops and informed viewers the other had been captured. But he didn't say *which* cops had done the shooting and the capturing.

When asked why the priest was at the Mainardi home in the first place, Pinto frankly admitted that he didn't know. And as to Lauro Tadesco's role in the affair, that was still under investigation.

The chief's performance was followed by a series of reactions to the murder.

A spokesman for the National Association of Bishops said Father Vitorio's death was a tragic loss and so forth and so on, the usual *nil nisi bonum*.

This was followed by a montage of comments from some of Father Vitorio's former students, none of whom seemed to have acquired a turn-the-other-cheek attitude from associating with their former mentor, and all of whom expressed satisfaction that at least one of the killers had paid with his life.

The next face to appear on the television screen caused Arnaldo to choke on his breakfast coffee.

ROBERTO MALAN wasn't a Catholic, didn't represent the State of Amazonas in the chamber of deputies, and had nothing to do with the death of a priest in Manaus. But there he was, in a tight close-up, speaking from his office in Brasilia.

"*Rede Mundo* wouldn't have gone to him," Hector said. "He must have—"

He stopped short when Silva held up a hand.

". . . not of my faith," Malan was saying, "but Father

Vitorio was a man whose service to the poor demanded respect. Certainly, he had mine."

"Five will get you ten Malan never heard of him before he got knifed," Arnaldo put in.

"No bet," Silva said. "Now will the two of you kindly shut up?"

Malan paused and continued. "Brazil has, this day, lost a good shepherd. It's not only a loss to his flock, it's a loss to our country as a whole."

"Does he talk like that in person?" Arnaldo asked.

"No," Silva said.

The deputado leaned forward. He looked straight into the lens. His skin began to redden in anger. His voice took on a tone of righteous indignation.

"His death," he said, "is an outrage, made all the more outra-geous because it was entirely avoidable. Yes, avoidable! So who, in the end, are we to blame for Father Vitorio's demise?"

Malan left viewers in no doubt he had the answer to that, but he took another pause, building up the expectation.

"The Almeida brothers, certainly," he said, "and the nefarious—"

"Nefarious? Oh, *please*," Hector said *sotto voce*, and raised his eyes to the ceiling.

"—person or persons who employed them. But they're not the only ones. Others contributed to Father Vitorio's death. They didn't contribute by shooting him, or ordering him to be shot, but they're guilty just the same. They're guilty of gross negligence."

"Here it comes," Arnaldo said.

"And who are these negligent incompetents? My fellow Brazilians, they are the federal police! Yes, the federal police! Those same federal police who let the mass murderer,

Claudia Andrade, slip through their fingers not twenty months ago. If the federal police had been truly zealous in their efforts, dedicated in their comportment, efficient in their methods, they would have apprehended Claudia Andrade long ago. And if they had taken the initiative to suppress the dastardly exploitation of minors, with which the death of Father Vitorio Barone is undoubtedly linked, he would be alive today instead of—"

Click.

Silva put down the remote control. "I give him fifteen minutes," he said.

Hector scratched his head. "Who?" he said. "Who do you give fifteen minutes?"

Nelson Sampaio was on the line in less than ten.

"Did you see Roberto Malan's interview on *Rede Mundo?*"

His voice was higher-pitched than usual. He sounded, Silva thought, like someone was squeezing his scrotum.

"Yes, Director, I did. Grandstanding, I think they call it."

Sampaio, who was prone to doing quite a bit of grandstanding himself, glossed over Silva's critique.

"Why, Mario? Why would he go and do a thing like that?"

"I assume," Silva said, "the deputado has become impatient with us in general and with me in particular. I've kept him waiting for news about his granddaughter. He can't go public with that, so he chose another opportunity to make us the whipping boy. He knows the escape of the Andrade woman still galls us. He knows it would be painful to reopen the wound. What he *doesn't* know is it's all connected: the death of Father Vitorio, the disappearance of his granddaughter, Claudia Andrade, they're all tied together."

"Claudia Andrade? She's involved?"

Sampaio was silent for a moment. Silva thought the director was going to insist on more details.

But he didn't.

"Shouldn't we tell Malan what we already know?"

"Not yet."

"Why not?"

"The only way to appease him is to tell him something concrete about the whereabouts of his granddaughter. I'm not yet in a position to do that."

JUST BEFORE lunchtime, Lefkowitz came to call. He settled into a chair in Silva's suite, and while he mopped his brow Hector went to fetch him a guaraná from the little refrigerator.

"I didn't want to use the telephone," Lefkowitz said, removing his glasses and wiping off sweat with his handkerchief. "The chief has a tap on it. I know that for a fact, because I'm the one who put it there. He's also instructed that all contact with you guys is to go through him. He's going to be pissed if he finds out I was here."

"If he does, it won't be from us," Arnaldo said. "We're giving the chief the mushroom treatment."

"Keeping him in the dark and feeding him a lot of shit, huh?"

"You know them all, don't you, Lefkowitz?"

"Just the really old ones. Has he told you about the prints?"

"Not a word," Silva said.

"I figured as much."

"Was I right?"

"Yes, Chief Inspector, you were. That Andrade woman left her prints all over the house."

He took a long draught of his guaraná.

"Anything else?"

Lefkowitz smacked his lips and nodded.

"There were three cars on the street near Carla's, sorry, *Claudia's* place. One was registered to a lowlife by the name

of Delfin Figueiredo. Soon as you left, the chief and his buddies were all over it."

"You and your people weren't invited to participate?"

"Nope. The story's going around there was money found.
They split it among themselves. Lion's share for the chief, of
course."

"Of course," Silva said. "You see him do it?"

Lefkowitz shook his head.

"And nobody else would be willing to testify they did. The
chief scares people. Now as to the blood, it's gonna take a
while to get the DNA results."

"So you can't tell us how many victims there were?"

"Not yet, but I can make an educated guess."

"So, guess."

"At least a dozen."

THE PACKAGE arrived about an hour after Lefkowitz left. It
was wrapped in brown paper, bore no stamps, no return
address. Silva's name was on the front, neatly written with a
felt-tipped marker.

"Dropped off at reception by some kid," Arnaldo said.
"Desk clerk never saw him before."

The package contained a single VHS tape, no note, no
label.

The hotel's convention center had a VCR, but it was
broken. In the end, Arnaldo had to go out and buy one. It
was almost six in the evening before they had it hooked up.

The tape opened with a close-up of Claudia Andrade and
maintained that visual all the way to the end. The composi-
tion was so tight that her pores were prominent, so tight that
no clue to her surroundings was visible. The recording could
have been made anywhere. The camera captured her head-on,

foreshortening her prominent nose. There was a smile on her face. She looked quite attractive.

"Sorry I missed you," she said. She paused to let the significance of the remark sink in. Missed killing them, she meant. "It's so difficult to hire decent help these days."

Her smile faded and her eyes turned hard. "Your attentions are getting tiresome. You need something else to worry about, so I've arranged it. Deputado Roberto Malan is going to get a little package. After what I saw on *Rede Mundo*, I'd hazard a guess that he dislikes you almost as much as I do. What I've sent him is going to make him dislike you even more."

The screen went black.

"Bitch scored another goal." Arnaldo said, his face grim.

"Game's not over," Silva said, hitting the stop button.

Hector looked from one to the other. "What the hell was she talking about?"

"She killed Marta," Silva said. "She killed her, made a video of it, and mailed the damned thing to Marta's grandfather."

Chapter Twenty-six

BENTO ROSÁRIO SCREWED OFF the cap and took a tiny sip of water. It loosened his tongue from the roof of his mouth, but did nothing to assuage the dryness in his throat. Still, he had to conserve the little he had. There was less than a centimeter left in the bottle, barely enough for a healthy swallow.

If Silva doesn't show up sometime soon, he thought, *I'm gonna have to decide between thirst and a bullet.*

Just then, a mosquito bit him behind the right ear. He reacted instinctively.

Slap.

A mistake. One of the taxi drivers heard the noise and looked toward the bushes where he was hiding. Bento forced himself to lie perfectly still. After a while, the taxi driver went back to his newspaper.

A tour group, headed by a woman with a name tag pinned to the lapel of her bush shirt, came out of the Hotel Tropical. She passed between two taxis and led her charges toward the pier, where the excursion boats were docked.

He wiped his forehead. Partly, it was because of the heat, but he would have been sweating even if the day had been cooler.

Bento Rosário was scared to death.

The turnaround in Bento's life had come with dizzying speed. It was his own fault. It would never have happened if he'd followed his uncle Tarcio's advice.

"Working for the city is like being in the army," Tarcio had said.

Bento had never been in the army. He'd escaped compulsory military service because of his flat feet. He had to ask Tarcio for clarification.

"You keep your head down," Tarcio had explained, "do what you're told to do, never take initiatives, and never, ever, volunteer for anything."

Tarcio knew what he was talking about. In the army he'd risen to the rank of master sergeant, and now he'd been on the city payroll for almost three decades. Currently, he had a cushy sinecure in the sewer department, which gave him contacts throughout municipal government. But you needed more than contacts to get a job in Manaus. Contacts only put you in touch with the people who had jobs to give. You still had to bribe them to get one.

When Tarcio told him about the opening, Bento had been anything but enthusiastic.

"Clerk for the municipal police?" he'd said to his uncle. "Sounds boring."

Tarcio hadn't liked that. Hell, Bento knew for a fact that he didn't even like *him*. He thought his nephew was a prissy little pain in the ass, had told him so more than once. He wouldn't have lifted a finger to help if Bento's mother, Tarcio's kid sister, Arlette, hadn't bullied him into it.

"It's the only thing going," Tarcio said, "and it's a hell of a lot better than mucking around in other people's shit, which is where I got my start. Take it or leave it."

Bento knew what his mother would say if he didn't take it. He didn't want to put up with that.

So Tarcio had pulled the strings, and Arlette had paid the bribes, and the next thing Bento knew he had his very own seat behind one of three identical desks in the cellar of the delegacia central.

Alberto Coimbra, his new boss and the head clerk, was a

benevolent despot who didn't look too closely at the time Bento started in the morning and seldom complained if Bento came back half an hour late from lunch, both of which were big pluses. Bento had always found it difficult to wake up early, and he loved long lunches.

Another plus was that Coimbra generally left everybody to do their own thing. He didn't go hanging over your shoulder, double-checking every damned piece of paper and file. The last thing Bento had expected was that he'd incur Coimbra's wrath by taking a bit of initiative. Tarcio had clearly told him initiative was a no-no, but what did Tarcio know? There was a considerable difference between the sewer department and the municipal police, right?

Wrong. Coimbra had been furious.

"Why didn't you talk to me first?" he'd said, his face so close to Bento's that Bento could feel little drops of spittle while Coimbra was shouting at him. "Do you have any idea what you've done?"

"I just answered a query. I thought you'd be pleased. I thought—"

"You're not paid to think. You're paid to *do*. *I'm* paid to think."

Bento didn't get it at first. All he'd done was respond to an E-mail from the federal police in Brasilia. The E-mail had a photo attached. The federals wanted to know if they had a file on anyone who looked like the man in the photo.

Simple.

And easy for Bento, who had a good eye for faces.

He'd started with the "A's" and, within minutes, he'd come up with a match. The guy's name was Damião Rodrigues, but somebody had misfiled his jacket under the A's instead of under the R's where it belonged.

By the time Coimbra got back from his afternoon coffee

break, which usually involved cachaça instead of coffee and generally went on for an hour or more, Bento had already shot off a reply to the federal cops and put a copy of that reply onto Coimbra's desk. Coimbra's reaction had been swift and terrible.

First, he looked at the E-mail. Next, he unlocked a drawer of his desk, took out a piece of paper and ran his finger down the page. Then his face turned red.

He sprang to his feet and came storming over.

After Coimbra spat all over him, Bento took the wise course and apologized for thinking. But Coimbra wasn't having it.

"Apologies don't cut it," he said. "This is more serious than you know. I have to see the chief. Don't move until I get back."

Bento hadn't moved.

Five minutes later, Coimbra swept back into the room, took him by the arm and led him up to the chief's office.

"We already got an answer to your fucking E-mail," the chief said.

Those were the first words the chief had ever spoken to him. Bento had never even been introduced to Chief Pinto, much less seen the inside of his office. He didn't get much of a chance to see it that day either. The chief didn't tell him to sit down.

"You, Rosário, are a first-class fuckup. I should fire your ass right now."

"But . . . why?"

The chief looked at Coimbra.

"He wants to know why," he said. "Jesus."

"Jesus," Coimbra echoed.

The chief looked back at Bento.

"Because you fucking ignored your instructions, that's why!"

"You're supposed to come to me first," Coimbra said. "You're supposed to come to me whenever any outsider asks for information from our archives. You've been told that."

Bento hadn't been told any such thing. Coimbra was covering his ass. Bento opened his mouth to defend himself, but when he saw the way Coimbra was looking at him, he shut it again. If he lost his job, it was going to reflect on his uncle Tarcio, which meant his uncle Tarcio was going to be pissed. And not only that, his mother's hard-earned money would be right down the drain. It was time to eat crow, and he did.

"I . . . forgot," he said.

Again, the chief looked at Coimbra. "He forgot. He fucking forgot."

Coimbra shot his eyes toward the ceiling as if asking God for patience.

Pinto shifted his attention back to Bento. "Clean out your desk," he said. "Don't leave anything behind. You're on unpaid leave until further notice."

"Unpaid—"

"Leave. Something wrong with your ears?"

"No, Senhor. Ah . . ."

"What?"

"May I ask the chief when I might be permitted to come back?"

He'd addressed the chief, but used his title, like he'd seen in war movies. *You piss anybody off, for any reason, you act like you're in the army*, Tarcio had told him.

Coimbra and the chief exchanged a glance. The chief hesitated then said, "You never heard of Damião Rodrigues, and there was no file, right?"

"*Sim*, Senhor," Bento said, smartly. "Unknown name. No file."

The chief grunted.

"All right," he said. "Find someplace where you can stay. Don't tell anybody where it is. I don't want those federals to go looking for you, but if they do, I sure as hell don't want them to find you. Call Coimbra in a week or so. If everything has blown over by then, you can come back. If not, you stay away longer."

Bento tried to be a good cop. He may have been only a clerk, but he liked to think of himself as a cop, and a cop followed orders. He went to his desk, cleaned it out and left the building. Joel Lopes, his new best friend, tried to ask him what happened, but Bento told him he wasn't allowed to talk about it.

Only later did he realize what it all meant. It meant there were felons to whom the chief was extending his protection. It meant, in short, that the chief was a crook. But, at the time, Bento was so shocked he didn't take time to think. He simply went home, packed a bag, and told his mother he had orders directly from the chief. He wasn't permitted to tell her where he was going.

She wouldn't have approved if he had.

He went to Samuel, his mother's ex-husband, Bento's stepfather for almost five years. Samuel had no children of his own—none he could be sure of, anyway. But it wasn't from lack of distributing his seed. Samuel was a man who couldn't be content with one woman, so he always had several at a time. When Arlette, Bento's mother, found out about what she thought was Samuel's second extramarital affair, although it was really more like his fifteenth, she'd thrown him out. Literally.

Samuel worked in a fish shop, and never lifted anything heavier than a pacu. Arlette worked in the central market, shifting wooden boxes of vegetables. She was half a head taller than Samuel and thirty kilograms heavier. The night she evicted him, he went flying from the front door of the house and halfway across the street, hit his head on the cobblestones, and lay there, stunned, while she threw the contents of his dresser drawers on top of him.

Bento had been fourteen at the time. He'd adopted Samuel as a father figure and was sorry to see him go. So sorry, in fact, that within a month he'd gone to the fish shop, discovered where Samuel was living, and had been clandestinely visiting him ever since. So when Bento was ordered to go underground, Samuel's home was the logical choice. It was a little cramped because Samuel was living with a widow and her five children, but the widow was a friendly soul, and she did her best to make Bento feel welcome.

Bento was twenty-one years old, an only child, and had never lived anywhere except with his mother. After a week of being away, he'd come to miss her a great deal. He crept back to her house in the middle of the night and was about to tap on the door when a bullet smashed into the doorjamb above his head. Nobody had ever fired a shot at Bento Rosário. He didn't, at first, realize what it was. Then another shot rang out. That one missed as well, probably because the street was dark, and the shooter couldn't draw a proper bead over his sights.

Bento took off like a gazelle. He knew every alley, every back street of his neighborhood, which his pursuer apparently didn't, so it wasn't long before he'd gotten clean away. He hadn't dared to go back that night, or even the next. Bento couldn't think of a reason why anyone would want to kill him. He concluded that the assault had been a robbery attempt. But that was before Samuel brought the newspaper home.

On the morning of the third day after the shooting incident, Samuel had been using a sheet of two-day-old newsprint from the *Diário de Manaus* to wrap a fish for a waiting customer. He'd just about finished the job, when an article less than ten centimeters high caught his eye.

WOMAN MURDERED, the headline read.

Samuel read further and his jaw dropped. He wrapped the fish in another sheet, took off his apron, and asked one of his colleagues to cover for him. It was less than a five-minute run to the widow's place. Samuel found his erstwhile stepson watching a cartoon show on television and shoved the article, now reeking strongly of fish, under his nose.

Below the headline, and after giving Bento's mother's name and stating her age, the journalist went on to write:

> . . . was tortured and murdered sometime in the early hours of the morning, probably in an attempt to get her to reveal the whereabouts of her valuables.

Bento was devastated. What kind of valuables could thieves hope to find in the shack of a box-shifter who worked in the Municipal Market? It didn't add up.

But there was another explanation that made sense: that they'd been trying to get her to reveal Bento's whereabouts. Originally, the chief had wanted him to go away for a while. Now, it looked as if he wanted him to go away permanently. Bento was frightened, so frightened that he was staring at another article on the page for at least a minute before it registered: Mario Silva, the *well-known Chief Inspector of the Federal Police* was in town and staying at the Hotel Tropical.

And right then and there, in the midst of his fear and grief, Bento experienced an epiphany: the federal police had dropped him in the shit; the federal police were the ones who were going to pull him out of it. He needed protection. He needed to get to Silva.

Chapter Twenty-seven

"I HAVEN'T SEEN IT myself," Nelson Sampaio said, shifting his telephone to his other ear, "and after the deputado's description of the contents, I'm quite sure I don't want to." He was referring to the videotape Claudia Andrade had sent to Roberto Malan. "He called me within a few minutes of looking at it," the director went on. "I have to tell you, Mario, his comportment was most . . . extraordinary."

"Extraordinary?"

"You'd expect him to be distraught, right? Break down, release some of the sadness he must be feeling. But he didn't. All he did was to threaten and bluster."

"Threaten?" Silva said.

"And bluster," Sampaio said. "He wants your head, Mario. He said it was your fault. He said you failed. He's going after our budget allocations, told me that if I didn't get rid of you immediately, he'd cut everything to the bone. It's his committee, Mario. He's a powerful man. He can do that."

The director paused.

Silva didn't say anything.

After a second or two, the director continued, "I like you, Mario, I really do. And I don't blame you for what happened to the girl, but he does."

"Hmm," Silva said.

"You've got to understand my position, Mario. It would be wrong to prejudice the whole organization just because of one man. You've got to think like a team player here."

"You want me to resign?"

Sampaio sighed.

"I think it would be best for all concerned," he said.

"Tell him I want to see him."

"What?"

"Tell Malan I want to see him."

"See him?"

"I'll do a quick in and out. I'll come down there on Wednesday night, see him the following morning, and return in the early afternoon."

"Wednesday, as in the day after tomorrow Wednesday?"

"Yes."

"He's an important man, Mario. You can't expect him to adjust his schedule on such short notice."

"That's why I'm giving him until Thursday morning. Tell him it's in his best interest."

"That sounds like an ultimatum."

"Let him take it any way he likes."

The director was a worrywart, but he was a politician, and he wasn't stupid.

"You've got something on him, haven't you?"

"I have no idea what you're talking about."

"Yes, you do. All right. Thursday morning. I'll tell him, but I'm warning you: as far as Malan is concerned, the issue is already resolved."

"Not by a long shot," Silva said.

BENTO ROSÁRIO was getting desperate. The sun was approaching its zenith. The heat was intolerable. His water bottle was empty. The comfort he got from being in the shade of the bushes was offset by the fact that those same bushes blocked the breeze from the river. Worst of all, Bento was now convinced that one of the cab drivers wasn't a cab driver at all.

When, five times, the man's vehicle had come to the head of the rank, he'd driven off without a passenger. And each time, after a short interval, he'd returned to join the end of the queue.

The other drivers were as aware of this strange behavior as Bento was. They weren't treating him as one of their own. No one had exchanged a word with him in all the time he'd been there, which was almost as long as Bento had been hiding in the bushes.

The man was wearing a jacket, and who the hell would wear a jacket in a place as hot as Manaus? That alone was suspicious. And something else boded ill: the driver's eyes were fastened on the front door of the hotel. He was watching it like a cat watches a mousehole.

"I NEED food," Silva said, glancing at his watch.

It was a little past one.

"I'm not gonna eat another damned fish," Arnaldo said. "And I'm not going to eat anything that tastes like fish."

"Which means you're either on your way to the airport, or you're going to starve," Silva said.

"Which means neither," Arnaldo said. "I am going to get a steak."

Silva and Hector looked at him.

"While you people," Arnaldo said, "confined your conversations with Lefkowitz to DNA testing and suchlike, I got him aside and questioned him about something of real importance."

"Food?" Silva said.

"Food," Arnaldo confirmed. "There is a restaurant in this culinary desert owned and operated by a Gaúcho."

Gaúchos were people from the State of Rio Grande do Sul, and the State of Rio Grande do Sul was famous for its beef.

"This restaurant," Arnaldo continued, "is less than ten minutes from here. The owner flies his steaks up from Porto Alegre. According to Lefkowitz, they are untainted by fish."

"Lead us to this marvel," Silva said.

The heat outside hit them like a Turkish bath. Arnaldo went over to speak to the valet. Hector reached for his sunglasses. Silva, wiping his forehead with a handkerchief, was the first to see a figure scuttle out from under the shrubbery and head toward them at a dead run.

He was a thin young man in dark shorts and a T-shirt, wearing tennis shoes, and carrying what appeared to be an empty water bottle. One of the cab drivers caught sight of him, got out of his car and put a hand under his jacket, a move that attracted the attention of the federal cops. All three of them reached for their weapons. The driver took in the situation, got back into his cab and took off down the drive with a screech of rubber.

By that time, the young man was in front of them, panting from the effort. He reached out a hand and took Silva by the wrist.

"You're Silva, aren't you?" he said. Then, without waiting for an answer, "You people have gotta help me."

Bento Rosário started talking right there on the street. He was still talking when they were shown to a table in the Recanto Gaúcho, the restaurant suggested by Lefkowitz. He paused long enough to drink an entire bottle of mineral water, asked for another, and continued his story.

The three federal cops nursed glasses of beer. Silva and Hector sat where they could keep on eye on the entrance. Arnaldo chose the other side of the table, next to Bento, and covered the door leading to the kitchen.

Bento finally took a break to scan the menu. He ran his finger down the offerings and frowned.

"Hey," he said, "what's the matter with this place? They don't serve fish."

FROM THE restaurant, they went directly to Manaus's sole federal magistrate, a man by the name of Rosenblatt. After being sworn to secrecy, and listening to Bento Rosário's story, Judge Rosenblatt issued a fistful of warrants and wished them good luck. He too was no fan of the chief's.

Silva told Arnaldo to call Brasilia from the judge's chambers.

"Get Gloria up here," he said. "We can't do this alone. We're going to need her."

Gloria Sarmento, a woman who, according to Arnaldo, had "more balls than a pool table," headed ERR1, one of the federal police's elite hostage rescue teams.

"Gloria isn't going to like it," Arnaldo said. "She hates Manaus."

"Tell her to bring six of her people," Silva said. "We shouldn't need any more than that."

"Which six?" Arnaldo said.

"Let her choose."

"No, no, no," Arnaldo said. "What if she brings Diogo Carmo?"

Diogo Carmo was one of those people who couldn't finish a story. You'd meet Diogo in the hallway and he'd say something like, "On the way into the office this morning I stopped off for coffee, and speaking of coffee, have you ever bought coffee at that little shop down among the warehouses in Santos? Oh, yeah, Santos, that reminds me, how about that game between Santos and São Paulo last Thursday? You know, Thursday, the same day. . . ."

And so on and so forth. He drove his colleagues nuts.

Silva considered for a moment, then shook his head.

"Gloria won't bring him," he said. "Diogo has the same effect on Gloria as he does on everybody else."

"Gloria," Arnaldo said, "might get so pissed off about coming to Manaus that she'd pick Diogo just to—"

"I get the point," Silva said. "Tell her not to include Diogo."

From Judge Rosenblatt's chambers, they went directly to the municipal dock, where they rented a boat. They told the owner/captain to moor the vessel in the mouth of an out-of-the-way tributary, turn on the air-conditioning, and leave them alone in the cabin.

While Hector took a handwritten statement from Bento, Silva made calls from his cell phone. One of them was to the reception desk at the Hotel Tropical. There'd been two calls from Chief Pinto and one from Silva's wife, Irene. He ignored the messages from the chief and was lucky to catch Irene still relatively sober. He told her to expect him the following evening in Brasilia.

"I'll pick you up at the airport," she said. "We'll share a cocktail when you're safely home."

"Don't start without me," he said.

AT ELEVEN o'clock that night, the three federal cops took the boat back to the municipal dock. They left Bento aboard and packed themselves into a cab for a quick trip to the airport. Gloria and her people arrived on time, aboard the 11:30 P.M. flight from Brasilia. It took three more cabs to carry the personnel and equipment. Thirty minutes later, they arrived at the headquarters building of Manaus's Municipal Police.

Silva assigned men to oversee the operations of the switchboard operator and the radio dispatcher, then assembled the rest of the small nighttime staff. He identified himself, showed his credentials, and waved a paper.

"This," he said, "is a search warrant for this building and these"—he waved two other papers—"are arrest warrants for Chief Pinto and Coimbra, the guy who runs the archives. Under no circumstances are you to attempt to contact them. Nobody leaves the building. All calls, incoming and outgoing, are going to be monitored. Turn in your cell phones to the little lady with the big gun and line up to submit yourselves to a body search, men on this side, women over there."

His listeners were more accustomed to pushing people around than being pushed, but they did it. An examination of Alberto Coimbra's desk revealed no list of what might have been protected felons. They moved on to Pinto's office, where the search for any kind of incriminating evidence proved equally disappointing.

"Only one more chance," Silva said. "Where the hell is Lefkowitz?"

"Here, Chief Inspector," Lefkowitz said, coming in through the doorway, rubbing the sleep out of his eyes. One of Gloria's men had commandeered a police car and picked him up at home. They'd made record time in getting there.

"I seem to recall you tap telephones," Silva said. "Are you any good at it?"

"I'm a virtuoso."

"Good. I want you to tap the chief's."

"His home?"

"His home."

"Got a warrant?"

"I do." Silva showed it to him.

Lefkowitz grinned. "It'll be a pleasure," he said.

"When you're finished there," Silva said, "go to Coimbra's place and do the same thing. Here's his address. Arnaldo will meet you there. Hector, take Enrique and follow Lefkowitz to the chief's home. Keep an ear glued to his calls. If he gives you probable cause, break in and slap the cuffs on him. If he sticks his nose out the door, and you think he's going to make a break, do the same."

COIMBRA, A bachelor who lived alone, was awakened from a sound sleep by the pounding on his door. He grabbed the phone next to his bed and made a desperate call to the chief.

The chief's wife and two kids were in Rio, visiting his mother-in-law. The woman next to him in the king-sized bed was the maid. She picked up the telephone and handed it to him.

"Chief?"

"Coimbra? It's three-ten in the fucking morning. What's so import—"

"The federals are pounding my door."

The maid slipped her hand down from Pinto's stomach to his groin. Angrily, he brushed it away.

"Merda! Where's your copy of the list?"

"Under my mattress. I brought it home after Carvalho missed his shot at Rosário."

"Destroy it. Now!"

And Coimbra would have, if Arnaldo hadn't put the earphone aside and broken down his door.

The chief's first outgoing call was to a *Sargento* Carvalho, but all he did was to ask him for a telephone number, which he promptly called. It turned out to be the cell phone of Carvalho's boss, *Tenente* Jordão. "What the hell's going on?" The chief was getting angrier by the minute. "Did I give you an order to kill those goddamned federals, or didn't I?"

"Sorry, Chief, but we can't kill them if we can't find them. They left their hotel at lunchtime and never came back."

"Go to Coimbra's place. He says they're there, pounding on his door."

"Merda. They must be tooled up for an assault. I've only got two men with me."

"So get some more," the chief said and slammed down the phone.

The tap bore additional fruit. Calls provided links to two more of the chief's accomplices. He berated the first one for having allowed Bento Rosário to fall into the hands of the federal cops.

"You saw him, for Christ's sake. You saw what he was doing. All you had to do was to shoot the bastard."

"I told you, Chief, there were three of them, and they all—"

"I haven't got time for this. Get your stuff together and get out of there. If Rosário recognized you, they'll be at your place next. Hell, they might be on their way over there right now."

PINTO WAS locking his front door, when he heard the rustle of leaves. Hector stepped out of the samambaia ferns that lined the path.

"*Bom dia*, Chief," he said, "You're up early."

"Yeah, I am. Not that it's any of your business. What do you want?"

Hector crossed his arms. He wasn't holding a gun.

"To arrest you," he said.

"On what charge?"

"Racketeering."

"You'll never make it stick."

"Oh, I think we will."

The chief's hand dropped to the revolver on his belt.

Enrique, behind him, said, "Thumb and forefinger, Chief. Just the thumb and forefinger. Then hold it up so I can grab it."

The chief closed his thumb and forefinger around the butt of his Taurus. Then, in a last gesture of defiance, he tossed it into the bushes.

Chapter Twenty-eight

THERE WERE TWO CELL blocks in Manaus's delegacia central: a larger one, with ten cells divided equally on either side of a concrete corridor, and a smaller one, with two. The smaller block was on the second floor and reserved for female prisoners. The female cells were depressing and damp, but they were five-star accommodations when compared with the cells down in the basement. There, an area originally designed to hold a maximum of forty prisoners held almost two hundred men. They had to sleep in shifts, because there wasn't room for all of them to lie down at once.

The light, the little there was, came from five fluorescent tubes on the ceiling of the corridor. At one time, there'd been lights inside the cells as well, but after the bulbs had been smashed half a dozen times the warders had given up replacing them.

The prisoners were expected to clean their own cells, which they never did. The place was a dim paradise for vermin. The plumbing had long since given up the ghost, and the inmates were reduced to using buckets for human waste. The smell of unwashed bodies mingled with the rank odors of urine and excrement.

Arnaldo, to whom Pinto had been entrusted, pushed the chief through the door at the head of the corridor and followed along behind him, jangling a ring of keys as he went. The chief was still in uniform and his arrival was greeted by grim silence until the prisoners realized that his hands were cuffed behind his back. Then the jeering broke out.

"Who wants to share a cell with him?" Arnaldo said, taking a position in the center of the corridor, just out of reach of groping hands.

Everyone did, but one voice, deeper than the others, cut through the rest.

"Put that fresh piece of meat in here."

The man who owned the voice stepped forward into the dim light. His shaved and tattooed head towered above the shoulders of every other man in his cell.

"Friend of the chief's, are you?" Arnaldo said.

The man gripped the bars with hands the size of hams. His smile was pearly white against his dark skin.

"Oh, yeah," he said. "Me and the chief, we go back a long way,"

"Get me out of here," Pinto croaked.

"Give me a good reason why I should," Arnaldo said.

"I'll tell you everything."

"That's a good reason," Arnaldo said.

WHILE THE chief and Coimbra were giving their statements, and falling all over each other in an attempt to shift blame, Silva dispatched Gloria's team to find and bring in the men Pinto had called just prior to his arrest.

When Sargento Carvalho and Tenente Jordão found out that the chief and Coimbra were cooperating, they entered into the spirit of the thing. They talked about the bribes being paid to the mayor and the governor. They talked about their involvement in the drug trade. They talked about the traffic in underage girls and confirmed that the felons on the list taken from Coimbra had been paying for protection. Silva went from interrogation room to interrogation room, letting the confessions ring like music in his ears.

There was only one false note, one area of dissonance: not

a single member of the chorus had any information about the current whereabouts of the woman they'd known as Carla Antunes.

THE THREE federal cops went from the delegacia central to The Goat's boate. By the time they got there, it was half an hour after sunrise.

Rosélia received them at the front door, wearing a nightgown and suppressing a yawn. Her hair was in disarray. There were circles under her eyes.

"I already told you," she said. "I have no idea where he goes fishing. Somewhere on the river, that's all I know. So why don't the three of you get lost."

Silva waved a paper under her nose.

"What's that?" she said.

"A search warrant. Assemble the girls."

She looked from the warrant back to him.

"You're wasting your time," she said. "They don't know a damned thing."

The girls all looked as disheveled as Rosélia did. Silva addressed them as a group.

"We've arrested Chief Pinto," he said, "and some other cops along with him. They're going to prison, and so is The Goat."

"He's lying," Rosélia said, loud enough for even the girls in the back of the room to hear it.

"If any of you want to leave," Silva continued, "you're free to go. No one is going to follow you. No one is going to force you to come back."

Silence.

Silva tried again.

"Who knows where I can find The Goat?"

More silence.

"The sooner I find him," he said, "the sooner he'll be in jail."

One of the girls, olive-skinned and with a broken nose, looked like she was about to say something.

"You?" he said, pointing at her.

The other girls turned to look at her.

Rosélia didn't look, she glared.

The girl pressed her lips firmly together and shook her head.

Silva sensed she didn't believe him. She wanted to, but she didn't.

The journalists he'd called hadn't believed him either. They'd told him they'd have to send reporters to the delegacia central to check the story out. That had been forty-five minutes ago. In Manaus, even the media moved at a snail's pace.

"It'll be on the radio any time now," Silva said, hoping it would. "Hector, see if that thing works."

He pointed to the audio system on the bar. All you could pick up in Manaus were local stations, and Hector chose one at random. They were broadcasting an old Roberto Carlos tune.

"You might be worried about where to go," Silva said, still addressing the girls. "There's a hospice in the city run by the Sisters of Notre Dame de Namur. I've spoken to them. They'll give you a place to sleep, give you food, help anyone who wants to do something else with their lives."

Not one of the girls met his eyes. They were all staring at the wall, or at the floor, or at Rosélia.

"When I leave here," Silva said, "I'll be taking Rosélia with me. You have nothing more to fear from her."

Rosélia shot him a nervous glance.

As if on cue, Hector turned up the volume on the radio.

A breathless female voice replaced the music:

*. . . were arrested at their homes in the early hours of this morning.
Formal charges have yet to be brought, but we've been informed
that Chief Pinto and his associates will be accused of racketeering,
extortion, and murder. The federal police . . .*

The girls' voices overwhelmed that of the news reader.
Hector lowered the volume.

The girls fell silent, and every face turned toward Silva.
They were looking at him differently now. Some of them
were smiling.

"This woman," he said, pointing at Rosélia, "says she doesn't
know where The Goat is. I think she might be lying, but there's
nothing I can do about that. She has the right to remain silent.
As for you girls, we'll leave you alone for a few minutes to
reflect upon what you want to do, whether you'd prefer to stay
here, or try to return to your homes, or take advantage of the
offer being made by the good sisters of Notre Dame de Namur.
My men and I will be outside, waiting for your decisions."

Rosélia suddenly realized what Silva was up to. "Take me
with you," she said.

Silva shook his head.

"I'm sure the girls will be grateful for your . . . advice."

Rosélia froze. The girls moved in to encircle her. One of
them picked up a heavy glass ashtray.

Silva led his companions to the door.

When they were outside, he said, "Two or three minutes
will probably do it."

Two or three minutes did.

THE GOAT was sunbathing when he heard the sound of the
engines. Cautious, as always, he swept up his clothes and
satellite telephone before retreating into the brush above
the beach.

The boat that swung into view from behind a neighboring island was gray, and so were the uniforms of the half-dozen men he could see on deck. Two of them were holding machine pistols. The helmsman spotted The Goat's boat and made a beeline toward it. When they were about fifty meters away, he lifted an electronic megaphone. There was a crash of static, and The Goat's name rang out across the water.

"José Luis Ignácio Braga. Come out of the cabin with your hands up."

The sailors started hanging out fenders. The naval patrol boat came alongside The Goat's cruiser. The girls, as they'd been instructed to do, remained below in the cabin, but Osvaldo came up on deck. When he saw the weapons, he raised his hands. The Goat took another step backward into the concealing foliage, turned on his heel, and started running toward the inflatable he'd stashed on the other side of the island.

The Yamaha sixty-horsepower four-stroke had an electric starter. It was almost too much engine for the little boat. Almost.

The navy men must have heard the roar when The Goat pushed the engine to full throttle, but he was shielded by the island, so they couldn't see him. And, at his top speed of almost seventy kilometers an hour, there wasn't a chance in hell they'd be able to catch him.

BRASILIA

"MY ADMINISTRATIVE assistant," Malan said, "*Senhorita* Godoy."

Silva wasn't surprised that the deputado had left him cooling his heels for over thirty minutes, but he was surprised to find a woman in Malan's inner sanctum. Senhorita Godoy was somewhere between fifty and sixty, a thin-faced individual in a dark suit, with a blouse buttoned up to her neck.

"A pleasure, Senhorita," Silva said.

The pleasure, apparently, wasn't mutual. Senhorita Godoy said nothing at all. Her cold gray eyes squinted at Silva through a pair of rimless glasses. She had a small mouth and thin lips. The lips were pursed.

Malan's expression, in contrast, was almost jovial. Silva recognized at once that it wasn't so much his ultimatum that had secured him an appointment, as it was a desire on the part of the deputado to humiliate him. Malan kicked off their conversation with a vengeance.

"No use begging me to change my mind, Silva. It's made up and someone of your limited talent and ability isn't about to change it."

"With all due respect, Deputado, I think we should limit this conversation to the two of us."

Malan raised an eyebrow. "And I think not. I have no secrets from Senhorita Godoy. Anything you have to say to me, you can say in front of her."

Silva remembered her now. The Godoy woman was an important figure in Malan's church, a lady bishop or some such. It was said that the deputado kept her around because his coreligionists believed that anyone with Senhorita Godoy at his side must truly be laboring in the vineyards of the Lord. She was the mistress of the moral high ground.

"As you wish," Silva said.

He put his briefcase on his lap and opened it. "I have here," he said, "a number of documents from the Dutch police. This one"—he removed a sheaf of papers and put it on Malan's desk—"is the transcript of an interview with Frans Oosterbaan, an associate of an Amsterdam businessman named Arie Schubski. And this one"—he removed a second sheaf and put it alongside the first—"is a list of Senhor Schubski's clients provided by the aforenamed Senhor Osterbaan. There's one name on the list, one in particular, to which I'd like to draw your attention. He's an individual who lives right here in Brasilia, one who regularly receives DVDs mailed to him from the Netherlands."

While Silva had been speaking, Deputado Malan had been turning pale. Senhorita Godoy apparently hadn't noticed. She was looking at Silva with a slightly bored expression, as if she was wishing he'd get to the point.

Deputado Malan's next statement took her entirely by surprise. "Leave us," he said.

She turned to look at him. "Are you addressing me?" she said, thin eyebrows climbing toward a frizzy hairline.

"I am," he said.

Her pale skin turned red in embarrassment. She took in a deep breath, released it with an unladylike snort, and rose to her feet.

"Hurry up, hurry up," Malan said.

"I'm not accustomed—"

She got no farther.

"For Christ's sake, get out," he said.

Gathering what dignity she could muster, Senhorita Godoy made for the door and slammed it behind her. Malan took his head in his hands and looked down at the desktop, massaging his temples with his fingertips.

"This could ruin me," he said.

"It certainly could."

The deputado took a deep breath and looked up. A tear of self-pity appeared at one corner of his left eye.

"I don't expect you to understand," he said, "but I can't help myself. It's an addiction, like alcohol or drugs."

The tear started rolling down his cheek. He took a handkerchief out of his pocket and wiped it away.

"Like alcohol or drugs," Silva repeated.

"So help me God. I'd never do anything like that myself. I just like to . . . watch it, that's all. If I don't buy that *merda*, someone else will. It's not like I'm a one-man market, inciting those criminals to do what they do."

Silva remained silent.

"The reason you're here," Malan said, "it's money, isn't it?"

"Partly," Silva said.

"I knew it! You and your holier-than-thou attitude! Silva, the incorruptible cop! You have your price, just like everyone else. How much do you want?"

"For me? Nothing."

"What?"

"The federal police's budget allocation, Deputado. I not only want you to approve it as proposed, I want you to stand up in that committee of yours and fight for an increase of twenty percent."

"I'm only the chairman. I only have one vote. I can't guarantee—"

"Oh, I think you can, Deputado. I didn't say fifty percent, I didn't even say thirty percent. I'm a realist. Twenty percent will do us very nicely, and I'm sure you can get it."

Malan's tears had dried up, as if they never had been. This was something he understood. This was politics.

"Suppose I can. What else?"

"Stop demanding my resignation. Call my boss and tell him you were overwrought by your granddaughter's murder, that you overreacted, that you want me kept on the case. Then tell the same thing to the press."

Malan rubbed his chin. "I can't do it."

"Of course you can."

"I'd be reversing myself."

"Politicians do it all the time."

"You don't understand the political implications."

"I understand them perfectly well. Consider the alternative."

"You're a bastard, Silva."

"And you, Deputado, are a sanctimonious hypocrite. But you're a powerful man in this country, and from now on you're going to be *our* sanctimonious hypocrite."

Malan didn't react to the insult. Worse things had been said to him, even worse *of* him. "Sampaio know about this?"

"No."

"Who else does?"

"Only two of my trusted subordinates."

"And I have your word it will go no further?"

"You have my word."

Malan reached forward and swept up both sheaves of paper. "I'll keep these," he said.

"The names of the other Brazilians have been excised," Silva said.

"I had no intention of—"

"Of course you did."

Malan looked offended.

"And those are only copies," Silva continued

Malan narrowed his eyes. "The originals," the deputado said, "will only be of use to you as long as they, like this conversation, are kept in the strictest confidence. We have a deal. Now, get the hell out of my office."

SILVA CALLED the director from the airport.

"I just got off the phone with Malan," Sampaio said. "What, in heaven's name, did you say to him?"

"I reasoned with him, Director, pointed out the error of his ways."

"He said he's not only going to support our budget request, he's going to push for an increase of twenty percent."

"Yes, he mentioned that."

"And he's no longer calling for your resignation."

"He mentioned that too."

"What do you have on him, Mario?"

"Have on him?" Silva asked innocently.

HECTOR AND Arnaldo were waiting when Silva got back to Manaus.

"We found The Goat's boat," Hector said. "The girls, and a henchman of his by the name of Osvaldo, were on board, but The Goat managed to get away."

"How?"

"They were anchored off a sandy beach. He went ashore to swim. When he spotted the patrol boat he hightailed it over to the other side of the island and took off in an inflatable. Osvaldo said he had it stashed over there in case of emergencies."

"Any idea about where he might have gone?"

"Rosélia says he didn't take much money with him, so he can't afford to run far."

"A man like that has money stashed somewhere. You can count on it. So Rosélia's still being cooperative, is she?"

"She wants him caught as much as we do. She was the only one who knew where he was, and he'll hurt her if we don't pick him up."

"Five will get you ten," Arnaldo said, "that he's pissed at Claudia as well."

"No bet," Silva said. "And speaking of Claudia . . ."

"No sign of her. God knows how she does it, but she's dropped out of sight again."

"Her boat?"

"Hasn't turned up. There are all these tributaries with over-hanging trees. It's like trying to find a needle in a haystack."

"Get one of those heat-sensitive video devices. Put it in a chopper."

"We've got one," Hector said. "It doesn't work well in this climate. Not with all of those trees. Claudia's got a scientific background. She probably knows that. And, if she does, she will have chosen a place where the canopy is thick."

"The boat is still her best bet to get out of here. Maintain aerial surveillance all night long. Maybe she'll stick her nose out of her hole."

"I can't believe that bitch got away again," Arnaldo said.

"She didn't," Silva said. "Not yet."

Chapter Twenty-nine

HANS HAUSER PULLED THE visor of his blue cap low over his dark glasses and struck a pose in front of the mirror.

"Where do you think you're going?" Claudia said.

"Into town. I'm going stir-crazy on this fucking boat."

"It's too dangerous," Claudia said.

"Hell," Hans said. "It's dangerous just sitting here."

He was right about that. By now, she must have heard the helicopter a half dozen times, flying around in circles up there like some demented insect. One of those times it had passed directly overhead. She'd sat on her bunk, her palms sweating, until the sound of the motor had vanished in the distance.

"Besides," he said, "it isn't like I'm leaving you without protection. Otto's gonna be here."

"Yeah," Otto chipped in. "We got it covered. Tonight it's him, tomorrow me. We decided."

The boat was moored to two trees, in a minor tributary, some thirty kilometers east of the city. The location was decked over by a canopy of vegetation that made it invisible from the air.

"I don't think you get it," she said, looking from one to the other. "I don't want either of you going anywhere."

Hans reached for a bottle of cheap cologne. "Stop wasting your breath," he said. "I'm going."

"And I'm going tomorrow," Otto said.

"I pay you to—"

Hans didn't let her finish.

"You don't pay us at all," he snarled, catching her eye in

the mirror. "Once you start dishing out the money, you can start giving orders again."

"I told you," she said. "I *have* the money. I just don't want to run the risk of going to get it. I promise—"

"Your promise," Hans snarled, "is the only reason we're still here."

He splashed some aftershave into one armpit of his shirt. The stuff smelled like cloves.

"You could at least make an attempt to change your appearance," she insisted. "Cut your hair. Shave off that moustache."

Hans splashed the other armpit.

"I like my moustache," he said.

And he left.

THE HULL heeled and began to rock as someone climbed aboard the boat. Claudia awoke with a start. Footsteps sounded on the deck overhead. She grabbed her pistol and pointed it at the door.

"Who's there?" she said, when the footsteps reached the main cabin.

"Who the fuck do you think?"

Hans's voice. He sounded drunk.

She glanced at her watch. It was six-thirty in the morning, time to get up. Claudia had always been an early riser. She climbed out of bed and unlocked the door to her cabin. There he was, standing in the saloon, smelling of cachaça, staring at her out of a pair of bloodshot eyes. His hat was turned around, the visor projecting over the back of his neck.

"Point that gun somewhere else," he said.

She lowered the Glock, put it on the table and started making coffee. Otto, who slept in the saloon, sat up in his bunk, rubbed his eyes, and yawned.

"What time is it?" he said.

"Six-thirty," Claudia told him. "Time to get your fat ass out of bed."

An early riser, yes, but not a morning person.

"I thought the first bus was at eight," Otto said, sleepily.

Claudia saw Hans' eyes flick toward her pistol. She made a grab for it, but wasn't fast enough. Hans snatched it up, took a step backward, and pointed it at her chest.

"The Goat was looking for us," Hans said, talking to Otto, not to Claudia. "He had two capangas with him. Get some rope."

"The Goat? Jesus Christ! He must be pissed," Otto said.

"He *is* pissed."

"What did he say?"

"Get the fucking rope, and I'll tell you."

THE GOAT showed up an hour later. He was alone.

The first thing he did was to rip off the tape they'd put over Claudia's mouth.

It stung like hell. She licked her lips and tasted blood.

"You got any idea what you did to my life, you lying bitch?"

"It wasn't me," she said. "It was that prick, Silva. He's the one to blame, not me."

"I don't see it that way. What you did with all those people in São Paulo, that was just sick."

The story was all over the media by now. She'd heard it on the boat's radio. The Goat must have seen it on television. She wasn't Carla Antunes any more, she was Claudia Andrade, accused of mass murder and organ theft. There was no use denying it.

"You don't understand," she said. "What I was doing in São Paulo was—"

He didn't let her finish. "What you did to the girls I sold

you, that was sick too. Silva was right to go after you. You deserve everything you're gonna get, you crazy—"

Hans cleared his throat.

The Goat turned to face him.

"What?" he said.

"The rest is between you and her, right? You got the money you promised me? The ten thousand? Me and Otto, we got to be going."

"Oh, yeah," The Goat said, "what I owe you. I got it right here."

He reached under his shirt. But when his hand came out again it was holding a pistol. In one flowing movement he raised it and shot Hans through the heart. Otto was still standing there with his mouth open when The Goat put a bullet into his forehead just left of center.

Claudia's ears were ringing from the reports. Her nose filled with the acrid stench of gunpowder. The Goat turned on her, still holding the pistol.

"No," she said. "Don't. You don't want to shoot me. I've got money. We can make a deal."

The Goat shook his head.

"Fuck your money," he said. "And shooting is too good for you. I got something else in mind."

He put the pistol down and peeled off his shirt.

Next to the empty holster on his belt dangled a silk cord.

Chapter Thirty

THE FOLLOWING MORNING, A little after seven, the telephone rang in Silva's suite. It was Lefkowitz. He told Silva that Claudia Andrade was on a slab down at the morgue. Silva called Hector first, then Arnaldo.

"It couldn't have happened to a nicer girl," Arnaldo said.

THE MORGUE turned out to be a single-story concrete building, appropriately located on a dead-end street. There was one of those electronic keypads on the front door. Lefkowitz was standing next to it.

"Body was wrapped up in plastic sheeting tied with clothesline," he said, punching numbers on the pad.

The lock clicked. He pulled on the door and ushered them inside. They started walking along a dim corridor, lit at intervals by round globes. The place smelled like morgues everywhere—and of something else too. Silva thought it might be mold.

"You guys know Yamaguchi?" Lefkowitz asked.

"No," Arnaldo said, "but hum a few bars, and I'll try to fake it."

"That joke," Lefkowitz said, "was old when my grandfather was a boy. Yamaguchi is the medical examiner, and I gotta warn you: the woman has no sense of humor."

"Perhaps not with your tired routines, Lefkowitz, but with outstanding wit like my own—"

"Where did they find Claudia?" Silva cut in.

"Somebody dumped her at your hotel," Lefkowitz said.

"The night clerk saw it happen, right through the glass of the front door. He was behind the reception desk when this white Volkswagen van pulls up. The side door opens. *Bang*, she's on the sidewalk. *Slam*, they close the door. *Vroom*, the van takes off. It's gone by the time he gets outside."

"What time was that?" Silva said.

"A little after four this morning."

"Present for me?"

"Could be. Somebody kills somebody around here, they usually drop them in the river. According to my wife, who knows about such things, there are more than six hundred species of fish out there. That's more than they've got in the whole Atlantic Ocean. They make short work of any kind of meat."

"And the people in this town eat those fish?" Arnaldo said. "It's enough to make a man sick."

"You can say that again," Lefkowitz said. "You try the Recanto Gaúcho, that joint I told you about?"

"Yes, we did. That Gaúcho saved my life. I'm gonna remember him in my will."

"Tell me more about the body drop," Silva said.

"I took a couple of photos *in sitio*, then I had her brought back here. I unwrapped her right on Yamaguchi's table. She was nude."

INSIDE, DOCTOR Yamaguchi and her diener—the morgue assistant—were bent over Claudia's corpse. The diener was a woman, raven-haired, attractive, and pregnant. She looked to be at least eight months along. Her appearance clashed with the surroundings.

The medical examiner, on the other hand, blended in perfectly. She was a short Asian woman in her midforties with a studious expression. Under a disposable paper cap, her hair was pulled back in a severe bun. When she heard the door, she looked up, and light reflected off the thick lenses of her eyeglasses.

"You're the federals, right?"

She had no trace of a Japanese accent.

"We're the federals," Silva agreed.

"Stand over there," she said, gesturing with a scalpel, "and stay out of my way."

Hector, Arnaldo, and Silva went to stand in the place she'd indicated. It brought them within three feet of the table. Yamaguchi's surgical gloves were smeared with blood. She'd already made the Y-incision and was palpating the liver prior to cutting it out for weighing. Claudia's lids were open, the whites of her eyes shot with so many petechiae that they appeared to be red.

"The ligature marks around her neck are consistent with death by strangulation," Yamaguchi said. "She was also stabbed, once, through the heart. She's been dead about twelve hours. The stab wound was probably post-mortem, the killer making sure his victim was dead. There was considerable bruising around the genitals and anus. She was penetrated in both places by something at least eighteen inches long and at least three thick."

"Sounds like me," Arnaldo said. "But I didn't do it."

Yamaguchi straightened up and looked at him through her thick lenses. Then she looked back and forth between Hector and Silva.

"Who let the comedian into my autopsy suite?" she said.

"Thank you, thank you," Arnaldo said. "This is my last show in Manaus. Don't miss me in Brasilia and as soon as possible I'll appear in São Paulo. I hope to be there for the rest of my life."

"Semen?" Silva asked.

Yamaguchi nodded. "That also. But the bruising was caused by something else."

"I'll need a DNA analysis of the swabs."

"Who pays?" she asked.

"Send them to Brasilia. We'll do it there."

"Five will get you ten," Arnaldo said, "The Goat did it."

"No bet," Silva said.

"Who's he?" Yamaguchi asked. She must have been one of the few people in Manaus who'd never heard of The Goat.

"A boate owner with a score to settle," Silva said. "We had a score too. I expect he thought he was doing us a favor."

"And he was," Arnaldo said. "Let's hear it for The Goat."

"What kind of a cop are you?" Yamaguchi said. "This is a murdered woman we've got here."

"She was a tough person to love," Silva said.

"But somebody did, in a matter of speaking," Arnaldo said.

Yamaguchi speared him with her eyes. "You are a disgusting man," she said.

When the three federal cops left the autopsy suite, Lefkowitz was gone. Side by side, they walked down the dim hallway toward the front door.

"Normally," Arnaldo said, breaking the companionable silence, "I hate these places."

"So do I," Silva said. "Normally."

He paused next to an overflowing barrel of trash, took out his photo of Claudia Andrade, and tossed it on top.

Then he led the way out of the gloom and into the sunlight.

Author's Note

THIS IS A WORK of fiction based on some sad realities.

In Brazil, the prostitution of children has reached epic proportions, and the country has become one of the world's premier destinations for men seeking sex with minors. The trade is often carried out with the enthusiastic support of local law enforcement.

Visitors to cities in Brazil's north and northeast are often surprised to find eleven- and twelve-year-olds sitting on curbs, playing with dolls, while they wait for clients.

In January 2006, the Brazilian federal government completed an investigation of the police department of Manaus. It resulted in more than a hundred officers being expelled from the force and charged with crimes ranging from theft and extortion to kidnapping and murder.

In Belém, up until recently, seventy-seven of the one hundred and fourteen houses of prostitution were offering children from eleven to seventeen years of age. Five houses specialized in children exclusively.

At the same time, in Arapina, the "services" of girls as young as eight could be bought for ten Reais, about five American dollars.

Recent estimates suggest that at least a half million Brazilian girls under the age of eighteen are currently working as prostitutes.

As for snuff videos, despite evidence to the contrary, some people continue to regard them as nothing more than urban legends.

They aren't.